CRECHELING

D.J. BUTLER

WordFire Press
Colorado Springs, Colorado

CRECHELING
Copyright © 2013 D.J. Butler

ISBN: 978-1-61475-303-2

Cover Image Art by Dollar Photo Club

Cover design by Janet McDonald

Art Director Kevin J. Anderson

Book Design by RuneWright, LLC
www.RuneWright.com

Published by
WordFire Press, an imprint of
WordFire, Inc.
PO Box 1840
Monument CO 80132

Kevin J. Anderson & Rebecca Moesta, Publishers

WordFire Press Trade Paperback Edition April 2015
Printed in the USA
wordfirepress.com

PROLOGUE

The Camel's Back

Dyan ran.

She wasn't a natural runner. She wasn't tall, so her short legs didn't eat up the miles like Shad's or Cheela's. On the other hand, she didn't have Wayland's bulk to slow her down, or Deek's awkwardness with the physical world.

She was herself, Dyan, and she was at peace with the System.

She pushed up the slope ahead of her in the final seconds of pre-dawn darkness, towards the edge of the Creche that had been her world her entire life. The ridge was called the Camel's Back, named after a pre-Cataclysm animal that Dyan had only seen in ancient pictures, and like a camel it was humped up in rounded knobs. Dyan raced along a trail only a few inches wide, tall yellow grass whipping at her knees as she went, light running shoes barely making an impression in the powdery dry dirt of autumn in Buza System.

She heard the heavier thudding of Shad's feet behind her.

This was her last day as a Crecheling. The thought filled her with joy. She was a baby bird, about to peck its way out of its shell. This morning would come the Lot Letters, the Hanging—she shivered slightly—and then the Selection, and then she would join

Buza System as an Urbane, an adult and a complete person. She would belong.

Dyan stopped just under the crest of the Camel's Back, panting and leaning her hands on her knees. She turned and looked back at the Creche, deep in shadow and just beginning to stir. It was a complex of many buildings, nestled in the valleys of the low foothills that ran from the Camel's Back to the towering Jawtooths. She devoured the sight of the long low dormitories, carefully segregated into the boys in one canyon and girls in another, with the Magisters living in a third. She lingered on the instruction halls where she had learned of the Cataclysm, the Cogitant Council that had formed Buza System to drag humanity up from the ruins, and the shards and tatters of legend that made up the history and geography of the world before. She basked in glowing memories at the sight of the hospital and the engineering rooms, the farms and fields and orchards, and the crafting tents. She drank in the training fields, with equestrian courses for riding and target stumps for archery, and for the monofilament weapons of the Urbane—the whip and bola.

All these spaces and all these subjects had been her school, and her life. Other than short journeys out, accompanied by a Magister, Dyan and her Crechemates had never left the Creche. They had trained and studied and prepared, under the observation of the Magisters and the direction of the Cogitants, for a Calling the System would give them on a day they had all long awaited.

Now the day had arrived, and Dyan was about to leave the Creche behind.

"We'll be able to be Love-Matched," she said out loud.

Shad caught up her to her as she said it. He didn't answer, just stopped and leaned back, resting his hands on his hips.

"What do you think?" she asked him. "What will you be Called to do?"

He shook his head. "It doesn't matter. Whatever I'm asked to do, I'll be happy to do it."

"Me too," she said. They were both lying, and she knew it. But it was a gentle lie, and they shared it, and sharing it made her feel closer to Shad. "To each his Calling. And we'll be able to be Love-Matched," she said again.

"Look." He pointed. "I'll never get over this."

The sun cracked over the Jawtooths, the brilliant white rim of a blazing disk. A new day. Dyan laughed with excitement. She straightened herself, turned, took the remaining steps to the height of the Camel's Back that was the very edge of the Creche, and looked down at Buza System.

The System lay along the Buza River, white buildings, green fields, and trees heavy with oranges. Early morning traffic clopped along the System's wide avenues on horseback, coming in from Eyrie and Cowell in the west and Nemap in the south, on the Lull Sea where the Snaik and the Buza joined, before flowing over the Dam and into the unknown world west of the Treasure Valley. Beyond the Lull stood the Wahai, rugged and brown as the sun woke them up for another day.

Capitol in particular showed signs of early life, around the glorious Garden, the towering domed Council Hall, and the squat Prison. That would be for the Hanging, Dyan thought with a thrill in her heart.

Will my Calling be the right one? she wondered, and then forced herself to think the more correct thought: What will my Calling be? The sunlight felt prickly-warm on her skin, raising her mood even higher as she turned and began to jog towards the dormitories. Magister Zarah would be knocking on doors soon, with Lot Letters in her hand.

Dyan badly wanted to be a Magister herself, tending children in the Nursery and teaching them in the Creche. This had been her family, and she wanted to continue with it, as a nurturer and as a guide.

"There's something maybe I should tell you," Shad said.

Dyan laughed and broke into a run.

"Hey!" Shad blurted out, and ran after her.

She cruised across the tops of the hill to drop at a steep angle directly down towards the central space around which the girls' dormitories clustered.

"Blazes!" roared a girl's voice she knew very well, just as Dyan reached the bottom of the canyon and slowed her run to a sweat-chilled walk. "Who put porridge in my blasted boots?"

CHAPTER ONE

Dyan walked to the Hanging with a spring in her step.

She wasn't happy, exactly, but she was excited. Proud. Eager. No, she admitted to herself, she was happy, too.

The summer was fading fast into autumn, pulling down red and gold leaves in heavy sheets from the trees all along the Buza River, along the side of which Dyan walked with her Crechemates. Buza's sun-browned Gardeners dragged rakes through the yellow and crimson carpet, gathering the leaves up to take them off and burn them somewhere. Dyan knew they weren't Urbanes, and she wondered where they were from.

The Gardeners nodded as the Creche-Leavers passed, without raising their heads or meeting the youths' gaze.

"You're disappointed," Shad said. He had a deep, manly voice and had had it for several years. When he'd first stopped sounding like a boy and started sounding like one of the Magisters, it had been funny. Dyan didn't find it amusing anymore. It excited her. She looped one hand inside Shad's elbow to show just how much she didn't find his deep voice funny. He grinned at her, square-jawed and strong, with just a hint of asymmetry in his nose and one eyebrow that tugged perpetually upward, like it felt compelled to go exploring in his slightly shaggy hairline, and then turned his attention back to Deek. "I get it," he told his skinnier, big-eyed

Crechemate. "You thought they'd want you for a Cogitant, and you're disappointed."

Deek shook his head so vigorously it looked like a spasm, and kicked at a pile of leaves a young Gardener was shaping into a hump under a cottonwood tree. The Gardener's eyes flashed briefly, but one of his companions, an older man, stepped between him and the Creche-Leavers, hiding him and cutting him off.

"I'm okay being a Mechanical," Deek said. He held several rectangular chits of Scrip loosely in one hand and rattled them together. "The Council and the Magisters know what they're doing. They know what the System needs right now. Besides, no one ever gets Called as a Cogitant. Not right out of the Creche."

"I'm much better than okay," Cheela said, flashing her flawless white teeth and throwing back her shoulders in a way that threw her breasts forward. Dyan forced herself not to look at Shad to see exactly what he might be looking at. Cheela was taller than her and had perfect coffee-brown skin and hair that fell in rings onto her shoulders and down her back. "This is *perfect*. I always wanted to be an Outrider."

She already looked the part, in the travel gear she had taken to wearing even before the Magister had handed them their Lot Letters that morning. She had the hat, broad to keep the sun from her eyes, and a long coat and boots, slightly too much clothing for this day that was still on the heels of summer and warm. She wore her whip-handle openly on her belt, and had strapped a bola to each thigh. The only piece of the Outrider's traditional garb she wasn't wearing, other than the badge, was the large bandanna. Of course not, Dyan thought. That would cover her cleavage.

Dyan forced herself to smile.

She and Shad were not Love-Matched—they couldn't be, until they were fully out of the Creche and had become full Urbanes— but she liked him and she knew he liked her. After all, he had said he wanted to tell her something this morning.

"Nice hat, 'rider," Wayland quipped.

"Thank you," Cheela said, "or blast you, depending on how seriously you meant that."

"When have I ever not been serious?" Wayland protested. Dyan and her Crechemates walked towards Rose Plaza at a leisurely pace designed to accommodate Wayland. He was heavy, and walked slow.

"This morning," Dyan reminded him. "When Magister Zarah offered you your Lot Letter and you told her no thanks, you'd already had yours, you had been asked to join the Council."

"I was close," Wayland said. He wiped sweat from his balding head, which was slick and glistened in the morning sunshine.

"Healer isn't half close to Cogitant," Deek grumbled, shaking his head quickly again.

"Come on, you Landsy," Wayland argued. "It's at least *half*."

"Two weeks ago," Shad added, "when you pretended you were sick during lessons so you could sneak back into our dormitory and remake my bunk, with the sheets shortened."

"Hey, are you still holding a grudge about that?" Wayland asked. "I had no idea your sheets were so rotten that you'd kick your feet right through them."

"No," Shad agreed, "but you laughed pretty hard when I did."

"Besides," Wayland shrugged, "I gave you my sheets."

"I know," Shad muttered darkly, scratching himself under one arm. "I'm still delousing myself."

"This morning," Cheela threw in. "When you filled my boots with oat porridge." She put her hand on a whip, and Dyan's eyebrows both shot reflexively up her forehead. Cheela had to be joking, of course. The monofilament whip was one of the Urbanes' most deadly weapons. Using it without justification, and especially on a fellow Urbane, was a serious, serious crime. A criminal of almost any sort would be hung, but a whip-murderer would be publicly tortured first.

"Cheela ..." Dyan said.

Wayland threw his arms wide. "Why would you think that I had anything to do with that?"

"How could he even get into the girls' sleeping rooms, anyway?" Deek pointed out. His voice whistled a little bit, through the nose, which it always did when he got nervous.

Shad chuckled. "You'd be surprised."

"Yes," Wayland said, straight-faced. "How could I even get into the dormitories while they were actually full of sleeping girls and put a full bowl of porridge into each of the freshly-polished riding boots standing side-by-side in your closet? You know I have no access, and besides, I was running endless miles up and down the Camel's Back."

He winked at Dyan.

For a moment, Dyan thought Cheela would kill Wayland then and there. She drifted off Shad's elbow, moving to be able to jump in between them. Though that would be pointless, since the whip would slice her and Wayland in half simultaneously just as easily as it would slice through Wayland alone.

But then Cheela moved her hand away from the whip and relaxed her scowl into a grin. "You're just not worth it, Wayland," she said. "Tomorrow, fellow Outrider Shad and I will be roaming the Wahai and the Snaik in search of runaway Landsmen and other outlaws, and you and your juvenile pranks will be nothing but a memory."

"Until you get bitten by a rattler." Wayland beamed. "Or crushed in a fall or stabbed by one of the outlaws. And then I will be thrilled to exercise my Calling in your aid."

"Not tomorrow," Dyan objected, hating all the images that Cheela's words conjured in her mind. "After the Selection."

Shad squeezed her hand but didn't look at her. "There are lots of Outriders," he said to Cheela, "and lots of Squads. I don't think they'd put two new Creche-Leavers on the same Squad."

"However much they might both want it," Cheela snapped. Shad looked away and kept walking, but Cheela caught Dyan's eye, just for a moment. She had a flare in her gaze that might have been triumph.

The Greenbelt Path they'd been following, a dimpled strip of rubberized ceramic that ran all along Buza River through thick trees, stopped at the edge of Capitol Boulevard. It was a path their Magisters used to teach them the basics of Buza System geography, and this was the first time they had walked it unaccompanied.

Capitol was broad and busy with motion. Shad barely looked both ways for wagon traffic before dragging Dyan into the street, weaving in and out among horses as their Crechemates followed.

He pulled up sharply just out of hoof-reach but within range of the fierce stare of a Guardsman. The Guardsman was armed, not only with monofilament whip and bolas, but also with knives, and a long sword at his hip that must be a vibro-blade. A bow and quiver of arrows hung attached to the side of his saddle, behind his hip, and the tabard on his chest bore the symbol of Buza System officialdom, a stylized tree with five arms. He snorted at the youths, chucked at his big roan horse and pulled its reins, making it step around Shad as Shad tipped his head in deference.

"What I want to know," Deek said, bumping into Dyan's back and clattering to a halt, "is what *kind* of Mechanical I'll be. I mean, I accept that I have to be specialized, but if I'm going to do just one thing for the rest of my life I want to do something really cool."

"Like hydroponics," Wayland puffed, catching up.

Deek shot him a glare like a rattlesnake. "Do I *look* like a Landsman?" he snorted.

"Weapons?" Shad asked mildly, pulled at Dyan's hand again to lead them all forward.

"Meta-Systems," Dyan guessed. "You want to know how Buza works."

Deek blushed, pointing his beaky nose and emerald eyes at his walking slippers. "Well, yeah," he admitted. "If that's not too much like being a Cogitant."

"I don't think so." Dyan smiled at her Crechemate, and he smiled shyly back.

"No, the thing that's too much like being a Cogitant," Cheela said, with a sharp edge to her voice, "is *Magister.*"

Dyan shrugged and tried to pretend there wasn't envy in Cheela's words. "Hey, I'll probably get a Creche straight out of the Nursery," she said mildly. "I'll be wiping snot out of babies' noses and pulling them out of Buza River while you're chasing rustlers and runaways in the Wahai. I might not even really leave the Creche. Doesn't sound much like a Cogitant to me." But she had a warm feeling as she said the words.

"Kind of it does," Deek muttered.

Cheela smiled teeth. "I'll dedicate my second kill to you," she offered, "my lowly Magister friend. My first kill, of course, I'll have to dedicate to my Crechemate Shad."

"Kill or capture," Shad reminded her. "Kill or capture."

They reached the far side of Capitol's broad lanes and found Magister Zarah waiting. Around and beyond her, foot traffic continued to flow upstream along Buza River, into Rose Plaza where the Gallows Tree was. The sun was in its afternoon zenith and uncomfortably warm, and Dyan envied neither Cheela in her hat and coat nor the Magister in her ankle-length black cloak.

"You're almost late, children," Zarah said. Her face was stern, its usual expression, made sterner by the way she wore her iron-gray hair back in a bun at the nape of her neck and wore no cosmetics. Dyan thought of herself as sparing in the use of make-up, and even *she* had painted her lips.

Wayland grinned. "Isn't *almost late* better than *almost on time?*"

Zarah arched an eyebrow at him and turned to walk into Rose Plaza.

"Why are we *children?*" Dyan asked. "We've had our Lot Letters."

"You're not Blooded yet," Magister Zarah said. She seemed unusually terse, so Dyan let the matter drop.

"After the Hanging, then," Cheela said with satisfaction.

The Magister didn't answer.

Rose Plaza lay along Buza River in the heart of the System. It was a large array of rose bushes of every color, part of the Garden, arranged in a symmetrical pattern that wasn't a maze but vaguely hinted at one. In the center of the Garden was the Yard, in the center of which stood the Gallows Tree, a five-armed scaffold, arms pointing out and spaced evenly around the central column. The Gallows Tree was the image reproduced on the Guardsmen's tabards, in the badges of the Outriders, on the medallion that every Magister wore on her or his breast, and anywhere else the Council and Buza System needed to mark its most solemn authority.

On every day of the year but four, the Garden was open to any Urbane who wanted to take a stroll, and Dyan and her Crechemates had taken many lessons from Magister Zarah there. In the grassy fields beyond the Garden, the Greenbelt, they had even practiced with whip and bola, a fact that explained many of the tree stumps, scarred limbs and blasted patches of grass-less earth along Buza River. On those four days, though, the Yard was off-limits. No one physically blocked access, but Crechelings were taught from a very young age that they were not permitted access to the Yard until they were Creche-Leavers, and then only on one day a quarter.

Dyan followed Magister Zarah past two tabard-empowered Guards, who frowned at the Creche-Leavers but nodded them through. Crowds filled the grassy spaces in the Garden and the ceramic paths, all facing inward towards the Tree, but at the sight of Magister Zarah's cloak and medallion of office and her five charges in tow, the crowd parted to let them pass.

At the front of the crowd, arrayed in a ring around the Gallows Tree, were knots of Creche-Leavers, each with an accompanying Magister. Zarah stopped.

"I guess we get a front-row seat." Cheela smiled like she was talking about getting the drumstick off a game bird. "Just this once."

"Hopefully just this once," Wayland said softly. "The other front row seats look a lot less comfortable." He nodded at the Gallows Tree itself.

Five condemned criminals stood on the platform of the Tree, one under each arm. They wore white trousers and tunics, and Dyan recognized none of them. There was no reason she should, of course. She knew the Magisters she had had during her life, and other Crechelings, Urbanes who were important enough to have been identified to her by her Magisters and guest instructors in the Creche. None of those people was likely to be standing on the Gallows Tree. Still, the sight of women and men with nooses around their necks and armed Guards behind them, as prepared as Dyan had thought she was for it, unsettled her.

"Magister," someone said behind her.

Zarah didn't move.

"Magister!"

Magister Zarah stood motionless, staring at the Tree. Dyan tugged respectfully at her cloak, but she stayed frozen.

"Magister!" A Guardsman struggled to push past the Creche-Leavers. "You're blocking the path!"

Magister Zarah snapped out of her reverie. "Come, children," she said, and started moving again. She led them across the Yard, close enough to the Tree that Dyan could have touched it if she'd wanted to, and into a vacant spot between two other Creches.

Shad nodded at other Creche-Leavers he knew well, from the boys' dormitory and from various joint exercises, and former

Crechemates. Dyan knew others, too, especially other girls, but she couldn't look at them. Electricity held her captive, a jolt of something that seemed to flow out of the Tree itself and sting her in her heart and stomach. It was the realization of the moment, the delivery of the promise of the morning's nerves and excitement. Maybe that was what had made Magister Zarah pause, too, she thought.

Maybe that was how death always was.

She knew, in a way that she suspected her Crechemates did not, that she was being brought here this day to confront the great mystery of death, and thereby become an adult. She thought that her sense of this necessity, and her Crechemates' obliviousness to it, was why she had been Called in her Lot Letter to be a Magister, and they had been summoned to other occupations. Not less important Callings, not less worthy ones, but roles that weren't so entwined with the growth of the soul, weren't so tightly wound into the fabric of the family that was Buza System.

She trembled, though the sun's rays were warm on her skin.

The Hangman pushed through the ring of Creche-Leavers and climbed the wooden steps onto the Gallows Tree's platform. The Hangman was a woman, burly and square. She wore a Guardsman's tabard, but her face was obscured by a hood, like a sack over her head, with holes for eyes.

She passed the lever that operated all five traps and stepped to the edge of the platform.

At the sight of her, all the crowd's ordinary murmur and rumble ceased, as if its collective windpipe had suddenly been stoppered.

"These five criminals die!" she shrieked. Her voice was surprisingly shrill, coming out of her barrel-like body. Shaped ceramic walls at the edges of the Plaza bounced the sound back so that everyone could hear her words, but Dyan had no need. She stood directly in front of the Hangman, and in her imagination the hooded eyes looked right at her.

Then she heard a tune.

"Death shows no mercy!" the Hangman continued. "The System can afford no remorse!"

Tension rippled through the crowd. Dyan looked at Magister Zarah, looking for an example of how she should hold herself for this experience. Expecting dignity and reserve, she was shocked to see a tortured look on the Magister's face and a single tear on her cheek.

Was this the reaction that was expected of her, too? She realized, to her surprise, that she felt a thick lump in her throat. Her eyes stung and she looked away. She looked randomly at anything, trying not to see the Tree and the condemned man on it, and when she looked into the crowd she found herself looking into a stranger's face.

The woman wore a Magister's robe and medallion. Her jowls and nose drooped in a matronly way, and one eye fluttered slightly. It was not a strange or a frightening face, but where every other face in sight was turned towards the tree, this unknown Magister focused squarely on Dyan.

Beside the Magister stood a man, and the sight of him made Dyan's breath catch in her throat. His face alone was striking—he was tall, with a strong, pointed nose and smallish ears—but that wasn't what caught Dyan's attention. The man wore a white tunic and trousers, and Dyan thought, seeing him in the Yard, how similar that clothing made him look to the condemned criminals. The difference was that on his chest, in black, was emblazoned the sign of the tree, and around his shaved head he wore a tight-fitting silver circlet, like a plain ring just above his thick eyebrows.

He was a Cogitant, a member of the Council. Dyan had never seen one of them so close, and this man stared at her.

And his eyes and face were cold.

Dyan heard the melody again, and she realized that one of the condemned criminals was *whistling*. She looked back at the Tree, which was the source of the melody, and then stared even harder. She hadn't noticed it before, but the man about to die looked *familiar*. He was a tall man, slightly stooped, with a thin beard. He looked out into space and whistled his tune.

And then Dyan realized she had heard the melody before. She felt her heart beat faster. What was that? She ran through all the songs she knew from the Creche in her head, martial songs, marches, hymns, nursery rhymes ... none of them matched the melody, the familiarity of which now seemed eerie, haunting.

"These die, but the System lives!"

Was that it? Maybe Dyan didn't know the man at all, but she had heard the melody before, and in recognizing it she had convinced herself that she recognized him.

Dyan sniffed. She looked up at Magister Zarah in time to see another tear fall.

Then, with a loud *CHUNK!* the Hangman pulled her lever.

The condemned fell.

CHAPTER TWO

Dyan's horse ate up the miles without effort, carrying her out of the Treasure Valley of Buza System and into the wilderness beyond. She was trained to ride—they all were, as they were all trained to fight with bola, whip, and vibroblade, like they were all trained in basic engineering skills, shooting a bow, and reading and writing, because you didn't know what your Calling was going to be until you got your Lot Letter. So all Creche-Leavers had to be capable of entering into the first stages of any Calling. Crechelings were apprentice-everythings in the System.

But horses, and tracking and hunting, and knowing the habits of animals, were more Shad's special gift than hers. It had been no surprise to Dyan that he had opened his Lot Letter and read "Outrider" to all his Crechemates. No surprise to her, but a great thrill to him. He'd picked her up off the ground and spun her in a three hundred sixty degree circle before putting her back down again. She was small, and he was a big man.

Cheela's assignment to the same calling was more surprising. She hadn't ever shown the same gifts. Or maybe, Dyan reflected as she watched Cheela ride easily over the tall yellow grasses and gray-green sage, slouched comfortably in the saddle, Dyan simply hadn't wanted to admit that Cheela was good at the same things Shad was.

And better at some. Dyan had once seen her shoot the jackrabbit out of a soaring hawk's talons from two hundred feet away. She hadn't needed the rabbit; she had only wanted to show Shad that she could do it. In front of Dyan.

The memory made Dyan want to grab Shad's elbow again, but on horseback she couldn't do it.

They passed a heavy Collector's wagon, inbound for the System. The wagon was ten feet tall at least from its bed to the tops of its poles, and all that space was piled high with sacks and bales of harvested crops contributed by Landsmen farmers. The Collector rode with a whip across his lap; one Outrider rode ahead and a second behind; and the wagon was flanked by four Guardsman. It was the fourth Collector they'd seen since leaving the System—the harvest was being brought in.

"An adult has choices," Magister Zarah said, snatching Dyan's attention back from the wagon. The Creche-Leavers rode shoulder to shoulder, a little ragged in their line, and she rode behind them, so they could all hear her voice without shouting or straining their necks. They had all read the maps, and the road to Ratsnay Station was well marked, so any one of them could have led the party. "You children have not had to choose anything. Your dormitories and food have been provided for you, you have had no say in your education, and even your Lot Letter designated each of you for a Calling without any decision on your parts."

"We're still children?" Cheela muttered, shooting a sidelong glance at Shad and shaking her head slightly.

The Magister continued as if she hadn't heard. "No decision," she intoned, "means no commitment, no risk, no price."

"Just the way I like it," Wayland added. He spoke loud enough to be heard by the Magister.

"Tomorrow, children," Magister Zarah said, "you will make your first real choice."

Shad rolled his eyes at the word "*children.*" He rolled them at Cheela, and Dyan felt a cold impact in the pit of her stomach, like she'd been punched by an icicle. Her jealousy warred with an intense curiosity at the Magister's words, and a sense of mild surprise. Something was happening here, something that felt large and inevitable but that she hadn't expected.

"Is it our Callings?" Deek asked. "Do I get to choose what kind of Mechanical I'll be?"

"Every single choice you ever make," the Magister said, "beginning tomorrow and for the rest of your lives, will have two attributes."

The sun, beginning to drift down on Dyan's right shoulder, was warmer than could really be comfortable, especially since Dyan was dressed in an Outrider-style traveling coat and hat. They all were. She took off her hat and wiped sweat off her forehead, squinting against the yellow glare.

"First," the Magister continued her lecture, "every choice will exact of you a price." Dyan had heard many explanation from Magister Zarah—and from earlier Magisters—while walking or riding, so in one sense this discussion of choices seemed very normal, very run of the mill. On the other hand, Zarah's words implied that everything was changing in the Creche-Leavers' world. Which, of course, it was.

Dyan gulped, remembering the sight of the unknown, whistling man falling to his death, his neck snapping instantly and his feet jerking for a few seconds, like the body of a slaughtered chicken.

"You mean in Scrip?" Deek asked.

"Some choices cost Scrip, yes," Magister Zarah agreed. Her voice was always stern and tough, but now it sounded truly hard, even bitter. "But for everything you choose, you pay a price by turning your back on all the other things you might have chosen."

"That's what Coolers are for," Wayland chuckled. "So I can have the iced cream today and still choose the berries tomorrow."

"Consider Love-Matches," Zarah said.

Dyan looked instantly at Shad. He looked down at his saddle, adjusting something with one hand, but he looked up and caught her glance after a moment. And smiled, a little.

"Oh, I consider them all the time!" Cheela snapped.

"A Love-Match is an exclusion." Something in Magister Zarah's voice made Dyan turn around and look at her teacher. The brim of her rider's hat obscured Zarah's eyes, but her mouth seemed to be twitching slightly at the corners as she spoke. "A Love-Match says *I choose this one and none other, and no other may choose me.*"

Dyan settled back into her saddle, facing forward again. "All those other possibilities are the price you pay for love," she said, understanding.

"The price I pay for being Called to be a Healer is that I won't be riding the canyons of the Wahai with bola in hand, looking for runaways," Wayland said. "Though that sounds like it's really a price paid by the Outrider Corps."

"All the other Callings are paying a great price for your gift to Healing," Dyan joked, and Wayland laughed. His whole body shook when he did so, which set the others to laughing, too, and spooked his horse. It broke into a jittery canter and rattled ahead several lengths before he could rein it in.

Dyan thought about the Magister's words while Wayland struggled, and when the Creche-Leavers had regained their formation, she shared her thoughts. "But that means that we've been paying prices all along," she concluded. "Only instead of prices of our own decisions, we've been paying the prices of the decisions of other people ... of the Magisters, I guess. Of the Council."

She looked back again and was pleased to see the Magister smiling. "That's right, Dyan," she said. "Your Lot Letter obviously marked you for the right calling."

"Yes," Cheela drawled, running fingers through her hair. "We're all pleased that Dyan gets to stay with the milkmouths."

"But I would have said that until now you have been paying the prices of the System's decisions," Zarah added. "Some things simply *are* the way they *must be*, with no question of fairness or how it might have been."

"Is that the second attribute of choices?" Deek asked. "That doesn't sound quite right."

"People," Zarah said, "are not as predictable or as regular as machines."

"They're not as dependable, either," Deek added.

"I'm glad to see your Lot Letter also reached the right recipient." Zarah laughed, a rare sound, and it made Dyan smile. "The second attribute of all your choices—beginning tomorrow—is that every choice you make will affect your relationship to Buza System."

Dyan felt a shiver down deep inside her, like the string of a musical instrument connecting her neck and her tailbone had just been plucked.

"For instance," Cheela yawned, "you could run away. And then the System would send Outriders to hunt you down." She patted the whip on her belt affectionately.

"You mean like the criminals this morning," Dyan said.

"Yes."

They rode in silence for a minute. This was the Magister's way, Dyan knew, of giving her Crechelings—her Creche-Leavers, now—time to consider and absorb a new point.

"The Hanging is an extreme case," the Magister picked up where she had left off, "as are outlaws captured by Outriders."

"Killed," Cheela said.

"Captured or killed," Shad added.

"But every single choice you make strengthens the System or it weakens it," Zarah continued. "Or it strengthens one part of the System at the expense of another."

"So Wayland devotes Healing resources to one Urbane at the expense of another," Deek said by way of example.

"You must consider the System and your relationship to it with every action you take," the Magister said, which sounded like agreement. "And with every action you take, the System will be considering you."

"The System's not a person," Deek added quickly. "It's just a collection of interacting things. Institutions, individuals, devices."

"Is it so obvious to you," the Magister asked in return, her voice quiet and subdued, "that there is a difference?"

"Of course you have to consider the System," Wayland said. "If you commit crimes against it, you get killed."

Magister Zarah was quiet again for a while. "The System," she said slowly, "kills to protect itself, and all the people who are its charges. Sometimes it has to kill criminals. Sometimes it has to kill the wicked, or the weak."

"What do you mean, *sometimes*?" Cheela grinned like she was imagining herself as a Hangman, and enjoying it.

"Sometimes the System has to kill good people," Dyan said, reaching the logical conclusion of Zarah's line of thought. "And the strong."

They rode in silence for a long time after that. Off to their right, they passed occasional crumbling walls of brick, and long stretches of shattered grayish pavement.

Buza System lay on the north side of the broad Treasure Valley, along a river and pressed against the lowest hills of the Jawtooth Mountains. To its south the land rose steadily, passing through a broad gate between a westward-jutting ridge of the Jawtooths and the easternmost of the Wahai Mountains. Beyond that gate lay a sea of grass and sage that was bright green for approximately one month of each spring, and otherwise lay yellow and gray under a hot sun, fit only for jackrabbits, coyotes and antelopes.

Out in this wilderness lay Ratsnay Station, the Creche-Leavers' destination. Ratsnay Station wasn't beyond the wilderness—as far as Dyan knew, *nothing* lay *beyond* the wilderness, and the entire world lay blighted, burnt and devastated—and there was no way to get through it that didn't involve a hard ride. Outriders, Cheela repeatedly informed the others, made this ride in a single, casual day.

As the sun fell below the jagged shoulders of the Wahai, casting golden-red shadows through the dry grass, Magister Zarah called for a halt. "There's a way station on that knob of earth," she told them, indicating the bulbous end of a long ridge that rose above a loop of track a mile long.

"I'll check it out," Cheela volunteered. She straightened her back and raised her heels to race off, but Dyan noticed that she still looked at the Magister, as if for permission.

Zarah nodded. "Go with her," she said, nodding to Shad.

Shad shrugged at Dyan and she smiled back, but he didn't look terribly bothered.

"How *did* you do it?" Dyan whispered to Wayland as the Outriders-designate rode ahead.

"Do what?" His eyes sparkled.

"Get into the girls' dormitories while we were sleeping."

Deek snorted.

"I didn't," Wayland admitted.

He looked so sincere Dyan almost believed him. "Then who did?" she asked.

"I went in the night before, during dinner."

Dyan considered. "That can't be right. The rooms would have smelled like oat porridge all night."

Deek grinned. "Not if you sealed the porridge in plastic bags that would slowly dissolve through the night."

Dyan laughed out loud. "You imp! Where did you get dissolving plastic bags?"

Deek laughed too, and almost fell off his horse. "If only you were a Mechanical, I could tell you!"

The three of them rode slowly up a gravelly trail that wound around the hill to its top, pulling ahead of Magister Zarah as their chuckles dissolved into comfortable silence. They arrived long after Cheela and Shad, who had split up and climbed the slope at different points, converging on the top of the low peak at the same moment. The crown of the rise held a chest-high log stockade, just like every other way station of Buza System Dyan had ever seen, and she expected, cresting the knob, to see Shad and Cheela tethering their horses and preparing a fire.

Instead, when she pushed up onto the gold-grassy space beside the stockade, she saw Shad and Cheela standing their horses shoulder to shoulder, gazing across the plains at the setting sun.

Dyan felt profoundly unsettled. Distracted, she slackened her grip on her horse's reins, and the animal skittered a few feet to one side. "Vixen," she muttered.

"*Ahem*," Wayland cleared his throat from behind Dyan. "I think we are *still* not allowed Love-Matches. And if we are, fellow Crechelings, I should tell you that I've had my eyes on Shad for some time."

Deek gained the summit, followed a few moments later by Magister Zarah.

"What about it, Magister?" Wayland asked. "Do Cheela and Shad get a Love-Match as a reward for their scouting work?"

"As a reward for their scouting work," Zarah said, her eyes shadowed pits in the twilight, "Cheela and Shad get to sleep sheltered from the wind. As, hopefully, do I."

The word on the Magister's lips made Dyan realize that she was right; at this height, the wind cut across the hilltop cruelly. With the sun down, the desert would soon be cold. She shivered and pulled her riding coat closed across her chest.

"Actually," Cheela said, "as an Outrider, I would suggest—"

"Outrider-designate." Zarah was calm, but her voice held authority.

Cheela looked down, abashed. "Outrider-designate," she agreed. "As an Outrider-designate, I would like to suggest that we camp further along the ridge."

"Oh?" Zarah arched an eyebrow at Dyan's Crechemate.

"We should light a fire in the stockade," Cheela continued, "and camp without one ourselves. That way, if any outlaws or renegades or runaways approach us in the night, they'll be drawn to the fire and not our real position."

"Should we be worried about outlaws, renegades, and runaways so close to Buza Station?" the Magister challenged her.

"We should beware of outlaws, renegades, and runaways everywhere, Magister," Cheela said. She had a childish, submissive, respectful expression on her face that made Dyan irrationally, for just a moment, think how satisfying it would be to kick the other girl's teeth in. "Being close to Buza System, or even in the Treasure Valley, is no guarantee of safety."

Zarah nodded. "I'm pleased to see you've paid attention to at least some of your lessons," she said. "Lead on."

Cheela led the way eagerly, and Shad turned his horse to follow her.

Dyan snapped her reins to urge her own mount forward, and when she thought she was out of earshot of the others she leaned in close to him and whispered. "You told her to say that. You're the one with the wilderness skills. All she's good at is killing things."

Shad shrugged. "She wants to impress the Magister so much." He didn't look sorry in the slightest.

"*You* could impress Magister Zarah instead," she suggested.

"Does it matter?" he asked, and spurred his horse onward.

"I thought ..." Dyan floundered.

She couldn't find the words, but of course it mattered. It mattered a lot. Yes, Shad was leaving the Creche, and Magister Zarah would no longer be his Magister. Still, she was *a Magister*, and he should want her good opinion.

Also, Dyan thought bitterly, why Cheela? If he wanted to help someone impress the Magister, why not her? Why not help *Dyan* look good? Had she been mistaken about Shad and his feelings for her?

She wanted to shout at him, but she knew it would be the act of a child, and she didn't want to be a child anymore. So instead she sat on her horse and watched his back as he rode up the ridge after Cheela, looking for a campsite that would be out of the wind and in sight of the hilltop stockade.

CHAPTER THREE

They are all celebrating the harvest," Magister Zarah said.

The party of Creche-Leavers rode down a long crackling slope of autumnal grass towards a stockaded settlement that must be Ratsnay Station. It squatted, bristling with the sharpened tips of pine logs, on the dam-end of a reservoir that shimmered silver in the late afternoon sun. All around the water, smoke began to trickle upward from large piles of wood.

Dyan hadn't said a word to Shad the night before, and only such words as were necessary during the day's ride that had brought them here. She felt saddlesore from the ride, cheated by Shad's sudden willingness to care so much about Cheela, and terrified by a mounting sense that to be an adult was to be very, very lonely. The other settlements they'd passed, all tiny, distant from the road and huddling behind protective walls, had only added to the sensation. The ruins dotting the wilderness made her feel even worse.

"Many of them are also celebrating the Selection."

"What is that, like picking the best of the crop?" Deek wanted to know. So did Dyan. They'd all known they were to participate in the Selection after the Hanging, but no one had ever explained what the Selection was.

"Yes," the Magister said, "if you mean the crop of new adults."

"It must be like the Creche-Leaving, then," Dyan intuited, happy for anything to clutch at that wasn't her own feelings.

"Much like it," Zarah agreed.

"Is there a Hanging?" Cheela asked.

"You'll see." The Magister spurred her horse forward, moving ahead of the Creche-Leavers for the first time. "You'll do more than see."

Two men rose from the grass. They were quick; one moment they hadn't been there, and the next, they were, springing up off their bellies. Dyan shrank back, startled at the suddenness of their approach and at their appearance. They wore leather shirts, stitched with row upon row of short animal bones, to make a sort of breastplate. Similar thick pads of leather covered the front of their legs and their arms, and their faces were painted with streaks of brown and ochre. Even without the paint and the leather, the men were deeply browned by the sun, much deeper than the people Dyan was used to seeing in the System.

They pointed long spears at the Magister, who brought her horse to a halt.

"Name yourself!" the taller man hissed through yellowed teeth.

"That *armor* wouldn't even slow down a bola," Cheela sneered.

"True," Shad said, "but it might help against a rock or a knife."

"What kind of idiot would attack them with a rock?"

"Or an animal's claws," Shad continued. "I don't think they're trying to protect themselves against us. I think they're armored against robbers and runaways. Remember, they aren't allowed bows, and they don't have whips or bolas. They make do with what they can get."

Dyan tried to imagine that Shad was sticking up for her against Cheela, but failed, and felt worse for having tried.

Magister Zarah held up her medallion with casual, deliberate speed. "We are here for the Selection," she said.

The men looked the Creche-Leavers up and down, grunted, and then stepped aside. "Magister," one of them said, tucking his chin to his chest in a little bow.

Zarah led them towards the water, and the people milling about the bonfires. As they drew closer, Dyan saw food and drink in abundance, makeshift tables created by laying boards on trestles, and musicians sitting on sawn logs and putting instruments in their laps. She saw dogs in abundance, playing among the celebrating people, and cats holding themselves aloof on rooftops and in the centers of tables.

A young man stood near the stockade gate wearing a black Magister's cloak.

"Children," Magister Zarah said. "Join the festivities. Stay close to the fires, and be careful what you drink—the Landsmen favor intoxicating beverages."

"Ew." Deek made a sour face.

"They work hard," Zarah said, "and live lives to be pitied. Beer is a small mercy."

"Yes, Magister," Dyan said along with the others, bobbing her head and turning to go.

"Dyan," Zarah said, and trapped Dyan's eyes with her own steely gaze. "Come with me."

Dyan followed Zarah and the other Magister inside the walls of Ratsnay Station. She kept a respectful silence, but the new Magister noticed her and introduced himself.

"Magister Stanton," he said. He was taller than Shad and thinner than Deek and he walked stooped over, as if he was inspecting the ground at every step over the five-armed medallion bouncing off his narrow chest. His face was very, very serious.

"Crecheling Dyan," she returned.

"Magister-designate Dyan," he contradicted her.

Her heart skipped a beat. "How do you know?" she asked. "Do you ... does everyone know?"

He laughed, the serious lines exploding into a tangle of mirth. "Nothing so terrifying as all that, Magister-designate. But my colleague has invited you into the conversation with us, which she would not do unless you were Magister-designate." He squinted at her fiercely, like an owl examining a mouse in its burrow. "Or perhaps a Cogitant-designate, though that would be a rare thing indeed."

"Magister," she squeaked, and then Magister Stanton brushed aside a hanging leather flap and led Zarah and Dyan inside a long one-story building.

It must be the schoolhouse. Crude benches and simple writing tables dominated the space in rows, and a great writing slate hung from the front wall, chalked with columns of numbers and model sentences. At the back of the room stood a carved wooden statue of a robed woman, her hands clasped together in front of her.

"Pay attention," Zarah told her. "You may be wiping snot from Crechelings' noses next week, it's true. On the other hand, you may be in a settlement like this one, wiping snot from the noses of Landsmen children."

From a table at the front of the room, Stanton picked up a small stack of cards and handed them to Zarah.

She leafed through them, scrutinizing each closely but not showing them to Dyan. "It is impressive," she murmured, "that their gene pool continues to throw up such intelligent specimens, even continuously thinned as it is."

"What?" Magister Stanton looked slightly offended, or maybe shocked.

Zarah smiled thinly at him and tucked the cards away somewhere under her cloak. "I do not express doubt, Magister Stanton," she said. "Only wonder. Is there anything I should worry about?"

Stanton frowned and recovered. "The boy Jak," he said.

"Troublemaker?"

Stanton shook his head. "Smart. That family regularly produces smart children. His older sister was Selected."

"You think he knows?"

"I think he suspects."

Dyan did not follow the conversation at all, other than to understand that someone named *Jak* must be watched carefully.

"Very well. Come out, and show me the parents. Dyan, stay close to me." Zarah inclined her head slightly to her fellow-Magister and left.

Evening's shadow fell over the settlement and the festivities began in earnest. When Dyan reached the reservoir shore again, in Zarah's wake, the air rang with the music of stringed instruments and thumped to the sound of sticks banged together or against hide drums. She passed Wayland and Deek at a table and saw the Healer-designate pressing a wooden cup into Deek's hand.

"Try this one," he said, grinning broadly.

Shad stood in a circle of Landsmen youth. The contrast between his fine coat and hat and their woolen cloaks and tunics was as stark as the difference between his lightly tanned skin and their nut-brown hides, but he grinned and cracked jokes. A pair of Landsmen girls edged closer to him in the group, smiling eagerly, until Cheela pounced on them, scattering them with bared teeth and, no doubt, some cutting comment that Dyan couldn't hear.

Dyan tried to ignore her Crechemates and focus on the Magister. Stanton introduced Zarah to three couples, one old woman, and a single burly man, each the parent or parents of one of the Landsmen youth who had been "Selected." Dyan didn't understand, but she knew that this was part of her own Calling, whether she was to follow in Zarah's footsteps or in Stanton's, so she tried to pay close attention. Each time, Zarah introduced herself as a Magister from Buza System. Their child, she said again and again, had been Selected. It was an honor, they should be proud. Also, since they wouldn't see their child again after tomorrow, they should be certain to say appropriate farewells tonight.

As Magister Zarah turned away from the old woman, a stray wash of firelight showed Dyan tears sliding down her cheek.

The tears shocked her, but then the entire process was astonishing to Dyan. She knew as a matter of science that she had parents, two adult human who contributed separate haploid gametes to create her in her initial zygotic state, whether or not the two adults ever met. She had no idea if they had, or who they were. How could she? Dyan's entire life to this moment had been the Creche and the Magisters, lessons about everything, and preparation for a Calling in the System.

A clapperless bell rung with a hard stick, insistent in its *ding-ding-ding-ding-ding!* silenced the musicians and made the revelers rotate and face in the same direction. Dyan realized that the bell had been rung almost in her ear, and when the Landsmen turned to look they were looking at her.

Along with the two Magisters and three old Landsmen, two women and a man.

"Children," Magister Zarah called, and Dyan's four Creche-mates joined them, arraying themselves to stand in a line with Dyan behind their Magister. Deek wobbled a bit when he walked, and he smelled sour, like vinegar.

"This is Magister Zarah!" bellowed one of the Landsmen elders, a paunchy, bearded man. "She's come from the System!"

29

An electric murmur ran through the crowd, mingling with the crackling sound of the bonfires.

"She has come for the Selection!" added the woman elder.

"Hear her!" chimed in their third colleague, a carrot-nosed man.

Zarah stepped forward, raising both hands over her head. In one, Dyan saw she held her glittering medallion of authority. In the other, she held the sheaf of cards Magister Stanton had given her.

"People of Ratsnay Station!" she called. Her voice rang against the wooden walls of the stockade and snapped back at them, creating a faint echo. "Every year you harvest your crops. You lay away what is good of your grain to bake your bread through the winter, spring and summer to come."

"Aye," the crowd murmured together. Dyan realized that it was an expected answer, part of the script. She tried to listen closer to the words, to memorize them. She might be reciting them herself, someday soon.

"And every year, you take the best of your crop and bake it into cakes and brew it into ale and celebrate. You celebrate what is good in your lives and the blessings of the System. You also celebrate against what is hard. You celebrate to help you bear up under your yoke."

"Aye!"

Many of the men followed each cry of *aye!* with a swig from a cup, pot, or bottle in their hands.

"Also, every year you raise another crop of young women and men."

An expectant hush fell over the crowd.

"And every year, the System harvests that crop. What is good among the crop is laid away at Ratsnay Station, to work, love, bear children, and live through winter, spring, and summer. What is best among the crop, the System harvests."

"Five!" wailed the bearded elder. "Five fingers on the System's hand!"

"Five is the number of death!" shrieked the old woman.

"Five is the number of life!" added carrot-nose.

"Aye!" the crowd shouted.

Dyan trembled, thinking of the Gallows Tree.

"I hold in my hand judgment!" Magister Zarah called. "Your youth have been winnowed and tried, and I hold in my hand the names of the five who are consecrated to the System. These names are not secret, they are known to you. Their fate is not secret, but it is sacred. The System needs new blood. The best among your children go to join the System."

"Aye!"

Dyan wondered if this was the source of Buza System's gardeners and other menials. Pieces seemed to be fitting together, and the thought that she was a Magister-designate made her heart beat faster. It was a little like being a Cogitant, whether you brought up Crechelings to know and love their roles, or brought in the new blood of the best and brightest Landsmen. She felt proud. A Magister was a leader, had an important part.

"I have come with five, and we will take five with us!" Zarah recited. "Mechanical-designate Deek, step forward!" Deek did, stumbling a bit, but staying upright. A few deep voices in the crowd chuckled. "Hamish, son of Goodman Soren and Goody Barrab, step forward!"

A grinning boy who could have been one of the Creche-Leavers himself but for his rough wool clothing kissed his mother good-bye and pushed forward. Dyan felt a twinge of something in her heart at the sight of the kiss, and ignored it.

"Deek," Zarah said, her voice softer now but still loud enough to be heard by everyone. "Look closely at this boy. Your task is to deliver him to Buza System, as the System requires. Will you undertake this task?"

Deek's eyes wandered and he blinked, but he managed to force out the one syllable required of him, "Yes."

"Healer-designate Wayland!" Magister Zarah called.

Wayland stepped forward, was matched with a young woman with missing teeth. Then Zarah matched Shad with a girl whose head had frizzy white hair like the spores of a dandelion, and Cheela with a boy with jug-handle ears and an expression on his face that might have been sullen.

"Magister-designate Dyan!" Zarah finally announced, and Dyan stepped forward.

"Jak, son of Rosyn, step forward!"

Jak, the boy about whom Magister Stanton had been worried, slunk slowly out of the crowd. He had big hands and a big head, Dyan thought, and he walked with his knees and feet forward and his chest sunken in, like he was shrinking from something. He came forward until he and Dyan stood face to face. The rest of the Landsmen youth, all standing in a row, stood at attention. Jak seemed to hang back a hair, and kept his hands in his pockets.

"Dyan," Zarah said. Dyan thought her voice sounded tender. "Look closely at this boy. Your task is to deliver him to Buza System, as the System requires. Will you undertake this task?"

"With all my heart," Dyan said.

Jak flinched.

Magister Zarah rested on a hand on her shoulder. "Not with all your heart, child. You do not need your heart to carry you through your obligations. The System does not need you to love it, and it does not need you to love your duties. It only needs you to carry them out."

"Yes, Magister." Dyan's face burned with shame, though Zarah's eyes looked, if anything, kindly.

"Will you do as the System requires?" the Magister asked again.

"Yes, Magister," Dyan said.

Zarah nodded. She turned back to the crowd and spoke, raising her voice again. "The Selection is complete!" she announced. "Tomorrow is the Harvest, when these five sheaves will be gathered in to the System! Tonight, now, is the time to celebrate!"

"Aye!"

More beer was swallowed, and the musicians began again, in earnest.

Chapter Four

 young woman chased a small child through the tall grass in the darkness. "Get back here right now, unless you want Guns to get you!"

The child shrieked and kept running.

"So what's it like in the System?" Jak asked.

He stood close to Dyan at the edge of the bonfires' light, above the Station and looking down at it. Dyan leaned against the thick, dried-out stump of a tree, shorn of limbs and needles and still taller than she was. Jak held pebbles in his hand, hefting them for weight, and as he asked the question, he hurled one high into the air, over the head of revelers, and silently into the waters of the reservoir.

"Haven't you been?"

Jak shook his head. "Not allowed," he said. "System men come out here and collect harvest tribute. Other than that, we see Magisters and Outriders. No one else." He whipped his arm casually and hurled another rock down into the water. "If I'd wanted to, I guess I could have ridden over and looked at it from the outside, but Holy Mother, that doesn't seem worth the trouble."

Dyan searched for words. "Well," she essayed, "Buza System is beautiful." She tried to think of what would be distinctive to this Landsman boy, how she could prepare him for his first sight. "There are parks. Trees everywhere, because of the river. The buildings are all white stone."

"Sure," Jak agreed slowly. "I've climbed the Jawtooths and looked down into it. That isn't what I mean."

Dyan tried to guess what he was thinking, and failed. "What do you mean?" she asked.

Jak turned suddenly and snapped his elbow again. A stone whizzed from his hand and thunked hard against something in the grass, something that suddenly rustled, stood up, and turned out to be a young man in leather-and-bone breastplate.

"Ouch," he grumbled, rubbing his forehead.

"If you're on guard duty, Eirig, you're doing a lousy job of it." Jak raised his arm as if to throw another stone. "Maybe I should report you."

Eirig raised his arms defensively. "What if I'm not?"

"Then you're missing the best party of the year."

"Does that bother you?"

"No," Jak admitted, and threw the stone in his hand. He nailed the other boy right in the center of his bone-stitched protection with a blow so hard it actually knocked him back a step. "But eavesdropping on my private conversation *does*."

"Okay, okay!" Eirig staggered away and down the hill, raising his hands in surrender. "I'm leaving!"

"Don't let your uncle drink all the beer!" Jak called after him. "I want to get hammered later!"

"I don't think there's any beer in the System," Dyan said. "Or wine or whisky. Healers dispense narcotics and other medicines when you need them."

"No beer?" Jak snorted. "If they'd told me that, I'd have tried even harder to bomb the tests."

That caught Dyan's ears. "You *tried* to do poorly?"

"Yeah," Jak said. "So what else? Are people in the System … nice?"

"They'll be kind to you," she said quickly. "They've always been kind to me. They'll make you feel right at home."

"You know, my sister was Selected a few years ago," Jak said. He stood slightly downhill of Dyan and looked into her face, so his was entirely in shadow and the expression on it was unreadable.

"I knew that, actually."

Jak was quiet for a moment. "So you know Aleen?" Dyan still couldn't see his face, but she thought he sounded surprised.

"No, I ..." Dyan cursed herself silently. She was trying too hard to act like a Magister, like someone important and in the know, and had given him the wrong impression. "No, I don't really know anybody."

"I heard you don't have families in the System."

"That's true. The Council decided years and years ago that families were unnecessary, and reorganized the System to do without them."

"So who ... who raised you?"

"The Magisters. I've grown up in the Creche, changing Creche-mates every two years. That's why I don't know anybody. Unless they're a fellow-Crecheling or a Magister. Although as of ... well, yesterday, I think, I'm not a Crecheling anymore."

Jak shook his head. "I think if I'd been raised by Magister Stanton, I'd have killed him or myself long ago."

Dyan was shocked. "You don't mean that."

"You're right," Jak agreed, "I don't. What I mean is I would have punched him in the face and left the Creche."

"You can't leave the Creche," Dyan said. "It isn't done."

Crunching footsteps in the grass warned them of someone's approach, and they both turned to look.

"Milt," Jak said, nodding to the jug-eared boy who'd been Selected along with him. "I didn't know making friends was a talent of yours."

"It isn't," Milt agreed. His voice was sour and terse. "But she promised to show me something amazing."

Jak barked a short laugh. "I bet she did."

"Cheela," Dyan said. She was happy to see her Crechemate with the Landsman, because it meant that other girl wasn't with Shad. But then, neither was she.

"Step away from the tree, Dyan," Cheela said. She stood squarely downhill from Dyan, her feet planted apart and under her shoulders, her long coat pulled back behind her, her fingers flexing above her belt. "You too, Jaik."

"Jak," he said.

"You've been watching too many funvids about Outriders," Dyan told her Crechemate. "You don't need to call me out, whatever problem you think you have with me."

Cheela was quiet for a moment, which was ominous, given that her back was to the fires and her face was entirely in shadow. Then she hiccupped. "I'm not calling you out," she replied. "I'm calling out the *tree*."

Dyan scrambled out of the way. Jak was a little slow to move, and wore a puzzled look on his face, so she grabbed his wrist and pulled him with her.

"You've been drinking!" she accused Cheela.

Cheela ignored her. The dark girl in the Outrider get-up stared down the tree stump fiercely. "You've escaped for the last time, you dirty renegade," she growled.

"Duck," Dyan whispered.

"What's she going to do?"

"Just in case." She pulled Jak with her, down into a crouch.

"Draw!" Cheela shouted. The big-eared boy Milt fell back in surprise, she grabbed a bola off her hip, instantly elongating its monofilament cord with the slightest pressure from her fingers as she simultaneously whipped the weight-end of the bola around once, releasing it in the direction of the tree—

and the bola disappeared into the shadow of the grass, hitting the hillside with a soft *thump*.

"Got you, you dirty dog," Cheela muttered. She pressed a button in the bola's holster and the bola flashed red in the darkness so she could find it. She passed to the uphill side of the tall stump and bent to pick up her weapon.

"So … you missed," Milt sneered. "Gee, that *was* amazing."

Cheela said nothing. Standing uphill of the tree, she reached out one arm, leaned against the trunk, and pushed it over. The log, sliced in two with an utterly clean precision typical of monofilament instruments but otherwise impossible, tipped forward—

whumph!

And slammed to the ground right beside Milt.

"Holy Mother!" Milt snapped. "You almost took my toes off!"

Cheela looked at her fingernails with exaggerated indifference. "You want to see something even more amazing?" she suggested. "Find me a big *rock*."

Dyan stood. She felt Cheela had crossed some sort of line, but she wasn't sure what it was. In her heart, she suspected she might have crossed the same line. As she groped for words to express her doubts, she heard a stern voice in the darkness.

"Children. Time to retire."

She turned and saw a caped silhouette standing on the hillside beside her, yellow firelight splashing against the Magister's black cloak of office. Zarah's hood was thrown back, and in the fire's shadows her face looked like it would suit a bird of prey.

"I don't think I'm one of your children," Jak shot back at the Magister. "And I think I'd still like to have a beer or two."

"You are not," Zarah agreed. "And you may."

Jak took Dyan's hand and squeezed it once. "Thanks for the tree," he said. "I guess I owe you one."

Dyan nodded, feeling under Magister Zarah's stare that more would be inappropriate. Jak and Milt turned and sauntered down the hill together towards the bonfires and the beer, and Zarah led Cheela and Dyan away from the stockade, back up the hill.

"Camping away from the fire again?" Cheela grinned as she asked the question, like it was a personal victory for her.

Dyan didn't care. She was astonished and fascinated by the events of the day. She had had no idea, leaving Buza System, that she would be immediately plunged into her Calling this way, and she was full of questions. Why were the others along? she wondered. They weren't Magisters. Was there some portion of this Selection process that they needed to see? Why hadn't they all been told about this part of their education sooner?

The question she decided to ask was about Jak. "Will the other Creche-Leavers ... I mean, the Landsmen who have been Selected ... will they receive a Calling? Are you carrying their Lot Letters? What will they do when we bring them back to the System?" She imagined Jak finding his sister Aleen, and how sweet the reunion might be. She wondered what it would be like to have a sister of her own.

"Child," the Magister said, not looking back, "we aren't going to bring them back to the System."

Dyan had nothing to say. Her mind reeled, and she focused on putting one foot in front of the other and following Magister Zarah up the slope.

Wayland, Deek, and Shad waited at the top, nearly a quarter mile away, under a steep butte wall. All six horses were neatly picketed within a short box canyon, and someone—almost certainly Shad— had already laid out bedrolls neatly, with packs piled against stiff brush to break the wind.

"Children," Magister Zarah announced, turning at the edge of the little camp to gather them all under her gaze. The bonfires were too far away to provide any real illumination here, but light from the moon and stars above cast a cold, pallid glow down over her features. Her eyes looked like bottomless wells of darkness for just a moment, and then she pulled her hood up over her head. "There is death in the world."

Wayland opened his mouth to say something, but stopped. No wonder, Dyan thought; the Magister's tone of voice made it clear that she did not invite questions at this moment. She *looked* like Death, perched at the top of the small campsite, shrouded in black from head to toe.

"There is no choice that is free of death," she continued. "Death is inevitable, death is all around you. Do you see it?"

"Yes," Dyan's Crechemates answered, but something in Magister Zarah's face made Dyan answer slightly differently.

"Aye," she said.

Zarah waited.

"Aye," added Deek, and then the others followed his and Dyan's lead, "aye."

"If you would guard life, you must wield death." The Magister's words seemed to echo out of a bottomless pit. "The hunter kills prey to feed her people. The farmer kills weeds and vermin to protect her crop. The shepherd kills the wolf to save the flock. Do you see it, my children?"

"Aye."

And Dyan *did* see it. And suddenly, horribly, she knew what was coming next.

"So the System wields death, to protect the life of the System. Guardsmen repulse attacks with violent force. Outriders track down renegades and bandits and bring them to justice. Criminals are hung. The System does not punish, my children. The System kills whom it must, to protect life. Do you see it?"

"Aye."

The Magister paused. Poised in her cloak against the stars, she looked like a vast darkness, like a blotting out of the light.

"You have seen the Hanging," the Magister said. "The System killed the worst of its own, in the name of life. You have seen the Selection. The System chose the brightest children of the Landsmen of Ratsnay Station. It has done this, too, in the name of life. Tomorrow, you will see a third thing done for life's sake.

"You will not only *see* it, my children, you will *do* it. Each of you has already been assigned to one of the young Landsmen. In the name of life, and at the order of the System, each of you will kill his ... or her ... Landsman. You will do this not because the young Landsmen are bad, not because they are criminal, but because the System requires it. Buza System requires it of you and it also requires it of them. Do you see it?"

"Aye."

"Aye," Dyan whispered, last. She forced herself to keep looking up at the Magister, now a terrifying shadow, an empty void into which the entire world around her seemed to be pouring at a lightning pace. She looked at Zarah, but she kept seeing Jak. She didn't care about Jak, Jak was nothing, but she didn't want to kill him. He didn't deserve to die, and she didn't want to be a murderer.

She saw the Hangman in her mind's eye too, burly and merciless, and she heard the condemned man's tune. She knew it, she was certain of it, though she still couldn't place her finger on what it was.

An elbow in her ribs snapped her out of her train of thought.

"Dyan!" Shad hissed.

She realized that she'd actually been humming the tune. "I'm sorry," she mumbled, mortified. She looked up at Magister Zarah, hoping to see a forgiving smile, or, even better, to hear a retraction. *It isn't true,* she wanted to hear, *you were being tested, but there's no need to go through with it. Tomorrow we'll ride back to Buza System with Jak and the others, and you can help him find his sister.*

She heard none of that, and she saw only the black silhouette of the Magister in her cloak.

And she realized that Jak's sister Aleen was dead.

"This is the Cull," the Magister intoned. "Tomorrow you will be Blooded. Tomorrow you will no longer be my children, but Urbanes, adults, fully-grown and Called into the System. "Do you see it, my children?"

Dyan couldn't hear the others respond. The world spun around her and her heart felt hard and cold, like a fist punched into the center of her chest.

"Aye," she whispered.

CHAPTER FIVE

The entire population of Ratsnay Station turned out to send off its best and brightest children—unknowingly—to their doom. Dyan couldn't look at their faces, and hoped that they took her staring at their feet for a sign of the lingering effects of alcohol. More than a few of the Landsmen looked groggy and sick from the previous night's beer-fest, including the Selected youth.

The Landsmen whistled and stomped their feet and cheered as the Magister rode away with ten children in tow, the Station's five brightest youth riding its five best horses. Conversation was muted by headaches, the early morning hour, and, at least in Dyan's case, by a heavy weight on her mind.

She had to kill Jak.

And he kept staring at her.

"What is it?" she asked him, trying to force a smile. "What's wrong?"

He shrugged but didn't look away. "I'm just wondering how Aleen must have felt when she rode away on this very same road. I think it was even the same Magister … what's her name?"

"Magister Zarah."

"Zarah," Jak chewed on the name. "That sounds right. I think it was your Magister Zarah who led her away."

"Are you looking forward to meeting her?" The words were charcoal in Dyan's mouth.

"I'm looking forward to this whole thing very, very much," Jak agreed.

Zarah led them by a different road, a thin trail that led west rather than north.

"This isn't the road to the System," Jak observed. Finally, he looked away from Dyan, at the cottonwoods and tall, dry grasses banking the road. "You're sure your Magister Zarah isn't taking us to join some pack of Wahai renegades?"

Dyan's mouth felt very dry. "The Magister is a teacher. Maybe she has something to show us."

"That must be it."

At midday they ate, parched corn and dried beef and water from a spring that bubbled from a seep above the trail and slid down over red rocks into the Snaik. Magister Zarah said little, and though conversation picked up among the Landsmen youth and the Creche-Leavers, it never became better than sporadic. Dyan felt the dark secret of the Cull divide the two groups of youth like a chasm.

As the shadows lengthened into evening, Magister Zarah turned the party off the trail across a great sheet of slickrock. Once they'd dropped over a swell in the stone and gotten out of sight of the trail, she stopped and tied her horse to a stunted juniper.

"Follow me," she said tersely, and struck out across the sea of sand and stone, her black cloak making her look like the shadow of some great bird of prey passing overhead. Dyan tethered her horse to the same tree and followed. She didn't want to look at Jak, and definitely didn't want to be close to him, but he pressed close to her, walking at her shoulder.

The sky was an empty blue, slowly darkening from a pale chalky shade into a richer azure that brought out the presence of the moon. The sudden appearance of a crisp border to the slickrock on Dyan's right, where the stone fell away sharply into a canyon, brought home to her the imminence of the moment of terrible truth.

Jak was unarmed, the Landsmen all were. It wasn't fair. It wasn't execution, it was murder.

Fairness had nothing to do with it. Magister Zarah had explained this all the previous night. This wasn't punishment, it was weeding the garden. It was the System's regulation of life and death within its human self.

The rock on Dyan's other side fell away, and she realized that they were climbing out along the edge of a promontory. Below them must be the Snaik River, and as she made the connection, she thought she could smell the water and the plant life it sustained.

The Magister reached the end of the promontory and turned. She stood and raised her arms to the sky, facing all the youth. "Children," she said—

Thump! Cheela hit the ground.

Dyan started to laugh, despite the obvious solemnity of the moment, but the sound caught in her throat. The jug-eared boy, the one matched with Cheela, stood over her with one arm raised above his head.

In his hand, he held one of Cheela's bolas.

"We know!" he shouted.

Jak slammed his shoulder into Dyan's side, knocking her staggering sideways. As she went, she felt his hand grab at her belt, and come away with her monofilament whip. She managed to regain her footing and not fall, but felt a vertiginous sucking in the pit of her stomach.

The other Creche-Leavers struggled briefly with their counterparts, then pulled away, fists up.

The world was still for a long moment.

"Who knows?" Magister Zarah asked. "What do you know?"

"*We* know!"

Dyan spun around at the sound of the new voice behind her, and saw Eirig, the boy who had been sneaking around in the grass the previous night. He was mounted and he led a second horse by its reins. He held a bundle of spears in his arms across the saddle, five of them, tied with a leather thong. He wore a coil of rope around his chest, shoulder to hip.

"I heard you last night," Eirig said. "I'm not going to let you kill my friends."

"What do you plan to do?" Magister Zarah was surprisingly calm.

Dyan looked Jak up and down. He held her whip in his hand, but obviously didn't know how to use it. His finger was nowhere near the button that would release the monofilament and turn the device from an inert club into an unstoppable slicing instrument of death. Before he could figure the weapon out, she was confident she could cut him down with a bola.

Which she didn't really want to do.

Shad punched his counterpart, the girl with the white hair, in the jaw. It was a sudden attack, snake-like and quick, and she fell to the stone and lay still.

Jug Ears pointed a finger at the Magister. "One more move, *Outrider-designate*," he sneered, "and I cut your precious nursery master in half."

Cheela climbed to her feet, rubbing her jaw and glaring.

"Don't do that," Zarah said. "You'll only hurt yourself."

Jug Ears laughed. "Are you going to tell on me?" he asked. "Are the Guards going to come riding down from Buza System and catch me? You won't leave here alive, and if by some miracle of the Holy Mother you do, by the time you've told anyone in Buza, all of Ratsnay Station will know the truth."

"That would be a grave mistake." Zarah looked completely calm. Dyan's heart raced like a galloping horse.

"Of course it would!" Jak snapped. He still focused on Dyan, whip raised, and she felt like he was yelling at her. "Then the System would lose its yearly tribute of blood, and the Station would stop losing all its natural leaders."

"Anyone you tell," Zarah explained quietly, "you mark for death."

"You do this at every settlement?" Jak demanded.

"The System does."

"And all the Systems do this?" Jug Ears pressed.

Dyan snorted. "There are no other Systems."

"We'll rise up!" Jak shouted. He shook the whip in his fist as he said it, and Dyan worried he'd accidentally activate the device.

"You'll die," the Magister said. "You'll all die. Your families and friends. Your mother, Jak. Better that you surrender yourselves peaceably, isn't it? Choose to sacrifice yourselves to save the rest of the settlement."

"Save them for what?" Jak wanted to know. "For more sacrifices next year?"

"Yes," the Magister agreed, "but only five. Five is the number of death."

"Five is the number of life!" Jak spat back bitterly.

Zarah nodded.

"You killed my sister," Jak accused her.

Magister Zarah hesitated. "I was a Creche-Leaver many years ago," she said finally. "Far too long ago for me to have killed Aleen."

"We're leaving!" Jak yelled. "Anyone tries anything, the Magister dies!"

Magister Zarah just shook her head.

Deek's counterpart, who was still grinning like an idiot, and the girl with missing teeth bent to scoop up their unconscious friend.

"Enough!" Cheela snapped, and went for her other bola.

Dyan jumped and grabbed for her whip, nervous that Jak might accidentally activate it and turn her into mince. Instead, he clubbed her in the face with it, hard. She stumbled back.

The world spun, but she still saw Jug Ears. He managed to finger the right spot because the monofilament's weight ejected from the body of the weapon.

But he was holding it all wrong.

He spun the bola around his head, Cheela dodging sideways to get out of the way and Shad jumping at Magister Zarah. If he'd released it at that moment, Jug Ears might have sliced Shad and Zarah both to pieces.

But he kept swinging. A second time around his head, and then Dyan hit the ground hard.

A third time around his head, and Shad tackled Magister Zarah, knocking her out to the ground and falling on top of her.

Jug Ears released the bola. The weight was behind him, though, the momentum was all wrong—

the bola whizzed off into space, over the lip of the canyon—

and Jug Ears stared down at his own chest in horror. For a moment, he looked fine. Then blood began to seep through his wool shirt in a perfectly straight line across his torso, from hip to shoulder.

"Wow," Deek muttered.

Jug Ears collapsed in a fountain of blood, head, shoulders and arms falling one direction while the rest of his body fell another.

"Go!" Jak yelled.

He grabbed Dyan and threw her out of his way, in the direction of her Crechemates. She was too stunned to resist, but aware enough to be surprised at how strong Jak was. He certainly didn't look as muscular or big as Shad, but he threw her like she weighed nothing. She tumbled into Cheela and they collapsed in a tangle, and then Jak was on his horse.

The grinning boy charged at Magister Zarah, a spear in hand. Shad's whip jumped into his hand, quicker than Dyan would have expected, and with a single smooth crack of it, the grinning boy's head fell from his shoulders. His body kept running for the half dozen paces it took it to charge off the edge of the cliff and disappear.

"Get off me!" Cheela cursed, pushing at Dyan.

The girl missing teeth ran at them both, holding a heavy rock over her head. Dyan didn't see the bola in motion, but she saw the girl's hands suddenly separate from her wrists, and the rock bounce off her head as it fell. The girl looked at her own blood-pumping stumps in confusion, and then a second throw sliced off the top half of her head.

"Sorry," Deek muttered, scrambling after his bolas. "Bad aim!"

The white-haired girl stirred, and struggled to sit up.

"Jone!" the boy Eirig shouted, and spurred his horse towards her.

"No time!" Jak raced past his friend, grabbing the reins of the other boy's horse and pulling him along in his wake.

Wayland lumbered forward with another spear in hand—somehow, in the confusion when Dyan wasn't watching, the spears had been scattered around the promontory—Eirig must have tried to arm his friends—and impaled White Hair, Jone, from behind. She sat up facing Dyan, and Dyan saw the steel spearhead protrude from her chest in a sudden spurt of blood and a look on the girl's face that resembled disappointment, and then she crumpled forward, dead.

Shad raced to intercept the two mounted boys, whip lashing.

Jak threw himself off his mount, saving himself—

but in the process, the horse lost its head completely. Its charge carried it in Shad's direction and its head fell at his feet, tripping him. He lurched aside in a maneuver that was part dodge and part stumble, thwarted from making a further attack.

Cheela threw Dyan off and snapped off a quick shot with her bola. The boy Eirig and his horse both took the blow, right through its neck and his arm. The animal exploded into an exsanguinating mess of dead meat. Eirig hit the ground hard, screaming.

Jak pulled his friend to his feet and they both ran. They left the arm behind.

"Stop him!" Magister Zarah called, rising to her feet.

Dyan pulled a bola from her belt, raised it over her head to throw, but couldn't quite bring herself to do it.

Jak slammed the butt of his spear into Shad's face as he passed the other boy, knocking Dyan's Crechemate to the ground with a heavy thud. Then he ran at the Magister, spear up and aimed at her chest.

She stood unflinching. Dyan saw acceptance in her eyes, and didn't understand it.

But, however conflicted and terrible she felt about the Cull, she couldn't let her Magister die. She snapped off her bola, not at Jak—

but at his spear.

Her throw sliced off the tip of the weapon, turning it into a staff of a club, and then her bola vanished out into space. Cursing, Jak pummeled Zarah once with the wood and then turned, leaping out into midair over the edge of the cliff—

and disappearing from sight.

Eirig followed him, and his scream seemed to echo forever.

Dyan was standing, though she wasn't sure when she had stood up. She bent over and vomited, throwing up into the sand and the blood.

"Are you alright?" she heard Shad ask.

She looked up to smile at him and felt punched in the stomach. He was asking Cheela.

"I'm angry!" her Crechemate snapped. "That Landsy stole my bola, and then he didn't even have the decency to stick around so I could kill him."

"No," Wayland agreed. His voice sounded far away and his eyes didn't quite focus. "But he did a pretty thorough job without your help."

"Which leaves us with a problem."

Dyan heard the Magister's words and felt an uncomfortable premonition. She wiped sour bile from her lips and stood up. She was unsteady on her feet and would have liked Shad's arm to lean on, which made the fact that he was supporting Cheela doubly bitter.

Magister Zarah stood with her back to the cliff and her arms at her sides. On her face she wore an expression Dyan had never seen on her before: fatigue. She looked tired, and maybe a little sad. "Wayland," she said. "Shad. Deek. You are all Blooded. You are no longer my children, you are not Crechelings. You are adults and Urbane. Welcome to the System."

Dyan suppressed another urge to throw up.

"Cheela," Magister Zarah continued. "Dyan. There are two fleeing Landsmen who must not be allowed to escape. You are not yet Blooded."

She arched her eyebrows at them wearily, and gestured over the cliff behind her.

CHAPTER SIX

Dyan stumbled down the draw, Deek's bola on her leg replacing the one she had lost in saving the Magister. The orange stone walls scratching towards the indigo sky on either side of her expressed neatly the tunnel she felt she was in. Magister Zarah had talked about choices, but she had none. She couldn't refuse to kill Jak—*kill the Landsman*, she forced herself to think—because that would make her a rebel against the System. Rebels were criminals. They were executed for the good of the System, and if they managed to escape, they lived short, brutal lives as desperadoes in the Wahai. So Dyan had no meaningful choice.

Would it be different when she was Blooded?

Cheela was ahead of her because she was faster, tall, strong, and long-legged to Dyan's short and slight. No wonder Shad was attracted to her, Dyan thought.

She tried to shut down that train of thought, too.

The ravine was choked with boulders and treacherous to descend. Ascent would be even harder. Dyan heard Magister Zarah and her other Crechemates following behind at a more relaxed pace. She hoped that when she got to the bottom she would find the two Landsmen dead, and the ordeal would be over.

But would it? Or would it just start again, from the beginning? Or would Dyan have failed, and would she become an outcast, or be executed, removed as a failure from the System in order to protect the successful life inside it?

She shook her head and dropped six feet over the crumbling lip of a jagged rock onto powdery sand. No, she should hope that Jak was in great pain and dying anyway, so she could put him out of his misery and still be given credit, still become Blooded.

Ahead of her, Cheela splashed into water. Dyan cursed, realizing suddenly that if there was only one survivor of the fall, and Cheela killed him, or if the Outrider-designate simply killed both boys, Dyan would be a failure and an outcast anyway.

And then Cheela would have Shad all to herself.

Dyan nearly jumped down the last twenty feet of steep slope and landed in cold shallow water on her hands and knees. Forcing herself up, she staggered around the base of the cliff and found Cheela standing with her arms crossed over her chest, surveying the scene. The canyon walls were high, mostly unbroken by ravines, handholds or other ways of getting out. A river, wide and flat, wound around sandy hills silted up within the elbows of the canyon and small groves of desert trees that clung to them.

"They hit here," the other girl said as Dyan arrived, and pointed. "Where the water makes a deep pool under the edge of the bluff."

"The mud is still disturbed," Dyan agreed.

"All the better," Cheela snarled. "I'll kill my Landsy any way he comes, but I'd rather he be standing, facing me, and preferably armed."

Dyan stared at her Crechemate. "For honor, you mean?"

Cheela snorted. "For glory," she said.

Dyan splashed back to the bottom of the ravine. Magister Zarah stood above her, with Deek and Shad at her side. Wayland, Dyan guessed, hadn't been able to get this far down the draw.

"Are they dead?" Zarah called.

"No." Dyan shook her head as Cheela joined her.

"I'll track them," Cheela assured the Magister. She patted her whip. "They won't get out."

Zarah nodded. "If they do, you understand that Outriders will destroy Ratsnay Station."

"Do they have to?" Dyan asked. In her mind's eye, she imagined herself as one of the people of the settlement, being chased down by Outriders whose faces were hidden by bandannas and broad-brimmed hats. She remembered the jug-eared boy, slicing himself in half with Cheela's bola, and shuddered.

"The System kills," the Magister reminded her, "to protect life."

"We brought your things!" Shad called, and Dyan saw that he had saddlebags over one shoulder and a bow in his hands.

He grinned, but not at her, and then he tossed the saddlebags and bow to Cheela. She let the bags fall into the water and then picked them up, but she caught the bow neatly with both hands.

"Here's yours, Dyan!" Deek yelled, but Dyan's bags were already splashing into the water. She looked at him just in time to catch her bow, partly with one hand and partly with her head, the string snagging around her neck and almost choking her.

"We'll have to divide our forces," the Magister said. "We'll leave someone to cover this ravine, and we'll go to the nearest exits up and down river to watch them."

"I'll kill the Landsies," Cheela agreed.

"*We*," Dyan butted in, feeling she was being left behind. "*We will* ... we'll complete the Cull, Magister," she said.

Zarah nodded. "We'll meet again here, when it's over." She pointed above her head, to the site of the massacre.

The Cull, Dyan reminded herself.

Dyan picked up her saddlebags and slung them over her shoulder. The cold water felt good on her body now, in the last heat of the day, but she knew that temperatures would soon plummet, and she'd be grateful for her coat, as well as for all the supplies in the bags.

Magister Zarah turned to lead Shad and Deek back up the draw, and Dyan and Cheela plodded back out into the middle of the river. The last of the sun left the surface of the water even at the canyon's broadest point, retreating in a slow blaze of orange up the wall. Dyan shivered.

Without a word, they plodded together over to the sandy hill that filled the far corner of the canyon. Scanning its edges, they saw no tracks.

"We'll have to split up," Cheela said.

"They won't have split up," Dyan said. "Jak ... the Landsy Jak wouldn't leave his friend injured. They're together."

"Of course they are," Cheela sneered. "But we can't be sure which way they went, can we?"

And Dyan knew instantly which way Jak had gone. Downstream meant back to Ratsnay Station, and Jak would never have done that. That would only bring danger on his people, and his mother. Upstream meant the Wahai, where everyone knew people could live, because people *did*. Renegades and outlaws, and Dyan had been trained to think of them with fear and disdain, but Jak might feel differently. He might think of the Wahai outlaws as people who might take him in.

He probably did.

"I'll go upstream," Cheela said. Without waiting for an answer, she turned and headed for the shallowest part of the river.

Dyan hesitated, but only for a second. She plunged after her Crechemate, calling, "I'm coming with you!"

Cheela snorted in disgust, but Dyan let her think what she wanted. Going downstream, she knew, was a waste of time. It prolonged the inevitable, maybe, or it led to life as a solitary outlaw. It didn't lead to Jak, or back to the System, or to recognition as a full Magister.

The girls trudged upstream, bows in their hands and bags on the shoulders. The saddlebags held their arrows as well, in tubes of leather attached to the side of the bags and snapped shut at the top against inclement weather. Dyan hoped her arrows were still dry, after their fall into the river.

If they were real Outriders, Dyan knew, they'd have infrared goggles in their saddlebags, too, and other really useful devices, instead of just blankets, food, pure water tablets, and a few basic medical supplies. Of course, real Outriders in pursuit of renegades would be mounted and in large numbers.

But Jak was unarmed. Well, practically. He and Eirig had spears, but Eirig was badly injured, and maybe even already dying. They'd be easy to capture, once the girls found them.

Capture or kill, she heard Shad say in her head.

No, not capture. Just kill. And she again saw Jug Ears, slicing himself neatly in half and collapsing into the sand.

"Are those swallows?" she said idly, seeing small black shadows flitting in quick circular motions overhead.

"Bats," Cheela huffed at her. "You should know that."

"You're right, I should." Dyan felt embarrassed for having forgotten something so obvious. She watched the little beasts dive through clouds of evening insects, gorging on their prey and returning again and again to the cliff face. Their home seemed to be a ledge high up inside a chimney in the canyon wall, and Dyan wondered how the infant bats were fed. Maybe the adults were flying back to them even now and regurgitating half-digested bugs into their open baby-bat mouths.

The canyon wiggled left and right, back and forth, like a snake's trail, which was no doubt how it had its name; the Buza River, on which the System lay, flowed in a much straighter, lazier line across the north end of the Treasure Valley. Dyan knew enough about geology to imagine that maybe in a million years, or ten million, the Treasure Valley might be the top of a plateau, and the Buza River might have cut deep, winding channels like the Snaik.

In the next bend, the canyon wall was pierced by an arch that cut over into the next loop of the canyon. Within the natural bridge, the ground rose up to a tumble of boulders, large chunks of stone that had fallen out of the arch itself over the millennia. Cheela stopped and looked up into the shadowed arch in the last deep blue light of evening before darkness fell. Already, the first stars twinkled in the zig-zagging visible sky above them.

Dyan pulled her hand-held light stick from her saddlebag and snapped it on the sand around the base of the arch. "No footprints," she confirmed. "Are you thinking this might be a good defensible place to stay the night, and continue searching in the morning?"

"I'm not staying the night anywhere," Cheela growled in a whisper. "I'm killing those Landsies before the sun comes up. She pointed at the river upstream. "I'm wondering if they might have gone around the bend, and then snuck up into the arch as a way to ambush us, or get behind us when we pass."

"We have to split up," Dyan suggested softly. "One of us go under the arch, and one of us follow the river. Could be dangerous. Could be a trap."

Cheela nodded, a specter in the reflected glow of the light stick. "I don't really trust you for either job," she said. "But I guess I'd rather you took your light and splashed your way around the bend, making as much noise as you can. I'll sneak up under the arch."

"Do we need a code?" Dyan whispered. "Like a whistle, or something?"

Cheela laughed under her breath. "If you hear the Landsies screaming in pain, that's a signal that I found them. Otherwise, I didn't, and I'll see you on the other side." She pressed herself deep into the shadow of a boulder at the river's edge and hissed through her teeth. "Now go!"

Dyan obeyed. She kicked the water as she went, and when she came across a long stick protruding like a signpost from a sandbar in the middle of the river, she plucked it out and carried it with her, striking the water with it.

Her shoulder was sore from the saddlebags.

And, she realized, *she* might be the one walking into the trap. Jak and Eirig might be waiting in the furthest point of the bend with their spears, ready to stab her to death. She kept hitting the water and kicking up big sprays of it with her boots, but she stared into the gloom around her and poked it with the beam of her light stick, trying to spot boulders, caves, thickets, or other likely places in which to mount an ambush.

She realized that she was humming.

Puzzled, she listened to herself. It was the tune hummed by the hanged man, the song she was beginning to think of as the Gallows Song, though it still had no words.

Or did it? She tried to relax into the song, let her unconscious mind do the work and find whatever words went with the melody that she might know. "Mmm mmmm, she married a soldier," came from her lips, but then the elusive thread slipped from her grasp and she couldn't think of any more.

Dyan realized that, in her intense concentration on the slippery melody, she had dropped the stick. Oops. Also, she had turned the corner of the bend and was almost to the other side of the arch.

At least no one had ambushed her; that was good.

Also, she hadn't heard any sounds of Cheela killing the Landsmen.

She sloshed to the steep, rubble-strewn slope at the bottom of the arch and scanned the sand and pebbles there for signs of disturbance. Seeing none, she looked up the slope for her Crechemate.

"Cheela?" she called softly.

"Snap!" Cheela barked from behind her, and at the same moment a pebble thumped into the slope beside Dyan. "You're dead!"

Dyan turned around. "If you really wanted to kill me, I think you could do it at any time."

"Don't forget it."

Dyan studied Cheela. The stars overheard cast a silvery sparkle of light down on her, but her face was entirely hidden in the shadow of her hat brim. She was taller than Dyan, stronger, and almost certainly faster. She was probably prettier, too. Dyan's hair and skin were too fair, she burned easily in the sun, and freckled, and she wasn't chesty and curvaceous like Cheela was.

"You didn't hate me when we were younger," she said to her Crechemate.

"I don't hate you now." Cheela's voice was hostile, despite her words.

"You want Shad for yourself."

"So do you. Does that mean *you* hate *me?*"

Dyan didn't know what to say. "Come on," she finally managed. "Let's find these Landsies." She plodded ahead, leaving the light stick off and wishing she had a horse.

The canyon curved under a busy rock seep, bristling with dark clumps of watercress. A heavy patter of *drop-drop-drop* mixed into the sluggish sounds of the river's water hugging its course, and then, gradually, another water noise rose in the mix, a heavy crashing.

"Rapids?" Cheela wondered.

They rounded another corner in the canyon, and Dyan's first impression was that the canyon had simply ended, in a tumult of water noise. When spray hit her in the face, she realized what it had to be.

"Waterfall," she said. Gauging its height in the darkness was a haphazard enterprise at best, but she tried anyway. "Thirty feet?"

"There must be a way up," Cheela said.

"There isn't." It was Jak's voice.

Dyan felt something sharp poke her in her lower back.

"Don't move," Eirig whispered into her ear. Over the silty stink of the river and her own sweat, she suddenly detected the iron-rich whiff of blood.

She turned her head slowly, slightly, in time to see Jak, his own knife at Cheela's throat, unclip her whip and both bolas from her belt and hips. He tossed all three items into the churning foam at the base of the waterfall, and then her bow. Finally, he stepped back.

"That's much better," he said.

CHAPTER SEVEN

What—" Dyan started, not even sure what question she meant to ask.

Jak slapped her across the face. "Shut up!"

Her cheek stung, and she said nothing.

"Easy, Jak," Eirig said. The one-armed boy took away Dyan's weapons, but rather than tossing them, he slung the bow over his shoulder and tucked the monofilament weapons into a big leather purse on his belt. He trembled as he did it, and where his skin brushed against Dyan's, he felt feverish. He dug into the pockets of her coat, too, and came up with her light stick.

"I'm sorry about your arm," she said softly.

"That's twice!" Jak barked. "The third time, I kill you. Now put your hands on top of your heads and walk."

Dyan did as she was told. After a second's hesitation, so did Cheela, and they sloshed back down the river. For the first time, Dyan felt the chill of the evening, biting into the skin of her legs and feet, wet inside their tall rider's boots, and blowing into her open coat with the stiff breeze.

She was puzzled at first about Jak's insistence on silence; no one could possibly be around to hear them, unless maybe the renegades of the Wahai had come this far downriver. But then she realized that Jak didn't know the Crechelings and the Magister had split up. For all he knew, the others were close by, following or watching.

They sloshed back around the arch, following Dyan's footsteps in the riverbed rather than climbing up and under the stone vault like Cheela had done. At the furthest bend of the river, she realized that Eirig was humming.

He was humming the Gallows Song.

"Shh," Jak urged him gently, and Eirig fell quiet.

The moon rose above the edge of the canyon wall, throwing silver light over the stone, sand and grass. Everything solid looked gray, and the river was a ribbon of dark blood at the bottom of it all. The moon's light made the shadows that remained look even more impenetrable. More walking, and they reached the bottom of the chimney where Dyan had mistaken the bats for swallows.

The moonlight shone down into the bottom of a chimney, and Dyan saw a rope dangling.

Cheela cursed.

Jak ignored her. "Can you still climb?" he asked his friend.

Eirig chuckled. "It's just an arm," he said. "It's not like I lost anything *important*."

Dyan thought of Wayland, who couldn't be serious about anything.

"Here's how this is going to work," Jak told them all. "Eirig, you climb to the top. I'm going to send the girls … the *prisoners,* up one at a time, and you tie them. I'll come last."

"Done," Eirig agreed.

"You'd better give me their weapons," Jak added. "Just in case."

Eirig handed his purse over to Jak and shimmied up the rope. He was surprisingly agile, given how tentative and feverish he seemed, and given that he had recently lost half his arm. But he gripped the rope with his feet and his one hand, and in short order was scrambling onto the ledge above.

"It's like that old riddle," Dyan said, remembering a brain-teaser a former Magister of hers had once told her. "You have a cabbage, a sheep, and a wolf, and you have to get them all across the river in your canoe, only your canoe only holds one of them, and you can't leave the sheep alone with the cabbage, or the wolf alone with the sheep."

Jak snorted. "Except in this case, the two wolves have to get the two sheep up the hill without leaving them alone."

"Ha!" Cheela snapped. "In *this* case, two really stupid sheep have gotten in way over their heads and kidnapped wolves. And if the sheep had an ounce of sense between them, they'd drop their weapons right now and run for the Wahai."

Jak laughed. "Give me the saddlebags," he ordered his prisoners. Dyan and Cheela did, and he slung them both over one shoulder. Their combined bulk made him seem small and frail, but he held up under the weight.

"Send them up!" Eirig called down in a stage whisper that echoed loudly in the chimney.

"You first, wolf girl," Jak prodded Cheela, and up she went.

"I don't hate you," Dyan said softly, watching Cheela's coat billow out and swirl in the moonlight. "I don't think you're a bad person. It's just the way things are. It's just the requirement of the System."

Jak spat into the river. "You Systemoids are totally crazy."

Dyan faltered. "Don't you ... kill sick animals, to protect the herd? Burn pest-infested fields?"

Jak's laugh was hollow and cynical this time. "Do I look like a weevil to you? Was my sister a sick animal? Or does your precious System just kill to remind everybody that it can?"

Cheela disappeared over the lip of the ledge.

"The herd is more important than individual animals," Dyan tried to insist. In her heart, she felt a pang of doubt about the truth of her own words. "The System isn't a bully. It doesn't need to prove anything to people."

"She's tied!" Eirig called down.

"Yeah? Tell that to my sister."

Dyan wanted to say something, but didn't know what.

"I thought so." Jak pointed at the rope. "Up!"

Dyan climbed. Being shorter and scrawnier than Cheela at least gave her an advantage at this, and she was quickly up the chimney to the height of the bats' ledge. The physical demands of climbing, and the attention it required of her, gave her something other than Jak's words to think about it, for which she was grateful.

The ledge was narrow, just a strip three feet wide and jutting up like a defiant lower lip over the river, but at its base the cliff face was cracked and the ledge slid back into darkness. Sour-smelling bat guano carpeted the ledge and the crack, and the furry creatures flapped in the gloom about Dyan's head.

Eirig crouched on the ledge, more rope coiled in his one hand and at his feet.

"Where's Cheela?" Dyan asked.

"I ate her." Eirig grinned, his expression revealed in a strip of moonlight that cut across his face. He nodded at the crack. "She's inside. Now come on, turn around, or I have to throw you into the river. Hands behind you."

Dyan turned around. She put her hands behind her back, trying to look as cooperative as possible, but also tensing her muscles. The Magisters had never taught her anything about escaping from bonds, but she'd seen a few funvids, and more than once the captured, outgunned Outrider escaped from her captivity by tensing her muscles while she was being tied up, so that when she relaxed them later she gained a little slack.

Eirig fumbled a bit in tying her up, but only a bit. Again, Dyan noticed the heat of his touch, and felt terrible.

Two days ago, she thought, getting her Lot Letter from Magister Zarah's hands and looking forward to being Blooded and becoming an adult, she hadn't expected anything like what had actually happened. The Hanging, yes. But everything after that had been a shock, a world-changing trauma.

As it must have been meant to be, she realized. As the System must want it; as the Cogitant Council and the Magisters designed it to be.

"Is she tied?" Dyan heard Jak call from the bottom of the chimney.

"Yeah!" Eirig called back. "Come on up!" Dyan heard the scuffling sounds of climbing in the chimney and then Eirig pulled her back, gently. "Lie down," he whispered. "You're going to need to roll sideways."

Dyan felt a little sick to her stomach, realizing that she was lying back in bat guano, but she steeled herself and did it. Then Eirig pushed her shoulder, and she rolled from shadow into darkness. She spun like a wheel several times, struck her head on stone, and then came to a halt against flesh.

"Cheela," she said.

"Get off me!" the other girl snapped back.

Bats shrieked about them. Dyan rolled away from her Creche-mate and tucked her face into the collar of her own coat for protection.

The cold beam of a light stick snapped across the two girls and Dyan struggled to inch away from Cheela. She managed to get herself backed up into a sitting position against a rough piece of stone, and then Jak scraped into the cave on his belly, climbing down through the same crack through which Dyan had rolled. He pulled the saddle-bags in behind him, and Dyan's bow, tossing them into a corner.

While Eirig crawled in, Jak stomped over to the girls. He flipped Cheela over first, looked at the ropes around her wrists, and grunted. Then he pulled Dyan forward, away from her boulder, and checked her similarly.

"Good job, Eirig." He dragged his friend to his feet. They were dirty and wet, and their ragged wool trousers and shirt made them look like oversized children, so much so that Dyan had a hard time not laughing.

"I'm just glad they had a light stick." Eirig looked pale and his voice quivered slightly as he spoke. "Now if someone goes to hold my hand tonight, at least I'll be able to tell who it is."

Jak sat beside the saddlebags and began to dig around inside them.

"Any good snacks?" Eirig wanted to know. He squatted in a corner and then rolled back, disturbing two fist-sized balls of fur that instantly flapped away, shrieking angrily. "I hear that food is always the first order of business for a Wahai outlaw." He wagged his eyebrows suggestively at Dyan. "I'm afraid that love can only come second for a rogue such as myself, my dear."

"Love's third," Jak disagreed, "if it even ranks that high. Our first order of business has to be medicine."

In the splashy, reflected light of her stick, Dyan looked around. The crack opened into a roughly cylindrical shaft, choked with boulders and rubble that ascended at a forty-five degree angle. The stink of bats was so strong she couldn't smell anything else.

"Here it is." Jak threw aside the saddlebags he was rummaging in, holding up a medikit. He pulled at it, twisted it, gnawed at it, but the kit wouldn't open.

"You have to pop the seal, idiot," Cheela growled.

"You could tell us how," Eirig pointed out.

"Why?" Cheela stared at him. "So that when you kill me, your boo boos will feel better?"

"Hey," Eirig objected, "I don't know that we plan to kill you."

"We do," Jak confirmed.

"I'm sorry I didn't slice your head off," Cheela said to Eirig. "I'm sorry you didn't bleed out, and I hope you die of infection."

"You started it," Eirig pointed out. "You tried to kill my friends."

Dyan felt sick.

Jak slammed the medikit against a boulder. With a hiss, it popped open.

"Nobody's going to die of infection," he announced, coming up with a tube of topical antibiotic.

Cheela closed her eyes and feigned sleep while Jak knelt to take care of his friend, but Dyan couldn't look away. She saw now that Eirig had a tourniquet around his arm, and that the wound at the end of his stump was bandaged with strips of wool that had been torn from Jak's shirt and were now soaked through with blood. Jak peeled away the bandages, smeared antibiotic ointment over the wound, and then wrapped it in gauze from the medikit. Eirig bit his lip the entire time, in obvious pain but not crying out.

"On the plus side," the injured boy said, "it's a clean injury. No bone fragments or anything. You have to admire the precision of an Outrider's bola."

"Outrider-designate," Dyan said. She said it automatically, not meaning anything by it, but Cheela obviously took offense. Without opening her eyes, she kicked Dyan hard in the shin.

"You'll want a painkiller," Jak said, digging through the medikit again.

"I'm fine," Dyan said, though it smarted enough to bring tears to her eyes. "I just wish my hands were free so I could rub it."

"I'd rub it for you," Eirig offered. "You know, if I had two hands."

"Funny," Cheela snarled. "I'd have thought one hand was enough to accomplish everything a guy like you ever does."

"Painkiller's not for you, Systemoid," Jak said, popping open a canister of pills. He tapped two of them out into his palm and gave them to Eirig, who swallowed them.

"Thanks." The injured boy leaned against the wall of the cave and closed his eyes.

"Stop calling me that," Dyan murmured, but too softly to be heard.

Jak stood and faced his prisoners. He looked tall, standing over them, and Dyan turned her face away.

"You look like you know what you're doing with the medikit," she said. She meant it as a compliment, though it sounded painfully tiny in the cave.

"In addition to carefully marking which of us should be slaughtered," Jak told her, "Magister Stanton occasionally dispensed minor medicines. I think it made him uncomfortable that I paid such close attention to what he was doing." He paused for long seconds. "Now," he said slowly, "tell me why I shouldn't kill you."

"Because," Cheela growled, "when the Outriders catch you, they'll make you wish you'd never been born."

Jak's laugh was hard and thin. "Too late. And if you mean they would *kill me*, that's obviously already on the table."

Cheela spat on Jak's shoes.

"We could plead for mercy," Dyan suggested. "For you, I mean."

"Mercy for what?" Jak asked. He looked amused. "I haven't committed a crime. All I did was do well on the tests in school."

"Kidnapping," Cheela suggested.

Jak ignored her and kept talking to Dyan. "You said it yourself, no one hates me, I'm not a bad person. The System just wants to kill me because I'm smart."

"That's not true," Dyan said, too quickly.

"You're right." Jak bowed and grinned. "It wants to kill me because I'm smart … *and a Landsman.*"

Dyan had nothing to say to that.

Eirig popped his eyes open. "We may need them," he said. "We may need hostages."

Jak scrutinized the girls. "That's a good reason to keep *one of them* alive," he admitted. "I don't see that a second hostage is going to make any difference, unless we literally use them as shields."

"Please do," Cheela snarled. "I'll beg the Outriders to cut right through me."

"I should warn you," Eirig said, his voice heavy and slow, "it's not as fun as it looks."

And then his head tipped back against the stone and he began to snore.

"I don't want you to die," Dyan said. She hadn't meant to say it, the words just popped out of her spontaneously. Before her mouth was even closed, Cheela shot her a look of pure disdain. "I mean, *personally*," she added, trying to cover her mistake. "None of this is personal."

"I, on the other hand," Cheela said, "am taking this all very personally."

"Good," Jak countered. He threw a silvery microfiber blanket from one of the saddlebags over Eirig, and then settled into a seated position against one wall of the cave under a second. He snapped off the light stick, plunging them all into cool darkness. "So am I."

CHAPTER EIGHT

Dyan awoke lying on her side, feeling dirty and stiff. The salty animal tang of bats filled her nostrils so much it seemed to her she could actually taste the little creatures on her tongue. Her neck was balled into a single knot of stressed tissue and the left side of her face stung from lying on sand and stone all night.

To her surprise, she could see.

Cheela slumped upright against a large rock, chin forward on her chest, sleeping. A silver-wrapped lump in the corner, just where Eirig had fallen asleep the night before, snored gently. There was no sign of Jak.

Dyan rolled onto her back and sat up. She ached, every part of her, saddle-sore or foot-weary or scraped or bruised.

The light, she realized, came from above, and it was daylight. The top of the slanted well in the bottom of which they lay was open to the sky, and when she craned her neck around to look, she could just see the tiniest sliver of blue. By the faint light she could see that the well was climbable, even comfortably so. She also saw clumps of brown lichen all over the walls that she hadn't noticed the night before. They looked like leopard's spots, and she was leaning very close to get a good look at one before she realized what they must be.

Bats.

She pulled away at the last second.

Dyan leaned down and squinted out the crack onto the ledge by which they had come into the cave. She could see daylight there, too, and no sign of the Landsman boy she had been assigned to kill.

Now was her chance to escape. She took a deep breath, closed her eyes, and exhaled. She tried to let all the tension and stiffness she felt flow out of her body with the air of her lungs, to deflate like a balloon, become limp and soft and relaxed.

When she felt so relaxed she was almost fluid, she tried to slip her hands out of their bonds.

And failed.

"Lying funvids!" she cursed.

Cheela jerked her head up. Even in the moment of her waking up, her eyes stared at Dyan with a hawklike expression that was hard to interpret as anything other than full of hatred. She looked around quickly at the cave and then back at Dyan. "Shh!"

Dyan nodded.

Cheela stood. She was wobbly on her knees, but she gritted her teeth with determination and pushed her back against the stone. Dyan followed her example, the effort bringing tears to her eyes. It felt like the long muscles of her legs ripped as she moved.

When they were standing, Dyan nodded her head at the crack exit and mouthed a message, *Jak's gone.*

Either Cheela didn't understand her, or she ignored Dyan. The Outrider-designate whispered back, very softly. "We kill the cripple and get out of here."

"With what?" Dyan whispered back.

For an answer, Cheela raised one rider's boot off the ground, showing Dyan its sharp and heavy heel.

Dyan flinched. "I don't know if I can do that."

Cheela shrugged. "Not my problem." She stepped across the scratchy sand floor of the well and stood over Eirig. Leaning against the wall with her shoulder, she dragged back the microfiber blanket with her boot.

Eirig continued to snore. His clothing was crusted with dirt, and beneath the dirt on his face, Dyan saw bruises. He looked like a little kid, innocent and grubby. Cheela raised her leg to stomp on the boy—

"Bad idea."

The voice was Jak's, and it was loud in the cave.

Dyan looked up and saw him perched above Eirig like a roosting bird. He had been hidden behind a rock, and now emerged to intervene. He held a spear in his hand. Once, Dyan would have laughed at the spear, which was the weapon of outlaws and cavemen in the funvids, but she had seen gentle, harmless Wayland poke one right through a girl the day before, and it didn't seem funny now.

"Wait," Dyan said. She didn't know to whom.

Cheela stomped—

thwack!

Jak spun the spear and cracked the butt of it into Cheela's forehead with a sharp blow that sent her reeling backward. She rebounded off the stone wall behind her and charged, growling, as if she might headbutt the Landsman. Jak kicked her in the face from his position on higher ground and then jumped down to their level.

"Stop," Dyan pleaded.

Jak pushed her with one hand, knocking her sprawling. As Cheela raged and stormed at him again, he swept her feet out from under her with the butt of the spear, dropping her onto her back with an *oomph!* of air rushing from her lungs. He pointed the spear tip into her face.

"Are we done?" he asked.

"You don't expect me to just give in, do you?" she wheezed between painful-sounding grunts.

"Funny," Jak said, his voice flat. "That's *exactly* what you seem to expect from me."

"Kill me, then," Cheela pushed him.

"I've got a better idea," Jak said. He dug into Eirig's purse at his belt and came out with the little canister of painkillers. "I should have done this last night." He knelt, straddling Cheela's stomach to pin her, and set aside his spear. Shaking out a handful of pills into one hand, he dug under Eirig's blanket and produced a flask of water. "Breakfast time," he deadpanned.

Cheela spat at him, pointlessly. She was almost his size, but he had her tied up and trapped. Jak forced the pills into her mouth, clapping the water to her lips immediately after. She gagged and struggled, but had no choice but to swallow or drown.

Watching her Crechemate forced to drink, Dyan realized how thirsty she was.

When the flask was empty, Jak stood up.

Cheela gasped for air, and rolled over onto her side and retched, but the pills stayed down.

"That was four times what I gave Eirig," Jak observed, "and he's still out cold."

"Umm umm mot," Eirig objected sleepily, but he didn't so much as roll over.

"She could die," Dyan pointed out. "She could overdose and never wake up."

"True," Jak agreed, flashing a grin that showed all his teeth. "Or someone could drag her out of her home under false pretenses, lead her out into the desert and try to chop her in half. Life's hard like that, isn't it?"

Cheela cursed him as he stooped and worked at waking Eirig, but he ignored her, and after a couple of minutes of struggling, she passed out.

"I had weird dreams," Eirig confessed, when Jak pulled him to his feet and shook off the last of his painkiller-induced slumber.

"Oh yeah?" Jak asked. "Were you on the run in the Snaik River valley?"

"Worse than that," Eirig said. "Someone chopped my arm off." He raised his stump as if to do something with his missing hand and shrieked.

Jak laughed. "Curse you, Eirig," he said to his friend. "Can't you take anything seriously?"

"What would be the fun of that?"

Dyan felt a sharp pang in her heart. She looked down at Cheela, snoring on the cave floor. Cheela wasn't her friend. At best, she realized, Cheela was her Crechemate, companion, and team member. Often, she was a rival. At worst, she was openly Dyan's enemy.

But Wayland and Deek were her friends, she thought stubbornly. And what was Shad? She missed them all, and she missed Magister Zarah.

"We take this one with us," Jak said.

"My name is Dyan," she reminded him.

"I don't care what your name is," he told her. "You don't *have* a name, as far as I'm concerned. You're our hostage and our shield."

"What about Cheela?" she asked.

"If you mean the other one," Jak said, pointed at Cheela's snoring form, "we leave her here. She won't wake up before we're back, and if we get into trouble, just maybe we can still use her as a bargaining chip." He picked up one of the microfiber blankets and tore at it, pointlessly.

"Where are we going?" Dyan asked, nervous to hear the answer. The Wahai, she imagined. Or maybe back to Ratsnay Station, where she'd be killed. "You won't be able to tear that, you know. It's practically indestructible, which is why it's so great."

"Is it so great, then?" Jak sneered at her. "Hmmn." He draped the blanket over a boulder and stepped away from it. From the purse he pulled out one of the bolas.

"Uh, careful." Eirig backed into a corner of the cave and picked up one of the spears, like that would help him if the bola went bouncing around the chamber.

But Jak held both the body of the bola and its counterweight carefully, and slowly drew the counterweight out two feet. In between there was nothing visible, but Dyan knew—they all must know—that there was a microscopically thin but extremely tough filament, so thin that at mere contact it would slice steel.

Jak gently looped his hands behind the corner of the microfiber blanket, and using the bola like a knife he slowly sliced off a long strip of it. When the blanket piece fell to the floor he slid the bola shut and grinned vindictively at Dyan.

"Oh," she said.

"What else is *practically indestructible*?" he asked, and then he wrapped the strip around her head. She heard the *ffft, ffft* of medical tape being torn off, and then Jak's fingers, running tape under her jaw and attaching the makeshift hood firmly to her head. Her mouth and nostrils were free, but she was totally blind.

"The System," she said. "And not just practically. I don't know what you're doing, but Cheela's right. Your best bet is just to leave us here and run for the Wahai. By the time anyone finds us, you'll be long gone."

"Sure," Jak agreed amiably. He grabbed Dyan's upper arm and dragged her. She immediately barked her shins against stone and stumbled. Her caught her, and kept dragging, and she knew they were moving up the tunnel. "And what happens next?"

Next? "I become a Magister."

"I don't care about that. What else?"

"Outriders chase us!" Eirig called. He was behind them. "We become bandit lords, and marry beautiful princesses of the Basku or the Shoshan."

"I don't care about *us*, either," Jak said darkly. His breathing was labored from the effort of climbing the slope; so was Dyan's. Her heart raced. "What happens to Ratsnay Station?"

Dyan was puzzled. "Why should anything happen to Ratsnay Station?"

"When the Outriders come," Jak spelled it out, "and my mother says she has no idea where I am, will the Outriders believe her?"

Dyan hesitated. "Maybe."

"And will they believe that the good people of Ratsnay Station had nothing to do with my escape?"

"Maybe." Her answer came slower this time.

"And will the System and its Outriders believe that the secret of their precious murderous Selection is a secret still? Or will they assume that they have to act to keep the secret?"

This time, Dyan couldn't bring herself to answer at all.

"Exactly," Jak said. He let go of her arm for a moment and she heard him scrambling. Then he grabbed both her shoulders from above and dragged her up a short ascent. "So when I disappear, the System might destroy Ratsnay Station, might it not? Not because the settlement is bad, not because it's criminal ... but because, how did you put it? You kill a sick animal to protect the flock?"

"That's not what I meant," Dyan objected.

"Sure it is," Jak said. "Only you didn't realize it."

A breeze struck Dyan in the exposed lower half of her face, and she felt sunlight warm her skin. They were out of the cave, she inferred, and the footing immediately became much easier.

"Where are we going?" she asked.

"To solve the problem."

Dyan's feet crunched through plant growth of some kind every few steps, and she was grateful for her boots. Some of those plants must be cactus. "Are you going to trade me?" she wondered out loud. "For the Outriders to leave Ratsnay Station alone?"

"Something like that."

She stumbled along for a length of time she had no way to measure, though it was long enough for her legs and feet to lose their stiffness and then begin becoming sore again. Jak and Eirig didn't talk, and once, when she tried to ask a question, Jak shushed her back into silence. Finally, they stopped.

"I'm going to take your blindfold off," Jak told her. "And then I'm going to stuff it into your mouth. You can understand that I'm doing this because I want you to see something, and I really, really want you to stay quiet. Can't you?"

Dyan considered screaming, but as she hesitated Jak ripped away the hood and, true to his word, jammed it between her jaws. The tape burned as it peeled away from her skin, and then he wrapped more tape around her gag in three big loops to hold it in place.

After the shadow of the cave and the darkness of the hood, the desert sun blinded Dyan. She blinked away tears, gagged, and felt faint. Sweat streamed down her body under her long Outrider's coat, and the sun scorched the back of her neck.

"Breathe through your nose," Eirig advised her. "We don't smell *that* bad."

The laughter that improbably bubbled up within her at his wisecrack made her gag again.

"Shh," Jak said, and dragged her to the ground.

Dyan looked around. The three of them crouched in a scalloped shell of sand, the upper seats of a natural amphitheater. Above them stretched sky, mostly blue and brilliant, though away to the west, coming off the Wahai, Dyan saw billowing clouds, heavy and gray with rain. They were heading her direction, she thought.

"Down there." Jak grabbed her by the back of her head and focused her attention.

Dyan and her captors squatted behind a pair of shattered boulders, and below them lay a red slope. The slope gathered and dropped like an angled funnel into a narrow canyon, choked with stones and gray-green desert trees. At the mouth of the canyon, raggedly punctured and dark with what might be blood, lay a hat. *Her* hat, Dyan realized, or Cheela's. Jak must have crept out and laid it there during the night, which surprised her.

But she saw something even more surprising. Her whip jutted out of a crack in the canyon wall. No, she realized, squinting. Not the whole whip, but only the handle. Which meant that the weight—her eyes flashed to the other side of the narrow canyon and spotted a counterpart crack—must be wedged into the wall on the other side. Which meant that an invisible ribbon of death lay across the canyon, six feet off the ground.

And then Dyan saw something that made her heart stop. Clopping steadily into view on his horse at the bottom of the canyon, stopping at her hat and looking down at it, came Wayland.

"Mmmmm," she tried to shout, *no!* Her gag was taped too tight, and her hands were tied securely behind her back. She tried to stand, but Jak and Eirig both grabbed her and pulled her onto her back.

Dyan kicked, aiming at Jak's face. She missed, and her boots slammed into the rubble, sending a shower of stones clattering into the canyon below. Jak drew back a hand to slap her and she lunged, rolling out from behind the boulder and skidding down the sandy slope on her belly.

"Mmmmm!" She strained against the gag. "Mmmmm!"

Footsteps behind her told her that Jak or Eirig or both were following her. She couldn't see anything but the red earth slamming into her face, over and over again.

"Dyan!" Wayland yelled. "Gee yap!"

She heard the drum of galloping hooves in the sand.

CHAPTER NINE

Dyan tucked her head to one shoulder and kicked her feet against the ground. She intended to throw herself forward in a somersault, to get her face off the ground.

It worked, but the violence of her spin, its lack of balance and its rough forward motion, ripped skin from her face. She choked, face full of sand and blood, felt her hair yanked as some of it caught beneath her tumbling body, and then saw the flash of sky again as her back came down on the slope, hard.

Whumph!

Dyan's lungs screamed. She couldn't get air in fast enough through her nose alone. Wayland, she reminded herself. Sliding down, feet-forward and on her back now, she raised her head and shook it at her Crechemate, a big, violent, obvious *NO*.

Wayland rode through the whip.

The heavy boy's eyes bulged in surprise as he died, but his forward motion kept both halves of his body together and riding in the same direction for several more lengths. Dyan skidded to a halt at the bottom of the slope, her ankles jarring painfully against sand-rooted tufts of desert grass. At the same moment, Wayland's dead mount missed its stride and collapsed forward, slamming into the other end of the same bar of sand. Its head slid smoothly off its neck, rocketing past Dyan and skittering away up the slope. Wayland's legs stayed in the saddle.

Wayland's torso slammed into Dyan, knocking her back against the sand and pebbles.

Her vision spun.

"That's how I want to go," she heard Jak say through a whirl of color and a rushing sound that filled her head. "In the arms of a pretty girl."

"You dream such small dreams," Eirig countered. "I'd like to die in the company of three, at least."

They grabbed Wayland by his shoulders and dragged him off. Dyan sat up, smelling the reek of blood, stomach churning. Jak and Eirig dumped Wayland's torso aside without ceremony, the heavy boy's arms flopping like fish on the sand.

"That's not quite how I imagined it would go," Jak said. He seemed surprisingly ambivalent about his victory.

Dyan retched. Throwing up with the gag in her mouth, she immediately inhaled her own vomit and began to choke.

"It worked, anyway." Eirig patted his friend on the shoulder.

Dyan threw up again, gagged, choked. She squirmed and kicked, and felt bile streaming from her nostrils.

Jak noticed. "Hey!" He threw himself to the ground and ripped at the tape. Dyan tried to breathe, but her airways were all plugged. She felt herself losing consciousness.

"Come on!" Jak yelled. Eirig jumped in, ripping tape from Dyan's face and, when Jak pulled off the last of the tape, tearing the wadded microfiber strip from her mouth.

Too late. Dyan drifted in gray nothing. This is dying, she thought.

Somewhere, far away, she heard yelling and thumping noises. She felt calm and peaceful, released from all the fear and trauma of the prior several days.

Was this how it had been for Wayland? she wondered.

Was this how it would have been for Jak?

She coughed, spitting lumps of something onto the dirt into which her face was pressed. Air flooded back into her lungs, and it felt cold.

"Again!" Eirig yelled. "I think she just took a breath!"

Something heavy was on top of Dyan. It pummeled her between the shoulder blades and she coughed once more. This time her cough sounded wet, and she retched, spitting bile in a puddle around her own face.

"Stop!" Eirig cried. He pressed his dirty face down close to hers. "She's breathing," he confirmed.

Dyan wept. Emotion roiled through her in thick currents, all mixed together so she couldn't separate the fear from the pain from the hope from the despair.

Jak, who had been kneeling over her, fell aside onto the sand, cursing faintly. "Sorry," he muttered softly. Dyan couldn't even be sure she'd heard him correctly. Then, louder, "I didn't mean for it to be like that."

Dyan bit off her sobbing. "You meant to kill him. Don't pretend it was an accident."

"I meant to kill him," Jak agreed. "But it was painless and quick, and I only did it because I had to. And he killed my friend. Jone never harmed a fly in her life, and he poked a spear right through her."

"Don't act like you have the moral high ground." Dyan let her face lie in her own vomit. "He didn't have a choice. He never had a choice."

"Neither do I," Jak spat. "But I still have to deal with the consequences of my actions. And so did he." He pulled Dyan to her feet.

"Ah, look, you're a sight," Eirig chided her. He dug into Wayland's saddlebags and found a water flask. Holding it to Dyan's mouth, he helped her rinse and spit into the sand several times.

"I won't gag you again now," Jak told her. "The others are miles away, so there'd be no point in screaming. Let's get back to the cave and collect your friend."

"She's not my friend." Dyan felt numb.

Jak nodded slowly. "Let's get her anyway." He turned and took a step towards the dead horse, bending to collect its saddlebag.

Dyan ran.

She lurched and staggered, almost falling at every step, but she propelled herself forward with all the force she possessed. Not to escape, not to get away—

she ran towards the whip.

"Jak!" Eirig yelled. The one-armed boy dove for Dyan, his hand outstretched. He almost grabbed her, but his fingers managed only to hook into the big hip pocket of her coat, tearing the threads and ripping the pocket clean off. His hand banged into her ankle, knocking her slightly sideways, but Dyan stayed focused on her goal. She couldn't see the line itself, of course, but she stared at the whip handle, willing herself to pass it, to end her own suffering.

This was a choice she could make, and a consequence she was willing to suffer.

Jak slammed into her from behind, pounding her face down again into hard sand.

"Blazes!" she cursed him.

"Yeah," he agreed, breathing hard. "And worse."

"You're just going to kill me anyway," she mumbled into the sand.

"True," he admitted. "But not right now. I might need you still."

The boys dragged Dyan to her feet together, gripping her tightly so she couldn't run. Her will was spent anyway, and she didn't try. Not even when Eirig stooped over Wayland's body, picking up his saddlebags and hat and kicking off his own tattered shoes in favor of Wayland's boots.

He saw her looking at him and shrugged apologetically. "My shoes are in bad shape," he said. "And the walking's rough around here."

Dyan nodded. Numb.

He put Wayland's hat on Dyan's head. "And your skin's already turning red."

Jak led them back up the canyon onto the mesa and Dyan didn't look back. She stumbled, trying to collect her thoughts and feelings while her legs marched mechanically. Jak walked a meandering path, sticking as much as possible to the top of large stretches of slickrock, and out of the sand.

To avoid leaving tracks, Dyan realized, and she looked down at her feet.

Her trousers were soaked in blood. Wayland's.

She started to cry.

"It's not that bad," Eirig said at her shoulder, and then he laughed. "Ah, who am I kidding? How could it be any worse?"

Jak stopped and squinted at both of them. With his eyes mostly shut against the sun, his brown skin looked like the bark of a tree.

He looked like he fit into the desert, like he was a wild thing, like if he just lay down he'd disappear into the sand and she'd never see him again.

She stopped crying. To avoid seeing her bloody legs, she turned and stared at the rolling red-brown horizon.

"We passed a spring on the way out here," Jak said slowly. "Let's stop there and clean up."

They crawled around the skirts of an immense knobby tower of stone, and at the far side of it, as Jak had promised, a trickle of water seeped from its base. The water ran through a series of sinkholes, each large enough to swim a pair of horses, towards a gap in the slickrock that Dyan guessed must be the canyon through which the river flowed.

"I'll untie you," Jak told Dyan, "if you promise you won't do anything stupid."

"If doing stupid things is the test," Eirig quipped, "you'd better tie *me* up. I never should have come after you in the first place."

"I promise."

Dyan hadn't realized how numb her arms felt until Jak untied her hands. The sudden return of blood to her limbs tickled, then stung like a swarm of bees crawling through her veins and stabbing her at every tiny, furry step.

Jak directed her to the second pool. "We'll want to drink out of the first pool," he said, and then he positioned himself between her and the river.

Dyan shrugged out of her coat and laid it aside. "You don't trust me." She hesitated, and then began to strip out of the rest of her clothing. Her trousers especially were so stiff with dirt and blood, she thought they'd stand up by themselves. When she was down to her underwear, she slipped into the water.

The freezing cold of it shocked her. She thrashed her arms and legs for warmth and gasped for breath, and when she had recovered her self-control she saw that Jak still stood guard, resolutely looking the other direction.

She dunked her head under the surface of the chilled pool, sighing with her whole body as the coldness of it gave relief to her scraped and tender skin. "I guess I must look pretty terrible," she said.

"Don't worry about it."

Dyan submerged herself again, enjoying the feel of the cold water prickling her scalp. She emerged from the water and deliberately looked away from Jak. She rubbed her arms and legs with her hands, scraping off sweat and dirt as best she could.

She splashed to the edge of the pool and dragged her trousers and shirt into the water. It isn't Wayland's blood, she told herself. It's just dirt. It's just another kind of dirt, and it will wash out.

"You're going to be walking in wet clothes," Jak told her. "I'm not waiting around for your things to dry."

Dyan shrugged and arranged her cleaner shirt on the stone at the edge of the pool. The rock was warm and the sun fierce, and she thought the garment would dry quickly. They weren't made of microfiber cloth, but of a fine, elastic weave that breathed, insulated, was sturdy, and cleaned well.

"Sounds fine to me," she said. "Sounds cool."

He shook his head. "You'll chafe."

She laid her trousers out beside her shirt. Not all the marks had come out of the thin, tough fabric, but the spots were more indistinct now, and looked less obviously like blood.

"You're going to kill me," she said calmly. It seemed like a fact now, unavoidable and almost meaningless. "Chafing won't bother me long."

Jak snorted, glared at her, and looked away again.

"Are you going to kill me last?" Dyan asked.

"Do you think you can talk me out of it?"

"No." She shook her head. "Just curious to know what I should expect."

"I don't want to kill you at all," he said. The earnestness of his voice made her look at him, and he was looking back. He looked serious. He looked sad. He looked desperate. "I have to do what I can to protect my mother."

"I don't have a mother," Dyan said, automatically. "Or anyway, I have one in a biological sense, but I don't know her and I doubt she knows me."

"That's how it is for you Systemoids, then?"

Dyan nodded, and found herself humming. She let herself enjoy it. The haunting, unknown familiarity of the tune was strangely comforting.

Jak looked at her curiously for several long seconds. "I guess I deserve that," he finally said. "Feels kind of grim, though."

"What's grim?" she asked. She dragged herself up the lip of the sinkhole. Her arms buckled and almost gave out, but when Jak offered a hand she refused it. She threw herself onto the stone beside her drying clothes and closed her eyes, luxuriating in the heat of the slickrock.

"That song."

"You know it?"

"Doesn't everyone?" Jak harrumphed. "Heard it since I was a little kid. Aleen used to sing it me. I think its darkness appealed to her."

Dyan forced herself to keep her eyes shut. "You don't like the words, I guess." To her surprise, Jak started singing.

"Sally, she married a soldier,
A captain named William Lee.
I guess in his fashion he loved her,
But Sally always loved me."

He fell silent.

"That's not so grim," Dyan pointed out. "That's just star-crossed love. *Married* is an old word, a pre-Cataclysm word, for a Love-Match. At least half the funvids in the System Library are about tragic romance."

"True." Jak paused, and Dyan forced herself to keep her eyelids screwed shut. "And I know what *married* is. Goodman and goodwife. The grim part of the song is where he kills her."

Dyan's heart beat so loudly, she almost didn't hear Jak's footsteps on the stone as he walked away.

When she opened her eyes, the two boys stood at the spring, filling water flasks. Dyan followed the trickle of water with her gaze through spillover pools towards the canyon, and considered running for her freedom. But she had no weapons, and no tools, and she was alone. All she could really hope to accomplish was suicide. An hour or two earlier, that would have seemed like a desirable goal.

Now, she found, she wanted to live.

Instead she pulled on her clothing, which was dry, and beat her coat against the slickrock to force the worst of the dirt and dust out of it. Then she walked to rejoin Jak and Eirig.

"I guess you'll tie me up now," she said.

Jak nodded, but when Dyan put her hands behind her back, he hesitated. "In front of you," he finally said.

"Thanks."

They crossed more slickrock together, great whale-backs of the stuff that surged up among juniper groves and drifts of reddish sand, and to Dyan it seemed the desert would never end. But suddenly, Jak grabbed her by the back of her coat, pulling her away from a pit that yawned open at her feet.

The cave mouth.

Jak led the way, spear in one hand and light stick in the other, to assist the daylight that managed to trickle down and get into the shaft. He kept shining his light back behind him to illuminate Dyan's steps. She was grateful, but didn't mention it.

She'd been too nice to him already, seeing that he only planned to kill her.

"Mother!" Jak cursed.

Dyan snapped out of her thoughts. Jak had hit the bottom, she realized, and was shining his light all around the lowest part of the cave.

"Bat bite you?" Eirig joked.

Jak cursed again, and slammed his palm against the cave wall, startling three bats into sudden flapping flight.

"She's gone!" he hissed, and he looked at Dyan. "Your friend Cheela's disappeared!"

CHAPTER TEN

Jak stared at Dyan, and she could only shrug.

"I don't know where she is," she said.

"What did she get?" Eirig asked.

Dyan shrugged. "What?"

Jak ran one hand through his hair. "I left one of the bags here. I don't remember what was in it, but no weapons. Maybe a utility knife."

"We should track her down," Eirig suggested.

Jak squinted up the shaft of the cave and grabbed Eirig by the arm. "Out the crack!" he hissed, his voice dropping to a fierce whisper.

"You think she's setting a trap?" Eirig followed Jak's gaze and so did Dyan, but there was no motion in the cave mouth, no silhouettes or other signs of Cheela.

"Wouldn't you?" Jak asked.

"I would," Dyan agreed. She squatted, crouching to wedge herself into the guano-filled crack again.

"Eirig first," Jak ordered, and Eirig obeyed. "We'll get her when it's on our terms."

"Someone else could be waiting for us on the river," Dyan pointed out.

"For *us*?"

"I ... I mean ..." she stammered, "for *you*."

Jak only arched one eyebrow at her.

When the one-armed boy had entirely disappeared, Dyan scurried after him, dragging herself on her belly and forearms, pushing with her knees to force her body forward through sour-smelling dust and slime. It would have been much easier with her hands untied, but she had no hope that Jak was interested in freeing her. She emerged into afternoon shadow on the ledge, and Eirig pointing his spear at her.

Jak scraped out last, coughing from the dust raised by the others' passage. He climbed to his knees to survey the river, upstream and down.

"Flare," Dyan said.

"What?" Jak was startled.

She pointed it out. A trail of smoke drifted in gray tatters into view past the lip of the canyon above them. Moments later, a twinkling green light appeared. It sank between the canyon walls, floating steadily downward on the breeze until it splashed down in the brown water of the river and *fitzzed* out.

"Probably Cheela," Dyan said. "She must think she has us trapped, and is calling Magister Zarah and the others."

"Why her?" Jak pressed. He had a hard, appraising look in his eyes. "Why do you think it's her, and not someone else? Why not an Outrider?"

"The flare was green," Dyan pointed out. "Only Crechelings are issued green flares, so it isn't an Outrider, unless it's some kind of trick. But I can't imagine why an Outrider would be launching a Crecheling's flare so close to us. It seems like a wild coincidence. So I think it must be Cheela. Or maybe ... maybe one of the others." She shuddered and closed her eyes, trying to block out a sudden mental image of Wayland, falling to pieces with a look of surprise on his chubby face.

"Deek," Jak said. "Or Shad."

Dyan opened her eyes and met his gaze. He looked serious and concerned. She nodded.

"Why are you telling me this?" he asked.

Dyan hesitated, then told the truth. "I don't know."

He nodded slowly, then gestured at the river below. "Time to jump," he said. "Eirig first."

"Why am I always first?" Eirig demanded. "It's the one arm, isn't it?" he waved his stump, the skin of which was angry and red but not bleeding. The System's healing ointments were not only antibiotics, they also stimulated cell growth to speed healing. "You pick on me because you know I can't stand up to you in a fist fight?"

Jak shook his head. "I pick on you because you're ugly."

He pushed Eirig in the center of his chest with one hand. The other boy, balanced at the edge of the drop, wiggled to try to avoid the shove but didn't have enough room. Scrabbling for better purchase on the ledge with his toes, he tipped over backwards and fell into the water below with a splash.

He came up flailing and gasping. The water at the base of the cliff was four or five feet deep, and he sloshed out to shallower stretches, glaring up at Jak. "Not funny!" he hissed, but he was grinning.

"Shh!" Jak motioned to Dyan. "You next," he said. "Bend your knees."

She stepped out into the air. She felt the sickening pull of gravity at her stomach and then she splashed into the cold water. The water that had been so harmless to Eirig was over her head, and when she kicked against the river bottom her boots sank into mud. She panicked, losing most of the air in her lungs.

Then a *splash* in the water beside her knocked her sideways, and when she righted herself again, Jak had his hands in her coat collar and was dragging her out into the warm afternoon air.

"Breathe!" he ordered her.

When she had regained her footing, he let her go.

"It's only deep in that one spot," he said. "Right at the base of the rock."

"There's another one." Eirig pointed at the sky, and Dyan saw a second green flare, slowly dropping. "Guess your friend got bored and fired another one."

"Guess again," Jak snapped. "That's coming from downstream. Run!"

He dragged Dyan and threw her ahead of him, staggering through the water.

Eirig huffed behind them. Each of the boys had saddlebags full of gear slung over his shoulder, but Jak was more fit, and Eirig's balance seemed thrown off. Maybe by his loss of his arm, Dyan thought.

"We could hide," Eirig panted.

"Not here!" Jak shot back at his friend. "She'll be out any second!"

Eirig looked like he might have been about to say something else, but instead he tucked his chin and ran faster.

"Stop!"

Dyan heard Cheela's call and her step faltered.

Thump!

Something struck Eirig in the back, knocking him forward and face-first into the water.

Jak spun and raised his hand, holding, Dyan realized, one of the monofilament bolas. She cringed away from it, remembering the mess Jak's friend had made of himself with his unskilled attempt at a bola attack.

Eirig foundered, and as she dragged him up by one arm she looked back. Cheela was armed with a leather sling. She had probably made it herself, Dyan guessed. Cheela raised her arm to her shoulder, swinging it around to launch a projectile—and Dyan realized that Cheela was looking at her.

Jak plowed into Dyan from the side, knocking the air from her lungs and pounding down on top of her and Eirig. All three of them splashed into the water, and Dyan heard a *whiz* and the sharp *crack* of stone on stone as Cheela's sling bullet smacked into a half-submerged boulder right behind the spot where she had been standing.

Dyan rose from the water first in a fountain of mud. She grabbed at Jak with her bound hands to pull him up, but he pushed her away. "Run!" he shouted at her, and turned to face Cheela.

Dyan looked at her Crechemate, and saw murder in the other girl's eye.

Not killing, not the resolution to do the necessary thing that Magister Zarah had talked about, but anger, hatred, and a desire to inflict pain. Cheela stared right past Jak. She was looking at Dyan.

"Come on!" Eirig grabbed Dyan's forearm and pulled her. She resisted.

Cheela put another stone in her sling.

Jak stared at her, raising the bola.

Cheela whipped the stone around and launched it—

Jak dodged, but not fast enough—

and the stone hit him in the thigh.

"Holy Mother!" He stumbled.

Cheela put another stone in her sling, and Jak whirled the bola.

"No!" Dyan cried. In her mind's eye she saw the monofilament, flashing impossibly where she knew it must be, and she imagined it slicing Jak into ribbons. She remembered his friend spinning the bola too long, releasing it too late.

But did she really care if Jak killed himself?

Jak got it right. One spin around his head, just like a sling, and he released the bola in Cheela's direction. Without waiting to see what came of his throw, he turned in Dyan's direction and sprinted. Dyan wanted to tear herself away, but she couldn't. Instead, she watched the bola.

Jak's aim was terrible. The weapon launched close enough to Cheela that she ducked, but she was in no risk. Catching herself in a crouch in knee-deep water, she turned to watch the path of the bola's flight.

It passed her and kept flying, and she turned to race after it.

"Go!"

Jak slammed into Dyan as if he wanted to tackle her. His impetus carried her along like a river current, and she lost sight of Cheela as he pushed her around the bend in the canyon. Her Crechemate knelt in the river, feeling around underwater with both hands.

Dyan's breath came hard, but she was surprised and impressed enough that she had to say something. "You ... you missed ... on purpose," she puffed.

Jak shook his head doggedly and didn't slow down. "I'd have been happy ..." his breath was ragged too, "to slice that ... vixen in half ... but I threw hard ... so if I missed ... at least it might buy us a little time."

Dyan felt profound confusion. She shut up before she said anything even more damaging, and thought furiously.

She didn't like Jak. He wanted to kill her, and she should escape at her first opportunity.

On the other hand, Cheela had tried to kill her. Or had she?

Even escape wasn't enough anyway. Escape from Jak just left her in the position she'd been in before; Magister Zarah ... the System ... wanted her Blooded. It wanted her to kill someone. It wanted her to kill Jak.

Who maybe, just maybe, had saved her life.

She kept running.

At the arch with the mound of boulders beneath it, Jak paused. Dyan's heart thundered and her lungs scorched the inside of her chest, but as badly as she wanted to rest, she wanted even more to stay out of Cheela's grasp.

Cheela catching up would be a reckoning. It would force a decision.

"Do you know any other escape tunnels?" she panted. "Caves, like the other one?"

Eirig shook his head. "We were hiding," he puffed. "We got lucky."

"The waterfall ahead is impassable," Jak said. He stared sharply up into the arch. "But we can use this spot to our advantage. If your friend comes at us from one side, we can leave by the other and get past her."

"But she's not alone," Dyan objected. She wondered whose flare the other had been. She didn't know if she was better off if it belonged to Shad or to Deek. "We saw a second flare."

"All the more reason to get into the arch," Jak nodded, as if her reminder had led him to a decision. "Better to split them up by forcing them to come at us two ways at once." He started scrambling up the rocks.

As an afterthought, he turned to look at Dyan. But she was already following, on her own.

The going was rough, and Jak forced a quick pace. He was more nimble than Dyan was, and when she stumbled over a boulder twice the size of her own body, two thirds of the way up the slope, he caught her by her bound wrists before she hit the ground.

"Kind of makes you glad to be tied up, I guess?" Eirig winked at her as she recovered her balance and breath.

Dyan didn't answer.

"Get in here," Jak hissed at them, and disappeared into the high saddle of rubble and stone beneath the arch.

Dyan followed, saw that Jak squatted low among the stones, and followed his example. Her legs trembled from the effort of running and climbing. After a moment of crouching, they gave out and she dropped onto hard sand.

When she could breathe normally again, she turned and crept on her belly to lie beside Jak and Eirig, looking down into the loop of the river from which they'd come.

"We just have the one bola left," Eirig said. It sounded like a complaint.

"Remember what happened to Yoel."

Eirig shrugged. "Ah, but you're not Yoel, are you? You snapped that thing off at her friend just fine. Almost beaned her."

Jak shook his head. "Don't kid yourself." He nodded at Dyan. "*They* ... I mean, *the System* does it on purpose, you know."

"Does what?" Dyan asked.

"Arms its people with weapons like that. Like the bola, like the whip. Like bows."

Dyan shrugged. "What do you mean, good weapons?"

Jak sighed. "I mean, weapons that are really hard to use. Weapons that can hurt the person trying to use them, if they don't have special training."

Dyan was puzzled. "What do you mean? Why does the System do that then?"

Jak looked at her as if unsure whether to take her question seriously. "It does that because we ... *we Landsmen* ... don't *have* special training."

"A bow doesn't require that much practice," Dyan objected.

"It does if you want to hit anything," Jak said.

"It also requires two hands." Eirig grinned. "So much for my plan to become a great hunter."

Dyan realized that neither of the boys had a bow anyway. "What happened to my bow? To the bow you had?"

"Broke," Eirig said. "Chasing you down the canyon. Small price to pay."

"So what do we have?"

"A bola," Jak listed their assets. "Arrows. Flares. Medikits. Utility knives."

"It's too bad you threw Cheela's weapons into the river," Dyan tut-tutted. "A whip and two bolas would have really come in handy right now."

"At the time," Jak reminded her, "Eirig wasn't doing very well. We couldn't take the risk of you overpowering him and taking your weapons back."

"I've always inspired confidence in my friends," Eirig said. "It's a special gift."

"Shh." Jak pointed.

Around the bend in the canyon came a single horse, bearing two riders.

"Blazes!" Dyan cursed.

The second rider was Cheela. Sitting easy in front of her on the horse, holding the reins and scrutinizing the canyon as they rode, was Shad.

CHAPTER ELEVEN

had stopped his horse at the base of the bouldered slope below the arch and looked up. Dyan strained her ear, but when Shad turned to talk to Cheela, it was in a whisper.

"Blazes," Dyan grumbled.

Cheela dismounted, and Shad urged his horse on at a trot into the bend of the canyon and toward the other side of the arch.

Dyan watched him go for a moment, and then returned her attention to Cheela.

Jak had found the field lens in his saddlebags and gazed through it at Cheela, spinning the dial around the outside of the lens to focus it tightly. "She looks proud of herself," he told them.

"She's going to be Blooded." Dyan didn't really want to discuss it. She felt miserable; in a no-win situation. Cheela and Shad would rescue her easily. Jak was right, she saw now. The System armed its people with weapons that were extremely powerful and that the Landsmen couldn't possibly use. Shad would bottle them up the far side of the arch and Cheela would climb up the near side, and Jak and Eirig had no way out. She looked around. Unless they could fly. "Cheela's anxious to become a full Outrider."

"Ah, that does sound nice," Eirig grinned.

Jak handed the field lens to Dyan. "Take a look. Myself, I'm sort of anxious to not be chopped in half."

"I have the advantage there," Eirig dug into the saddlebags beside him and found the other field lens. "For me, it would be *three* pieces."

Dyan looked through the lens. Cheela did look pleased with herself. She looked eager, sly, and sort of amused. As Dyan looked, and just before Shad disappeared around the bend, Cheela yelled up to her.

"It's not too late, Dyan!" she called. "Surrender! Maybe you can be forgiven!"

"I'm a prisoner!" Dyan hollered back. It was irrational, but she hoped Shad heard her words. She was shouting pretty loud, so she was pretty sure he'd hear the *noise* at least, but thought that the echoes might hide what she was actually *saying*. "Help! Rescue me!"

Shad turned in his saddle before entering the bend and looked up at her. She snapped the field lens around and focused on his face. She hoped to find confusion, disbelief, or sorrow reflected there.

But he just looked sad.

"I told him you attacked me!" Cheela shot back. "I showed him the bruises!"

Shad went around the bend and he and his horse disappeared.

Dyan looked back at Cheela. Her face was bruised. Also, her expression was smug, sneaky, and vicious. It was an animal-like expression.

Eirig laughed, but it was an uncomfortable sound. "I guess there's some tension between you two."

"Watch the other side," Jak told him.

Eirig scooted across the saddle to the Shad side, keeping low to the ground.

"Shad won't believe her," Dyan said.

"Yeah?" Jak pressed. "Is that how it always goes? The other girl's a big fat liar, and the handsome guy's on your side?"

"I ... I ..."

Jak didn't wait for her to finish. "Either check your girlfriend to see what weapons she's carrying or give me back the device."

"Field lens." Dyan looked through the lens and examined Cheela.

"Field lens," Jak repeated.

"I didn't say he was handsome. And she's not my girlfriend."

"The guy on the horse is in sight over here," Eirig reported.

"I can see he's handsome with my own eyes," Jak snorted. "And she sure isn't *my* girlfriend."

Dyan finished her survey. "Two bolas."

"No whip? You sure about that?"

Dyan checked again. "No whip."

"Not that it matters," Jak grumbled. "She might as well have Pistols."

"What's Pistols?" Dyan asked.

Jak ignored her question. "Don't take this the wrong way," he told her, "but now is not the time for old stories." He knelt beside an angular boulder, jutting upright like a tooth from the gum of the arch and leaning out in Cheela's direction. Experimentally, he put his shoulder against it and pushed. The big rock didn't budge.

"Whichever side of it you're on," Eirig added. "Horse boy has arrived."

Dyan scooted across to Eirig's side and looked.

Shad stood on a sandbar, across the canyon from the arch and from the water seep in the canyon wall beside it. He hitched his horse's reins to a gnarled pine, pulled the bow from his saddle and slung the quiver over one shoulder. He nocked an arrow and turned to look up in Dyan's direction.

Dyan stood. It was a risk, but Shad surely wouldn't shoot her. She held up her tied hands. "I'm a prisoner!" she yelled.

Shad raised his bow, lightning quick—

hands grabbed her coat from behind—

and yanked her backwards. An arrow rattled off the vault of the arch, lancing through the space Dyan had just vacated. She hit the ground hard and found herself staring up into Jak's face. *He* looked confused, disbelieving, and sorrowful.

"Cheela," Dyan gasped, sucking air back into her lungs. "She lied."

Jak shook his head. "I don't think you can blame this one on the System, Dyan," he said.

Eirig chuckled. "This one belongs to *love*," he smirked.

"Ironically," Jak pointed out, "your only hope right now is in me *not* freeing you. If I let you go, handsome guy believes dark and curly that you're the one who attacked him, and kills you on the spot."

"Kills or captures," Dyan said weakly, but she wasn't convinced.

"Not sure which would be worse."

Dyan wasn't sure either. "His name is Shad."

"I know his name."

Dyan dragged herself to the edge of the saddle, keeping low. "I didn't do it!" she yelled. "I didn't hit Cheela! I didn't do whatever else she told you—I'm captured by ... by these men!"

"Call us Landsies," Eirig suggested. "That always brings a tear of mirth to a Systemoid eye."

"Shut up!" she hissed at him.

"I've seen the bruises," Shad called back. "And there's no other way two unarmed Landsmen could have overpowered you."

"They snuck up on us!"

Shad shook his head. "Not on an Outrider." Was there a hint of doubt in his voice?

"I'm innocent!"

Shad shook his head stubbornly. He retrieved something from his saddlebags, and Dyan saw that it was a flare. He stripped its seal off, preparing to pull the ripcord and ignite the device. "I knew you were jealous, Dyan!" he yelled. "But I didn't think you'd go this far!" He raised the flare—

"Capture me!" Dyan yelled.

Shad hesitated.

"You're the one who always wants to capture, remember?" she called down to him. "Capture me! Take me prisoner back to Buza System. I'll explain!"

Jak and Eirig crouched beside her, watching intently.

"You sure you want to let her do this?" Eirig asked his friend.

"It's a distraction," Jak said. He had one of the field lenses to his eye and homed in on Shad.

Shad looked down at his boots, ankle-deep in the brown river water. When he looked up, his eyebrows knit together fiercely. "I can't." Dyan could barely hear him. "I promised."

"Holy Mother," Eirig cracked. "It's *true* love."

Dyan looked down at Shad and realized that she was staring at her own death.

He aimed the flare at the sky with one hand and yanked the cord with the other. With a sharp *pfffft!* the ball of green light snapped out of the flare tube and raced skyward. Then he nocked another arrow and stood waiting.

"Ha!" Jak spat, and dug into his saddlebags. He came out with three flares and held them to Dyan. "You know how to use these, I assume?"

She started to object that her hands were tied, but before she could articulate even the first words, he had produced a utility knife and cut through the ropes.

"I don't get it." She took the flares. "I didn't think you wanted to attract the others."

"I don't," he agreed. "I want you to shoot these at your girl-friend."

He scooted over to the other side of the saddle and Dyan followed. She looked down, and saw Cheela creeping up the slope. The flare had been Shad's signal to her that he was in position. He would wait with his bow and kill any of them who emerged.

"They're not really accurate like that," she said. "I don't know if I can hit her."

"If you can actually hit her, great," Jak agreed. "Mother, I think you might even find it personally satisfying to put a green fireball into that vixen's forehead. But at least keep her distracted."

"You trust me to do this?" she asked.

"The flare takes two hands to operate," he said, and nodded at Eirig. "Do I have another option?"

"I guess not."

"Wait until she exposes herself to try to throw at me," Jak suggested. "Then let her have it."

Dyan stripped the seals off all three flares. "What are you going to do?"

Jak pulled the bola, their last monofilament weapon, from the purse at his belt. "I'm going to do my best to kill her."

Cheela came low to the ground, moving from rock to rock with quick, planned motions, never exposing her body very long. Jak climbed up behind the tall, angular, leaning boulder, nodding to Dyan that he was ready.

Dyan aimed the first flare, squinting down it in Cheela's direction as if it were an arrow to the string of a bow.

Cheela paused a moment, crouching behind a gnarled, sunbleached tree trunk. She laughed. "You're just making it worse for yourself!" she called.

"I don't see how that's possible," Dyan countered.

Jak slipped around to the side of the boulder, exposing himself. He stretched apart the bola and its counterweight with his hands. He looked like he was trying to hug the rock.

Cheela stood, bola in hand—

Dyan pulled the ripcord. *Pffft!* A green spark the size of her fist exploded from the tube in her hand, spraying a sulfurous, stinking smoke into her face. She coughed.

Cheela yelped and fell back, scrabbling to get her balance on the rocks. As the smoke cleared, Dyan got a look at her former Crechemate and saw that the shoulder of Cheela's coat was singed. Dyan had hit her.

It felt good. She dropped the empty flare tube and pointed the second flare at Cheela.

Jak scooted back to safety behind the boulder.

Cheela got back into position behind her log, cursing.

Dyan laughed. "You could still surrender, Cheela!" she yelled. It was a ridiculous thing to say—did she really imagine that she was going to help Jak take her fellow Crecheling prisoner? But hitting Cheela with the flare had felt like a victory. It had given her hope, and she enjoyed the feeling.

In answer, Cheela threw a rock. Dyan didn't see it coming, and the stone narrowly missed her. Narrowly enough that if Cheela had thrown a bola instead, it would have sliced Dyan's head off.

Dyan stopped laughing, hunkered down, aiming the second flare at Cheela again.

Jak once more shuffled into an exposed position to the side of the boulder, hugging it with his bola extended.

This time Cheela threw a rock at Dyan first. The throw was left-handed, though, and Dyan didn't flinch. The moment Cheela rose from her crouch to fling a bola at Jak, she fired again. *Pffft!*

This second shot hit short of the mark, the flare spitting sparks in all directions as it struck the log in front of Cheela. The sparks, though, must have stung. Cheela held hands up to cover her face, and dropped back into hiding at the same time

Jak scooted around his boulder to shelter. "Help me!" Jak hissed to Eirig.

Eirig threw a quick look down at Shad and scrambled up to join Jak behind the boulder.

"Careful!" Dyan warned the boys. "Stay down, and behind the rock. You don't want either one of them to see you clearly."

What was she thinking?

As if to punctuate her advice, an arrow slammed into the boulder just over Jak's head. He squatted, getting out of the line of fire. Then he and Eirig put their shoulders to the rock and pushed.

Dyan felt a little thrill. She saw Jak's plan now, and she expected the rock to topple right over and cause instant headaches for Cheela, who crouched right in the stone's path.

Only the boulder didn't fall.

She looked back to the Outrider-designate, in time to see her swing her arm—

"Duck!" Dyan yelled.

Jak threw himself to the ground, dragging Eirig with him.

The bola sliced right through the big stone, whizzing through the space the two boys had just occupied. It spun between the saddle and the vault of the arch, then out into space on Shad's side of the river.

Good, she thought, and for a second she hoped it hit him.

Then she felt bad.

Jak snapped his fingers in her face, getting her attention. "One more time!" he whispered. "You ready?"

"The stone's too heavy," she told him. "Cutting through it isn't helping you. Blazes, it's cut through twice now, and the rock's just sitting there."

"Yeah," he agreed. "But Eirig's going to help me this time. Cover us!"

Dyan lay at the edge of the saddle again, pointing the last flare at Cheela. In the seconds during which Dyan had looked away, Cheela had crept another ten feet up the slope. She was daunting close now, with an easy shot at anyone who was exposed.

Jak and Eirig dropped in front of the boulder, one on each side. Dyan stood up, exposing herself.

Jak and Eirig looked like they held hands for a moment and then drew apart, and Dyan realized that they each held one end of the bola's monofilament line. Cheela might realize it, too.

"You lying cow!" Dyan shrieked.

Cheela looked at her and swung her arm.

The boys stepped back up into the saddle, slicing diagonally through the stone.

Dyan fired the last flare. It was a terrible shot, ten feet wide at least, and Cheela only grinned at it.

With an immense *crack!* a divot of stone sprang from the face of the boulder where Jak and Eirig had sliced it out. The stone slid, toppling and falling towards the slope.

Cheela threw her bola.

CHAPTER TWELVE

CRASH!

The boulder slammed into the slope. A noise like rolling thunder bounced off the vault over Dyan's head and filled her ears with echoes. She didn't watch the slope give way to landslide; the instant Cheela flung her arm forward to release her weapon, Dyan dropped.

The bola made a distinct hum as it whipped past her. Dyan felt a tug at her hair, and as she collapsed back onto the ground a cold panic flooded her.

Had her head been severed? Had she saved Jak and Eirig at the cost of her own life? Was she now dead, and just not yet aware of it?

She half-expected her skull to bounce away from her shoulders as she landed, but it didn't. With a painful thump to her entire body, the firm sand pounded all the air out of her lungs. Stunned, she barely noticed Jak and Eirig rushing over the rocks, out of the saddle, and down the slope towards Cheela, spears in their hands.

Blood rushed into her head and she rolled over, struggling to rise. She could run, she thought wildly. She could run to Shad and explain everything.

Only Shad didn't believe her. Shad had already tried to shoot her, and if she approached him now, he'd do it again.

Shad waited in the river below, to shoot her if she ran from Cheela. He must hear the same thundering of stone that Dyan did.

She wondered what he'd make of it. What signal would he have arranged with Cheela in case anything went wrong? Would it be more flares?

She couldn't wait to find out.

Dyan climbed to her hands and knees, then her unsteady feet, and finally she lurched out of the saddle, on the Cheela side.

Below her, in the deepening shadows of the afternoon, the slope was alive. It looked like a hill of boulder-sized ants, mad and swarming, all rushing downhill. Cheela stumbled near the river's edge, riding the swarm and struggling to stay on her feet. Jak and Eirig jogged towards her. They ran in the dissipating second half of the rockslide, and Dyan ran after them.

She caught up to them as they reached Cheela. The Outrider-designate stood in the river, coughing orange dust from her lungs and batting it off the sleeves of her coat. Her posture was ginger and tentative, like she might fall over at any second.

Jak pointed his spear at her. "We have a hostage again."

"I thought little Dyan here was your hostage," Cheela sneered.

"A hostage pretty boy cares about," Eirig explained. Then he shot an apologetic look at Dyan and shrugged.

"It's true," Dyan murmured. To Cheela she added: "You told Shad I hurt you."

"It might as well be true," Cheela laughed. "Look at you, running with the Landsies just like one of the herd!"

Dyan shook her head. "I only did what you forced me to do." In that moment, she wished she *could* be one of the Landsmen herd. Or one of any herd, actually. "What's the signal?" she asked.

Cheela bared her teeth. "I'm not telling you anything."

"There is no signal," Dyan said. "Kill her."

She didn't know, when she said the words, whether she meant them or not. They just came out, rising from training or experience or some deep-rooted emotions she didn't want to admit to herself.

Cheela, though, took her seriously. The Outrider-designate sprinted—

only she couldn't. She took one step and fell, screaming, into the water.

Jak stood over her, spear in hand, hesitating. "I'm in charge here," he said. He didn't sound completely confident.

Eirig looked back and forth between Jak and Dyan.

"Pretty boy's coming back this way any minute on his horse," Dyan said. Part of her, deep inside, wept at the sound of her own words. Shad! She shoved that part deeper down into the darkness and slammed a door shut behind it. "He's willing to kill me, and he's willing to do it because he's in love with her."

Jak nodded. "We run," he said. "Her ankle's broken, she'll slow him down."

"We run," Dyan agreed. "But first we get the horse."

"Help me get her on the sand."

Jak and Eirig dragged Cheela across the shallow river and threw her, roughly, onto a sandy bank of grass. Cheela struggled at first, but with every bump of her foot against the riverbed, she yelped, and the pain undercut her ability to resist.

Just as the boys pointed their spears at her face, Dyan heard splashing sounds in the bend of the canyon. She didn't have to look to know that it was Shad, charging in on his horse to save the day. Tears stung the corners of her eyes, and she ignored them.

"Give me the bola," she said.

Jak hesitated.

"The spears won't seem like much of a threat to him. And if you hold the bola," she pointed out, "he'll think you're just going to cut yourself in half with it, like your friend did. I know how to use it, and he thinks I'm one of you."

"Only you're not." Jak's words sounded like a question.

She looked into his eyes. "I am now. I don't have a choice."

Jak handed her the bola.

She stepped one pace back from Cheela, whimpering on the sand. "Give me space," she warned the boys in a soft voice. "If I have to use this, you don't want to be too close."

Shad reined his horse in midstream and stared at Dyan.

"I never would have believed it," he said. "I almost didn't believe it, when Cheela told me."

Dyan felt like a horrible gulf yawned at her feet, instant death and yet another forced choice. She had the bola in her hands now. She could kill Jak with it, and one-armed Eirig would be no challenge. She could tell Shad that Cheela was a liar, and she, Dyan, had been a prisoner who had now turned the tables on her captors.

She looked into Shad's eyes, about to begin an explanation. She stopped when she saw his expression. His eyes were full of love.

And he was looking at Cheela.

She looked at Jak. He had backed away and given her the space she had asked for. Now he looked at her, and his eyes, too, were compelling. He looked trusting, and nervous. And his eyes asked a question.

"Believe it," she said to Shad.

Eirig let out a soft sigh. She hadn't realized he'd been holding his breath.

"What happened?" Shad wanted to know. "Are you some kind of renegade?"

"What happened," she told him, "is that the System didn't give me any choice." She meant it as a defense, but when she said it she realized that it was true. And then she realized she had a chance to save other lives. "I told Jak and Eirig here what was going to happen. About the Cull. I helped them escape."

"Of course you had a choice." Shad shook his head impatiently. "You were Called to be a Magister. Your invitation from Buza System was to participate in the Blooding, become a full Urbane, and then teach children. It's what you always wanted to do, and the System offered it to you. And instead you decided to attack your own kind, go outlaw."

"The System offered me what I always thought I wanted," Dyan agreed. "But at a terrible price. I can't become the monster it wants me to be."

"The monster *I* am?"

She said nothing.

"So what now?" Shad asked. "You kill Cheela, I kill you, the Landsies ride home to Ratsnay Station as heroes?"

"Ratsnay Station," Jak hissed, "doesn't know anything about this. Ratsnay Station thinks I'm being taken to live the life of luxury."

Shad shrugged, indifferent.

"You give us the horse," Dyan said. "And we leave you here."

"And the weapons!" Jak added.

Shad laughed. "If I give you my weapons, you kill me."

"And if you don't," Jak said, "*you* kill *me*."

"You give him the bow," Dyan offered, pointing at Eirig. "And the saddlebags. And the horse. You keep your whip."

"Or else what?"

Dyan pointed at Cheela, who snarled back at her like a wild animal. "Or else I kill the blazing vixen."

"You wouldn't!" Cheela snapped.

Dyan stared down at her former Crechemate. Cheela's face was contorted by hatred and pain into something terribly ugly. Hatred, pain, and something else.

Fear, Dyan thought. It felt like an accomplishment to her.

"You lied and betrayed me." She stared at the taller girl. "You'd better believe I'd kill you."

"She'll die anyway," Shad said calmly. "If you take the bags, I have no way to get help, and it's a long way to carry her out."

"You could make a travois and drag her." Dyan's own voice sounded cold to her. "But we'll drop flares on the sand around the bend."

"I keep the medikit."

"Fine."

Shad narrowed his eyes. "How do I know I can trust you?"

Dyan raised the bola over her head, finger on the mechanism that would release the weapon's counterweight. One flick of her arm, and Cheela would be permanently out of her misery, sliced in half.

Shad threw his bow at Eirig's feet. "Fine." He dug the medikit out of his saddlebags, then dismounted and stepped away from the animal. He was closer to Cheela and Dyan both, his nearness reminding Dyan how tall he really was. His hand hung at his side, an instant's grab from the handle of his whip.

"Mount up, boys," Dyan told Jak and Eirig. She kept her eyes on Shad.

"It's a big animal, but it won't take us all," Jak answered. "I'm fastest. You and Eirig ride."

Dyan knew he was right. She backed away slowly, pivoting to the other side of the animal and mounting with one hand. She never relaxed her grip on the bola's trigger, and Shad never took his hand away from the whip. When she had the horse's reins in her hand, Eirig climbed up behind her, clutching a bow and spear.

Jak backed away slowly, and Dyan followed on the horse.

"You'll die for this!" Shad called after her.

"I'm dead no matter what I do!" Dyan laughed, feeling a rush of adrenalin in her battered body. It felt like freedom. "At least this way I'm choosing!"

She kept an eye on Shad as she rode away, Jak splashing at her side in the river water. The young man with whom she had once thought she might have a Love-Match knelt over his injured companion and tended to her foot. He was still working on it when Dyan rode around the next bend in the canyon and he disappeared from sight.

"Be careful," Jak warned. "Your other friends are still out here somewhere."

"Deek," she agreed, thinking that the shy, technically-oriented boy would be little threat.

"And the Magister," he reminded her.

"At some point," Eirig said, "even your Magister is going to have to admit that this has all just gone to blazes, and call in the Outriders."

"I'm not sure," Dyan mused.

As she had promised, she tossed the remaining flares they had—two of them—onto a dry bank of sand around the bend.

"So you've thrown in your lot with us." Jak kicked at the sand beside the flares.

Dyan laughed to put on a show of bravado. "I'll go it alone if I have to."

"I still have to kill them, you know."

"Why? If they don't have any reason to worry about Ratsnay Station, they'll leave the settlement alone."

Jak groaned uncertainly. "I don't know that for sure."

"You could never have been sure," Dyan pointed out. "Even if you killed them all, the System might still assume it was the settlement's fault and wipe it out. Or it might wipe them out, just to be on the safe side."

Jak rammed his spear into the sand and rubbed his face with his hands. "What do you suggest?"

Dyan scanned the walls of the canyon. They towered over her, immense and orange, like prison walls. She couldn't see beyond them, even in her imagination. She pulled off her hat to wipe sweat from her forehead and discovered that its crown had been sliced completely off. It took her a moment to realize that it must have been Cheela's thrown bola that had done it.

"What would you have done?" she asked. "Did you have a plan?"

"Kill you all," Jak said. "And then run for the Wahai."

"Is there any reason to do anything different?" she asked.

"The Wahai is terribly romantic, of course," Eirig agreed. "But don't you think the Outriders will assume we're hiding out around Ratsnay Station?"

"And then we're back to our original problem." Jak's voice was grim.

Dyan looked at the sand, scuffed and disturbed by Jak's kicking. "So we tell them where we're going," she suggested. "We leave a trail."

The afternoon had turned into evening and the bats were out when they reached the chimney leading to the cave.

Jak climbed up the rock with his back against one wall of the shaft and his feet against the other, and then let down rope. Dyan and Eirig climbed up—Dyan's muscles ached like they'd never ached in all her life, no matter how hard the training or exercise the Magisters put her through—and when Eirig bent to pull up the rope, Jak stopped him.

"We need to be followed," he said. "Remember?"

By the time they'd climbed to the top of the shaft and emerged again onto the mesa, the sun had fallen below the horizon.

"The Wahai is west," Dyan said. She looked at the stars quickly and pointed the direction. "We should make as much distance as we can tonight."

Jak shook his head. "We should make some distance," he agreed. "But if we run too fast in the darkness, we're going to find ourselves running over a two hundred foot cliff."

They walked slowly, several miles. This time, they deliberately walked on sand as much as possible, and kicked their way through thickets of brittle shrubs, and trampled grass. After an hour or more of tramping, on a high wrinkle of rock overlooking a tumble of wrecked stone walls and an inward-leaning grove of splintered timbers that must once have been a building, Jak called a halt.

He rubbed his eyes in the moonlight. "I'm exhausted. I'll stand the first watch, so I can sleep through the rest of the night."

"I'm not tired at all," Eirig yawned. "I'll stand a watch."

Dyan didn't think Jak had slept at all the night before, and Eirig's body, in addition to everything else it was going through, was using a lot of energy to heal his injury. Neither of them was in much condition to be on his feet any longer.

"Obviously," Dyan said, "I will stand the first watch."

Jak tended quickly to Eirig's arm again, smearing his stump once more with antibiotic and regenerative salve. Both of them fought sagging eyelids through the process, and then curled up under microfiber blankets in the shadow of a clump of juniper trees and were quickly snoring.

Dyan settled against a low ridge of stone. A cool breeze blew against her, and she opened her coat. The chill would help keep her awake.

She rubbed her wrists, chafed where she had been tied. The skin on her face and the back of her neck scratched and felt raw, and she guessed it had been burned by the sun. She thought about using some of the salve on herself, but decided to save it for Eirig. Besides, the pain would also help keep her awake. And in her heart, she knew she deserved all the pain she was feeling, and more.

"They're asleep," she heard a voice in the darkness. "Good. Now we can talk."

A black shadow detached itself from the ink of the night, and dropped its hood to reveal the lean face of Magister Zarah.

CHAPTER THIRTEEN

I'm armed," Dyan warned the Magister. "I could cut you down where you stand."

"Then I'll sit," Zarah said. "If I am to die, I'd like to do it comfortably." She settled carefully onto an arm of the same ridge of stone against which Dyan leaned.

"I could yell," Dyan told her, "and warn the others."

"So could I," Zarah agreed. "And if we are to tell of all the tragic and terrible things we might do, for that matter, I could have simply killed you in the darkness before you noticed me."

Dyan hesitated. Zarah didn't sound like she'd come to arrest Dyan. "How can you talk about *tragic and terrible things* so lightly?" she asked. "Do you know what happened to Wayland?"

"He was cut in half," she said instantly. "I was almost caught in the same trap myself, only Deek noticed the whip. Very clever."

Dyan was silent, remembering the sudden weight of Wayland's torso slamming into her body and the smell of his blood.

"If Cheela is to be believed, it was your doing."

"It wasn't," Dyan said. She wasn't sure she should be talking to the Magister, but she had to admit that if Zarah's purpose in coming had just been to kill her, she could have done it before Dyan noticed a thing. "And she isn't."

"I know." The moon shone on Zarah's face where she sat, giving it a soft, silvery glow. "She's in love with Shad, I see it. Young people do crazy things for love."

"I thought I was in love with Shad, once. It seems like a long time ago now."

"If ever you were in love with him," Zarah said softly, "then, on some level, you always will be."

Dyan bit back a sudden sob, managing to twist it into something like a cough. "Is it like that for everyone? That's terrible."

"Not for everyone," Zarah said. "But it's like that for some people, and I know you, Dyan. I've been watching you."

"You've been my Magister for four years."

"I've known you for longer than that." Zarah chuckled. "I knew you in the nursery, when you were a chubby little thing who wouldn't pick her feet up, so static electricity kept your hair standing nearly vertical."

Dyan laughed, slightly. She didn't want to wake Jak and Eirig. "I don't remember that."

"You wouldn't. Do you remember that you were the most tactile child in the nursery? That you insisted on touching all the other children, all the time?"

"No." Dyan lost herself a little in the images that Zarah was producing.

"The combination was a disaster." Zarah slapped her own knee in silent mirth, shaking. "You'd shuffle from child to child, shocking each of them in turn."

"That sounds like I was a mess."

"You were a human being. The difference can be difficult to spot."

Dyan didn't know what to say. She felt like she was being led into a teaching moment, but the point of it still eluded her.

"You're the kind of person who will love forever, Dyan," Zarah said. "You're also the kind of person who will always love easily. You have powerful empathy, the ability to know what other people are feeling, or at least to imagine what you would be feeling if you were them. It's a wonderful thing. It can give you great insights into people. It can also lead you into great disaster, and injury."

"I'm a human being," Dyan countered. "The difference between a human being and a disaster can be difficult to spot."

"You must realize that others don't feel as you do, and don't see as you do."

"What do you mean?" Dyan had had many conversations with Magisters over the years, including Zarah. They were frequently one-on-one interviews, but she'd never had a conversation this intimate before. She felt a little bit invaded. Zarah seemed to want her to understand something, but Dyan still couldn't see it.

"Take Cheela. You look at Cheela, and you see that she has feelings for Shad. How does this make you feel?"

"Betrayed." Dyan felt tiny. She wasn't enjoying this lesson very much.

Zarah reached over and patted her knee. "I'm sorry, Dyan. How do you feel about Cheela?"

Dyan shrugged, miserable. "Sad. It's bad luck for me that she likes Shad, and worse luck that Shad likes her back. I guess I envy her. How's her ankle?"

"She, on the other hand, sees you as a bug. She doesn't care what your feelings are. She couldn't imagine herself in your situation if she tried. If you two had traded places there on the riverbank today, she would have sliced you in half without a second thought."

"She did try to slice me in half," Dyan remembered.

"She doesn't care about other people's feelings because she can't really see them. Shad, by the way, is more like you. If those two have a Love-Match and it ends, Shad will remember it with happiness and pain years later, and Cheela will simply move on."

Dyan suddenly felt cold, and closed her coat. "That seems brutal."

Zarah shrugged. "It's a kind of person. Cheela isn't alone, and there are others who are similar in their small feeling for their fellow human beings, but more extreme. She lacks empathy."

"Maybe it would be nice to be that way," Dyan mused. "It would be nice to just forget about Shad."

"Cheela's lack of empathy is also a sort of gift," Zarah said. "It will make her a good Outrider. When she is tasked with bringing in an outlaw, it won't occur to her to wonder what the outlaw's feelings are. If she has to be harsh with him, or take extreme measures in capturing him, it won't bother her."

"Capture or kill," Dyan said sadly.

"Once the System has made sure of Cheela's loyalties, it can use her to great effect."

"That's what the Blooding is, isn't it?" Dyan asked. "It has nothing to do with the Landsmen, or maybe that's only incidental. It's about testing loyalty, and about hurting people in a way that makes them cooperative. Loyal. Submissive to the System."

"The System is complex and subtle," Zarah murmured. "Little of what it does can be reduced to single purposes. Yes, one of the purposes of the Cull is keep the Landsmen submissive. They lose their best and their brightest, the natural leaders of any rebellion. And they are in the habit of thinking that all their relationships, all their society, are subject to the consent and veto of the System. They submit.

"And also, another purpose of the Cull is to keep the Urbanes submissive. Every Urbane you have ever met ..." Magister Zarah hesitated, and a secretive smile played around her lips. "Every Urbane has submitted to the Blooding. That means that every Urbane shares the secret, common guilt. Every Urbane knows he is complicit, and knows he will submit to the very last crossable line. Every Urbane knows the secret of life—that it is cheap, and easily taken. So every Urbane also submits to the System."

"But the System is just people," Dyan said. "We could just change it."

Zarah was silent for a long time. "I have not come to talk with you about changing the System," she finally said. She sighed heavily. "Do you love that boy over there?" she asked.

"Jak?"

"I understand why you pretend to be surprised," Zarah said. "You do it for my benefit, and also for your own. You don't want to admit that a Landsman might have captured your heart. Especially one whom the System has designated you to Cull."

"It's horrible." Dyan's whisper was tiny.

"It *is* horrible." Zarah leaned in closer. "Life is horrible, Dyan," she said softly. "It is a series of terrible tragedies, and we choose the things we choose in life in order to soften those tragedies, and brighten the dull stretches between them. Do you understand me?"

"I think so."

"I'm like you, Dyan. I can imagine myself in your place. I can do it better than you can, because I am older than you. I've seen many things, experienced many things, stood in strange and unexpected places. Your gift is a Magister's gift, and the System is right to think that it can use you in that Calling to great effect."

"Once it can be sure of my loyalties," Dyan conclude. "Once it has placed on me the burden of collective guilt, and taught me that life is cheap, and that there is nothing so horrible that I wouldn't do it to save my own life. Once it knows that the thing I will choose to soften my tragedies and brighten the dull stretches between them is participation in the System."

"Life as an Urbane is not the worst life there is," Zarah whispered. "Urbanes have the best food to be had, and shelter. And medicine."

"And funvids," Dyan said bitterly.

"Distraction is a powerful and important thing," the Magister said. "And funvids can be considerably more than mere distraction."

"They don't teach you how to escape from having your hands tied," Dyan told her. "I know, because I tried."

Zarah chuckled dryly. "There are other things to be learned."

"So I'm finding out." Dyan huddled into her coat. The moonlight about her felt stern, and the stars cold and remote, and she wondered how Zarah could possibly be comfortable wearing only her simple clothing and cloak of office against the cold. "Magister Zarah, what are you doing here?"

Zarah sighed. "Most Creche-Leavers walk a pre-determined path," she said. "We show them blood, we lead them into the wilderness, we show them joy and community, and then we make them dip their own hands into the blood they've seen. We bring them back to the community sober and adult, broken down and rebuilt again."

"I see now that this is the heart of what a Magister does."

"It is. And you see that because it is in your gift to be a great Magister, a great builder, breaker, and re-builder of human spirits."

"But it went wrong this time."

Magister Zarah hesitated. "Something unexpected happened," she said. "Death has resulted, but death was always going to result, death always does result from the Cull. Some people have been Culled who were not supposed to be, and others, who were supposed to die, have not. Yet. But death still shows us that he is king, that he is the darkness around life's flickering match, the eternal silence around life's short, tuneless warble. No mysteries have been disturbed, no revelations cast into doubt. But a new path has opened. A different choice. Perhaps."

"For me," Dyan realized.

"For you."

"You're saying I have a choice."

"I am."

"I could come back to you."

"You would still have to be Blooded."

"What about Cheela?" Dyan asked. "She told Shad that I attacked her. She told you that I killed Wayland."

"You would have to do something sufficiently ... dramatic ... to convince everyone that Cheela was mistaken."

A thick, cold feeling of horror choked Dyan's windpipe. "I could Cull Jak and Eirig," she said. She wished the cold had rendered her completely numb, but it hadn't, and she felt sick at her own words. "For instance."

"Shad would remember that you spared Cheela when you could have killed her," Zarah predicted. "Others would be persuaded. Then you would cease to be a Magister-designate and become a Magister. You would soften the horrors of life with the pleasures of the System and the company of its people."

"Shad would still love Cheela."

"I don't imagine that Shad will ever forget the image of you standing over Cheela, threatening to cut her head off," Zarah said. "Do you?"

"No," Dyan agreed. "He won't."

"Nor would you ever forget Jak, a boy for whom you once had feelings."

"And whom I had to kill, to make my own life easier."

"Don't say *easier*. Say *bearable*."

"Would it be bearable?" Dyan asked.

"Eventually."

"And the other choice?"

Magister Zarah was quiet. "What do you think the other choice is?"

"The other choice to is to go with Jak and Eirig," Dyan said.

"There is life in the Wahai. There are outlaws, to be sure, but there are also the Shoshan and the Basku."

"Are there other Systems?" Dyan asked. "Other cities, like there were before the Cataclysm?"

Zarah shrugged. "If anyone knows the answer to that, it isn't I. I can tell you that in my travels, I have heard many rumors, and never anything more definite than a rumor. But there's something else I can tell you, something that will interest Jak a great deal more than the possibility that there might be other Systems."

"What's that?"

"Jak's sister Aleen is not dead."

Dyan inhaled sharply. "Is she in Buza System?"

"She escaped the Cull. That makes her an outlaw. I believe she is in the Wahai."

"So I would be like Aleen. I would fill my life with Jak."

"And he would fill his life with you. If he feels about you like you feel about him."

"I'm not sure."

"Maybe he isn't sure yet, either. There's time. You're leaving the Creche now, but you're still young."

"That might mean children," Dyan mused.

In the System, when a Love-Match resulted in the birth of a child, the child was turned over to the Nursery. Mothers delivered their babies and were not allowed to see them, not at all, not once. Dyan had witnessed more than one birth, through one-way glass and under Zarah's supervision. In the Wahai, she assumed, if you gave birth to a child you had to actually raise it. Which made every mother a Magister. It didn't sound horrible to her.

"But no funvids."

"This doesn't sound quite like the Blooding," Dyan said.

"No?" Zarah asked. "Maybe all of life is the Blooding. Maybe life in the Wahai will be its own Blooding to you, and that will be enough."

"Is that how the System sees it?"

"Or maybe my role as Magister is to prepare you for life, whether that is through the Blooding and transition to being an Urbane ... or otherwise."

That definitely wasn't how the System saw it. The choice to become anything other than an Urbane was a choice to run away. That meant being an outlaw, and a special kind of outlaw at that: a renegade. Renegades were hunted.

"Cheela might come after me," she said. "If I were a renegade, and she were an Outrider."

"Which she will be. She's not Blooded yet, but with her attitude, it's inevitable. For that matter, Outrider Shad might be sent to capture you."

"Capture or kill." Dyan considered. "Are you going to get another Landsman for Cheela to ... Cull, then?"

Zarah stood. "That isn't your concern, my child." She gathered her cloak about her.

"What is my concern?"

Magister Zarah disappeared into the darkness, her words drifting over her shoulder and reaching Dyan's ears on the cold night breeze.

"Your concern is to consider the consequences, and to choose."

CHAPTER FOURTEEN

Dyan let the boys sleep through the night, and they both slept hard. The more she thought, the less it seemed to her that she had anything to think about, and when Jak opened his eyes with the first gray light of dawn, she handed him a flask of water.

"I have something to tell you," she said.

"Thanks." He took the water and drank.

She told him that Zarah had said Aleen was alive. She had to lie about when she had heard it, of course. She couldn't admit that she'd let her Magister into camp the night before, and considered the possibility of murdering Jak in his sleep. Instead, she said Zarah had told her the night before the Cull.

He took the news quietly, without showing any visible reaction. Then he kicked Eirig awake and insisted they start immediately.

Dyan couldn't be sure, but she thought that Magister Zarah's words to her the night before had meant that if Dyan chose not to return to the System, and instead to flee with Jak to the Wahai, she wouldn't be followed. Or at least, she wouldn't be followed *now*.

Still, Jak went out of his way to hide their tracks and thwart pursuit, and she let him. She could have misunderstood Zarah, or Zarah could have lied. Or Cheela or Shad might pursue Dyan on their own, against Zarah's wishes. Or someone else might pick up their trail—outlaws or indigenes. So they walked on long stretches of rock, or single file on trails when they had to use them, and when the canyon walls dropped and the Snaik again became accessible, they crossed the river daily.

Jak and Eirig took rabbits with snares, and speared fish. Dyan shot a small deer with Shad's bow—with *her* bow. She knelt beside the animal's body and laid a hand on its neck to ask its forgiveness before Jak skinned it and cut up its flesh.

It wasn't the Blooding the System had intended, but it seemed sufficient to her. In her heart, she pronounced herself a Magister.

She and Jak were never alone together, except for brief moments when Eirig slipped away to check a snare or to deal with some bodily need. She cherished those times, and tried to smile at Jak even more than usual when Eirig was gone to show her feelings. He smiled back, but they never touched, kissed, or did anything that Dyan would have expected to do with a Love-Match.

Jak didn't talk about his sister, other than to mention to Eirig on the first day that he thought she was alive, and somewhere in the Wahai. But the closer they got to the Wahai, the more excited he seemed, the earlier he was awake each morning, and the further he insisted they all walk each day before resting.

They skirted around the broad open southern end of Treasure Valley before finally slipping into it at Nemap, on the shores of the Lull Sea, a week later. Like Ratsnay Station, Nemap was a settlement whose heart was a town enclosed within a stockade wall. Nemap was much larger than Jak's home settlement, though, and boats from its wharves plied across the Lull to visit Marsick and Cowell, and trading grounds of the Basku and the Shoshan on the Wahai-side shore. The Wahai themselves stretched up tall and brown on the other side of the Lull. The Jawtooths were visible on the opposite side of the valley, their tallest peaks capped with white snow.

Looking down from a high grassy ridge at the swarms of people moving in and out of Nemap, Dyan had a realization. "We're going to need new names," she said.

"Ah, if you're bored of *Eirig* already," said her one-armed companion, "you're going to be bored of anything else I can think of even quicker. My old dad had a better imagination than I ever did. I expect it had something to do with how much beer he drank."

"How much did he drink, then?" Dyan asked, recognizing the prompt.

"My old dad drank so much beer that the day after he died," Eirig told her, eyes glittering, "they went to cut his hair for the funeral and discovered that the stuff growing out of his scalp was *hops*."

Dyan laughed, and it was sort of funny. She wished she had an old dad to tell jokes about. "We still need new names," she persisted. "At least here, so close to Buza System. Maybe out in the mountains it won't matter so much."

"How about *Arik*?" Jak suggested. "I'll be *Jass*, and Dyan can be *Dana*."

"That's very fancy, my old friend Jass," Eirig said, "but of course we can't take Dana here into town with us."

Jak bristled. "Why not?"

Eirig laughed. "Look at you both, you're so excited to be having an adventure together," he swung his arms to mimic a marching pace, "choosing false identities and looking for Jak's sister, you've forgotten that Dyan here is dressed like an Urbane."

Dyan looked down at herself. It was true, she had forgotten, but everything about her clothing, from the hat to the coat to the rider's boots, marked her as being from Buza System. "Blazes," she cursed.

"You even swear like a Systemoid," Jak laughed.

"Sorry," Dyan snorted. "Blazes! There, is that better?"

"It is. But the clothing is still a problem."

"Going naked would be even more of a problem."

"Would it?" he asked, and Dyan blushed. Jak's eyes twinkled, and for the first time in many days she felt attractive.

"Come on then, you nitwits," Eirig said. "You hang out here naked. I'll go down and get the girl some decent clothing."

"I'll go," Jak insisted immediately. "I can ask about my sister."

"You can't go around asking if anyone knows *Aleen from Ratsnay Station*, either," Dyan said.

"Don't be silly, I know better than that. I'll say I'm looking for my cousin, who might be using any name, and describe her. The reason it has to be me is that the single best tool I have for finding Aleen is my face."

"What?" Dyan asked.

"She's a few years older than Jak," Eirig explained. "But other than that, people always said they could have been twins."

They sat down off the crest of the ridge and examined the remaining items in their saddlebags. When they had segregated out what they thought they needed from what they thought they could spare, Jak shouldered the bag full of their tradable goods: flares, one of the medikits, a light stick, a field lens, water purification tablets, some concentrated rations, several microfiber blankets. He gave Dyan an excited hug, gripped Eirig's arm, and then traipsed down the long slope into Nemap.

Dyan and Eirig sat and waited.

While they waited, Dyan whistled tunes. After she cycled through various Crecheling songs she knew, she found herself whistling the Gallows Song.

"Ah, I love that one," Eirig said.

"Do you know the whole thing?" she asked.

He sang.

"Sally she married a soldier,
A Captain named William Lee.
And I guess in his fashion he loved her,
But Sally always loved me.
Now I sit by this stone and remember
Her blue eyes and tresses of gold,
And how we said when we were younger,
We'd be together when we grew old.
Oh, sweet Sally,
Dear Mrs. Lee,
Your footsteps are gone,
But your memory lives on,
And you'll always be Sally to me.
The Captain was usually sober.
At night he was usually home.
On bad days he yelled and he beat her
Breaking her pride with her bones.
You know I was never her lover,
But not because I never tried.

She lay every week on my shoulder,
And whispered my name as she cried.
Oh, sweet Sally,
Dear Mrs. Lee,
Your whispers are gone,
But your memory lives on,
And you'll always be Sally to me.
He found us one day by the river,
Just talking, our feet in the foam.
Pulling his Pistol, he shot her,
And I ran to the forest alone.
Some say they drowned there together.
Some say he hanged from a tree.
I guess it doesn't much matter,
Since the Captain took Sally from me.
Oh, sweet Sally,
Dear Mrs. Lee,
Your kisses are gone,
But your memory lives on,
And you'll always be Sally to me."

It was a simple melody, but pretty, and by the end it had become haunting. Listening to the words, it seemed perfect that the hanged man had hummed this tune as he had gone to his death.

"I don't understand a lot of that," Dyan said, "but it moves me. It seems terrible and beautiful at the same time."

"What don't you understand?" Eirig asked.

"Just some of the words. What's a *missez*? You sing that over and over again, in front of a name, like it's a Calling. *Missez Lee.* And I don't know what a *pistol* is. Or a *Captain*. I think a *soldier* is a pre-Cataclysmic word for something like a Guardsman or an Outrider, and that makes sense in the song. And of course, the names are strange."

Eirig shrugged. "Old songs," he said dismissively. "Who knows? Maybe the words made sense to someone once. Maybe they were always gibberish. Like fa la la."

"Coo coo ca choo."

"Rock-a-bye, baby."

"Eirig," she asked him, trying to sound neither too frivolous nor too serious, "what about *your* family?"

"Well, there's my old dad," he said. "The first thing you should know about him is that stuff on top of his head, it isn't hair."

"Eirig!" Dyan punched him in the arm, and he faked a punch back at her—with his missing arm. When he missed and stumbled, she caught him and held him upright. "Be serious."

"Jak's my family," he said.

She furrowed her brow at him.

"Serious." He had a solemn face. "My old dad wasn't a drunk, he was a good man. But my mother died when I was young, and folks say my dad took it hard. He was a fighter and a scout, like an Outrider, I guess, only without all the fancy gear. I only have a few memories of him, and in my memories he's always just come home from some trip up the Snaik or into the Jawtooths, and he's filthy. And then one time he just didn't come home. He was out alone, so no one really knows what happened. Could have been a wildcat or a bear, or a Basku. Maybe he got on the wrong side of someone from the System, or maybe he just fell, broke his leg and died of starvation."

"How old were you then?"

Eirig shrugged. "Five, maybe."

Dyan looked at his stump. "Based on what I know of his son, I don't think something as little as a broken leg could have killed him."

Eirig grinned. "So, Jak's family raised me. His mom Rosyn, she was a fine old lady, but she had her hands full making a living with her own husband dead, so really, the only mom I knew was Jak's sister, Aleen. She's the only parent I remember well. She kept me dressed, and fed, and in school with the Magisters."

"And Jak kept you out of trouble."

"Ha!" Eirig thumped the ground with his fist. "That shows how little you know Jak. *He* was the one always getting into trouble. Whenever I went along, I ended up getting all the blame for whatever we did."

"So did you stop going along?"

"Nope. I just got used to being blamed."

"I don't know any parents," Dyan said.

"Yeah, I heard that," Eirig said. "I guess I have a hard time imagining what that means."

Dyan looked down at the slate gray Lull Sea with its toothpick boats, and the toothpick stockade wall around bustling Nemap. "It means that I remember the Nursery, but only a very tiny bit. It's hard to be certain the memories are even mine, really, and not memories I invented based on later visits to other Nurseries."

"I don't know what a Nursery is."

"Imagine rooms full of cradles. Magisters caring for little babies, other rooms to play in, toys, singing."

"Mothers?"

"No mothers. Like I said, I never knew my parents. I remember Magisters, and sometimes other visitors. I remember being observed through glass windows by adults. Not by anyone's mother."

"Until when?" Eirig asked. "I mean, I assume you didn't just leave the Nursery to come down to Ratsnay Station for the Selection."

Dyan laughed. "No. A child in the System is moved every two years. Two years in one Nursery, then two years in another, and then the child moves into a dormitory and the Creche. And every two years after that, a new dormitory and a new Creche."

"That's a lot of changing."

"Sometimes you have the same Magister more than once, or the same Crechemates. I think they want us to know a lot of people."

"Yeah, but nobody really well. I think they want you not to have a family."

He was right, Dyan thought, but she didn't say anything.

"What's a Creche?" he asked.

"Five kids together in school," she said. "Training. Experiments. Games. Contests. Everything you can do to get ready to be an Urbane. An adult."

"A Systemoid."

"A Systemoid," she agreed.

A speck in the stream of people and animals moving in and out of the Nemap gates individuated itself in the moment of turning off the road and moving up the long grassy slope in their direction. The speck became a blob as they watched it come closer, then a roan horse and rider, and finally Jak. Mounted.

He threw a bale of cloth on the ground when he arrived. "New clothes for everyone!" he said. "New saddlebags, too, that don't look like System issue. Some dried meat and fruit, a map." He dismounted. "This mare isn't the big Outrider beast you're accustomed to, but she should carry one of us at a time, and our gear. We can take turns."

"Your trading has been productive, Jass," Dyan told him.

"Thank you, Dana." He bowed.

"And your face, my good friend Ass?" Eirig asked. "I mean, *Jass*. Has your face accomplished everything it set out to do?"

"In fact," Jak said, "it has."

Dyan shivered at the news. "Really?"

Jak nodded. "A trader asked me almost immediately if I was any kin of that farmer, goodwife Alyra, over in Marsick."

Dyna gasped. She didn't know if she was more excited for Jak or for Eirig. Or maybe even for herself. If Aleena could be Eirig's family, maybe she could be Dyan's as well.

"What are we waiting for?" she asked.

CHAPTER FIFTEEN

I look Basku," Dyan said.

"No, you don't," Jak rejoined. "You're way too fair."

"And dirty." Eirig scratched himself.

"How dirty am I, then?"

"You're so dirty, that's not hair on your head, it's hops, growing in your scalp."

Jak cuffed him. "Do you have other jokes?"

"My old mom taught me never to use a new joke when an old joke will do. That's thrift."

"You didn't know your old mom."

"I meant your sister."

"You call goodwife Alyra *old*, and she may indeed teach you some new jokes."

"Ah, that's a risk I'll take to see her again."

Dyan rode. She wore a light wool serape over wool tunic and trousers. Jak hadn't been able to get new footwear for anyone, so she still wore her riding boots, but they were scuffed up enough that she didn't think anyone would give them a second glance. Her serape was woven in red, white, and green, the traditional Basku colors, and her red beret matched the red in the serape. She knew about Basku clothing and colors like she knew other things about the Basku, such as that they herded sheep, and ate spicy sausage and ewe's milk cheese with hard bread. She had learned these things from the Magisters. She'd seen the occasional Basku in Buza System, or on the road in field excursions, but she'd never actually spoken with one.

And now she looked the part.

The boys, on the other hand, had simple brown cloaks over their grey shirts and trousers. They had sturdy wool shoulderbags and they walked with their spears like staffs, which made them look like a lot of the Nemapi they passed on the road.

To avoid puncturing the disguise, the items they still had that looked like System manufacture—Dyan's coat, the bow and arrows, the bola, all the small devices—were tucked away out of sight. This made the bow a little inaccessible, because if she wanted to use it, Dyan would have to dig it out from under cloth camouflage and restring it.

"What I don't know," Dyan said, "is why I look like a Basku shepherd girl, and you two don't."

"I've never looked very good in girls' clothing." Eirig shook his head dolefully.

"You're worried that we don't match?" Jak laughed. "You and my sister should get along very well."

"I'm worried that our disguise looks ridiculous."

"I thought you'd like some color."

"I'd like not to get caught."

"Which is why this disguise is perfect. Some Systemoid Outrider tries to talk to you, you pretend you only speak Basku."

"What if one of the Basku tries to talk to me?"

"He'll know you're a fake. He'll probably be irritated that you're dressing like one of his people, and he might think you're ridiculous."

"I don't think I like the sound of that."

"But he probably won't turn you in to the Outriders."

Dyan considered that. "Fine," she decided. "But for my disguise to really work, I can't be traveling with two Nemapi scoundrels like you." She snapped the mare's reins and urged the mount on ahead, leaving the two laughing boys behind her.

Cresting a broad, slow rise, she saw Marsick below.

The Snaik here flowed not through the deep, rock-walled canyons as it did around Ratsnay Station, but through the middle of a broad valley, the bottom of which was forested. In the middle of the valley, the track Dyan was riding on hit the river at its widest, and she guessed it must be a ford. A knobby ridge overlooked the ford and was crowned with a stockade wall. The valley was littered with small farms.

Dyan let Jak and Eirig catch up, and the three of them rode to the nearest farm building. They found a burly sweating man, deeply bronzed, wearing only a pair of trousers belted under his prominent belly with rope, carrying bales of hay from a barn into a cattle pen.

"Goodman!" Jak called from the split rail fence.

"I'm busy," the farmer grunted. He heaved his bale of hay to the ground and ripped twine from it. Lowing cows drifted in the direction of the bale, and the farmer turned and rolled back towards the barn.

"I'll help," Jak said. Eirig followed him, and suddenly Dyan was alone, sitting astride the mare in the middle of the road, holding both their spears.

The rumble of male voices from the barn blended with the occasional buzz of bees and the distant cry of a hawk. Dyan surveyed the valley. The houses were built of chinked logs, but their yards were tidy and smoke rose from the chimneys. From her position on the road, Marsick looked pretty, alluring, and incredibly remote.

Eirig emerged from the barn first, a bale hoisted across his shoulders and steadied with his one hand. Behind him came Jak and the farmer, chatting easily now, and once the three of them had unloaded their bales and broken them open for the cattle, Jak thanked the farmer, and the boys picked up their spears and rejoined Dyan on the road.

"Across the river," Jak told her. "Left at the crossroads, in the canyon."

They descended into the valley. Dyan was so distracted by the people that she nearly rode twice into fences, and was only saved by the mare's natural and sensible balking. Finally, Jak took the animal's reins and led her.

What the people of Marsick did, Dyan thought, wasn't peculiar at all. They were just going about their daily business. They leaned over fences to talk to each other, they congregated on the wooden stoop of a building labeled *GENERAL MERCHANDISE AND*

POST—*YOU CAN ALWAYS GET IT OF ORVYL RICH, HE IS NEVER JUST OUT*, they pinned wet clothing to lines to dry. It was just normal life. But for some reason, Dyan found it fascinating, and she tried to figure out why.

She had seen Landsmen before. She had ridden through Nemap with more than one Magister, and of course, she had been to Ratsnay Station only a week or so earlier. Those had been different, though. Ratsnay Station she had seen at a special moment, she realized, because it had been the Selection, the harvest festival. She had seen bonfires, feasting and drinking. And when she had seen Landsmen on other expeditions, there had always been an invisible wall between her and them, the wall of the Magister's presence and Dyan's status as a System Crecheling.

Or, from the Landsmen's perspectives, a Systemoid.

Maybe they had been a little more guarded then. She had seen them salute the Magister and regard her with veiled distance. Now it was different. She was one of them. A stranger, maybe, and apparently a Basku, but someone who could be part of the community. As she descended down into Marsick, led by Jak's steady hand on the horse's reins, Dyan felt a curious warmth begin to grow inside her.

The Snaik was bigger here than by Ratsnay Station, much further across, but shallow. Dyan slid down off the horse to walk in the water. Eirig tried to insist that she get back on the horse, to which Jak only smiled broadly and kept walking. Finally, all three of them sloshed through the river together.

At the crossroads they turned left, and when the rutted track they followed spun off a branch into the narrow mouth of a canyon, from which drifted up a lazy spiral of smoke, they took the smaller path. The natural stone gate of the canyon mouth was supplemented by a rail fence, whose gate was held shut with a loop of braided leather rope. Jak unlooped the rope and then looped it behind them again. Past the gate, they walked through a bowl-like meadow surrounded by walls of stone and full of grazing sheep. On the far side of the bowl, perched on a shoulder of earth that nearly shrugged shut the narrow entrance into the next, higher stretch of canyon, was a cabin.

Jak practically skipped up the gravel path to the front door of the cabin. Wooden slats nailed together made the door, and it was hung with leather hinges hammered into the doorframe. Dyan had to race to catch up to Jak; she didn't want to miss his reunion with his sister. She wanted to be part of it. Eirig trailed behind with the horse.

Jak rapped hard on the doorframe with the butt of his spear. "Ho, the house!" he called. "Alee—Goodwife Alyra!"

Dyan heard a bustling sound within, and then a woman appeared in the doorway.

She might have been five or six years older than Dyan herself, but she looked much more than that. Her skin was bronzed and deeply lined, and there was gray in her dark hair.

And still, she looked just like Jak. She had his big head and hands, only somehow, where the oversized parts made him look gangly and uncomfortable, Aleena looked graceful and at ease.

Wild currents of emotion ran openly across her face. Her eyes widened, then screwed into tight beads. Her jaw fell open, her lips quivered, she ground her teeth. Her hands clasped and unclasped and clasped again.

"Aleena," Jak said, grinning. He looked like he was a dog that wanted to be scratched behind the ears for having fetched a stick.

"No," she finally said. "I'm goody Alyra, and if you're looking for a place to stay, I'm afraid you can't stay here."

"Aleena?" Jak looked stunned.

Eirig reached the door, leading the mare. He shook his head and said nothing.

"You might try Orvyl Rich's place, across the river. He rents a room in the back of his shop. Of course," her words came tumbling out, too quick, unnatural, "there's no work in Marsick anyway, now that the harvest is over, so you're better off moving along."

"Aleena ..." Jak spoke slowly. Uncertainty and confusion filled his eyes. "Aleena, I was Selected."

The woman burst into tears. "I'm not Aleena," she sobbed. "I don't know who you're talking about, but if you're hungry, I can spare a little food."

"Maybe we can come in," Eirig suggested. "Share a few jokes, like old times."

"No!" Aleena snapped. "No, you stay out here. I ... I'll get you a loaf of bread and some mutton."

She disappeared back into the cabin.

Jak shook his head slowly. "I don't get it," he said.

Dyan reached out and put a hand on his shoulder. She wanted to do more, but didn't know what.

"That's Aleena," Eirig said. "I'd bet my last arm on it."

Dyan tried to laugh, but neither of the boys seemed amused.

"I'm going in there," Jak said. He reached for the door—

"Ho, strangers!" boomed a loud male voice.

Dyan turned and saw the newcomer. He was a sturdy man, tall, with the bronzed complexion and leathery skin that comes from working in the sun all day, every day. His hair was long, oily and curled, like Cheela's, and he had a long black beard to match. He walked with a long staff, crooked at the tip, which she thought probably marked him as a shepherd. Only he wore a surprising amount of jewelry for a shepherd, rings on several of his fingers and a chain around his neck that looked like gold.

"Hello, Goodman," Eirig greeted the man.

Dyan waved a hand in greeting, uncertain if she should be pretending to be Basku still.

Jak nodded and looked at his feet.

"If you're looking for the owner of this place," the man said, "you've found him. I'm Narl."

"I'm Jass," Jak said. "These are Arik and Dana. We're traveling through. We thought maybe you had a place by a fire we could curl up in tonight. Even a shepherd's lean-to in the high pasture would be better than the trunk of a tree by the roadside."

"Basku?" Narl asked, looked at Dyan.

She nodded.

"No," Jak said, at the same moment.

"Hmmn," Narl said. "Well, I can do better than that, travelers. If you're willing to leave your spears outside so my woman doesn't feel nervous, I can give you a place by my own fire, and a bowl of lamb stew."

The door opened and Aleena emerged. She had a cloth bundle in her arms, and she had regained her composure. "Goodman," she said. "I was about to give these strangers a loaf and send them on their way."

Narl stroked his beard. "By all means, give them a loaf," he agreed. "But let's have them by our fire tonight. They can eat the loaf tomorrow on the road."

Aleena held out the bundle, but Jak didn't take it. Dyan tried to read his eyes, but found them inscrutable. Her heart ached for him. She imagined what it would be like to find her own mother and be turned away, and her eyes stung.

"Are you sure?" Aleena asked. "They seemed to be in a hurry." She offered the bundle again, and Jak kept his arms at his side.

Narl laughed, a sound like rolling thunder. "Would you make me out to be stingy and a bad host to these strangers, Goodwife?" he boomed. He gestured with his hands like he was sweeping Jak, Eirig, and Dyan into his cottage. "In, in!" he roared. "I can smell the stew from here, and I'm hungry!"

Dyan took the bundle. It smelled of fresh bread, and despite the strange tension in the air, her mouth watered. Aleena resisted, but when Jak made no more to intervene, she let go and Dyan took the bread.

The bundle made a crinkling sound as she pressed it to her breast.

"In!" Goodman Narl bellowed again.

Jak leaned his spear against the outside wall of the cottage and Eirig followed suit.

"What about the horse?" Jak asked. "May I hitch her somewhere?"

"She can't get out," Narl shrugged. "I suggest you take off her saddle and bridle and let her graze in the pasture. The sheep won't hurt her."

Jak lightened the horse's load and turned her loose with a slap to her rump. She trotted away into the pasture, and as Dyan ducked to pass through the cabin's low doorway, she saw the animal cropping contentedly at grass.

Jak set the horse's saddlebags, including the bow, on the ground outside the door. He and Eirig followed, then Aleena. Narl came last, and dominated the room. He was as large as any two of them, and he had to stoop to stand.

The room was lit by crude glass windows and by the yellow flames of the cooking fire. A black iron pot squatted in the fireplace, and the stink of many human bodies in a small space was overwhelmed by the savory smell of lamb and rosemary. A large wooden bedframe filled a third of the cabin, beneath a crawlspace reachable by a short ladder. There was a large table with four chairs, and animal skins on the walls and floor.

"Put your things on the loft," Narl invited them, "and let's eat."

Jak and Eirig quickly scrambled into the crawlspace, depositing their shoulder bags and cloaks. When Dyan climbed up by herself, she found a low, broad space, its wooden floor covered with several deer skins. She laid her serape and beret in a corner, and set Aleena's bundle on top of it.

The bundle crinkled audibly again as she set it down.

Not like cloth at all, nor like bread. It made a crinkling sound like paper.

Dyan furrowed her eyebrows and looked at the bundle. Quickly, not wanting to linger so long she attracted attention, she unwrapped it.

Inside were a beautiful loaf of warm brown bread and a folded sheet of paper. Dyan opened the paper and read the hand-written note on the inside.

YOU ARE NOT SAFE HERE, it read in block letters. *MY GOODMAN WILL TURN YOU IN TO THE OUTRIDERS. RUN AWAY, JAK. RUN AWAY AND DON'T EVER COME BACK.*

CHAPTER SIXTEEN

Holy Mother," Dyan murmured. She tucked the scrap into the waist of her trousers and stared around at their gear. She needed a way out, but she didn't see anything that looked useful. Maybe later they could slip away.

In the meantime, just in case, she grabbed the bola and put it into the top of her boot. Under the leg of her trousers, it would be invisible. Then, afraid she had already been in the loft too long, she slid back down the ladder.

"Do you have children?" Jak asked, as Dyan joined the others. He sat at the table with Eirig, a leather cup on the table in front of each of them.

"Sit down!" Narl called to her. He sat closest to the door, with a jug on his lap.

Aleena moved slowly around the table, setting bowls.

"Have some applejack, unless you think that won't sit well with your Basku stomach," Narl said.

Dyan didn't want to mark herself as a Systemoid by asking what *applejack* was. "Thank you," she said simply, and sat in the chair beside Jak.

Narl poured applejack into the cup in front of her. The alcohol smell of it stung her nostrils. "Or not-Basku, as the case might be."

"I'm not Basku," she said immediately, to fix her earlier contradiction with Jak. "I thought you were asking about my serape."

She took a sip of the applejack, swallowing it quickly and smiling, as if it weren't bitter and didn't burn her throat. "Thank you."

"I thought you looked awfully pale for a Basku girl," Narl nodded. Dyan wanted to laugh—to her own eyes, after her long days under the desert sun, the backs of her hands were now nut-brown.

"We don't have children," Aleen said.

"Don't need them for the sheep." Narl took what looked like a long, deep pull from the jug. "Don't like the idea of what they'd do to the Goodwife's body."

"You do all the work with the sheep, then?" Jak asked. His face looked a degree darker, and Dyan guessed he was struggling to contain at least irritation, and maybe rage, at the way Narl talked about his sister. "You give the sheep everything they need?"

"Got a hired man for the sheep," Narl laughed. "I give the *Goodwife* everything she needs."

Aleena set eating utensils on the table. She set knives and spoons in front of Jak, Eirig, and Dyan, but only a spoon in front of Narl.

Narl noticed. "Did we lose some knives, woman?" he grunted.

"Must have." Aleena made a show of looking on the cabin's long shelves and shaking her head. "Can't find them anywhere. Maybe Elber has them out in his shed."

"We'll ask, he'll be here any minute—I put the sign up for him to come in. In the meanwhile," Narl pulled a long knife from his belt and sank it tip-first into the wood of the table, "I can eat with this. More than a little blood has been shed by this blade, but it won't hurt the flavor." He laughed like a bull, throwing his head back and shaking his whole body.

"If you carry that as a shearing knife into the pastures," Eirig grinned, "I bet the sheep shear themselves out of pure fear."

"Oh, this is no shearing knife," Narl said. "It's a fighting blade. I still have it from the days when I rode scout for the Outriders. Up and down the Wahai, south to Ratsnay Station and beyond, far north into the Jawtooths—nowhere I didn't roam, on the trail of outlaws and renegades." His eyes glittered.

"Did you ever roam to another System? Besides Buza, I mean?" Dyan asked. She didn't care, really, she was trying to think of a way to get Aleena's note in front of Jak. Maybe distracting Narl was the way to do it.

"That where you're from, girl?" Narl grinned. "Some other System?"

Aleena carried bowls back and forth from the table to the fireplace, filling each with a big ladleful of stew and replacing it.

Dyan had been preparing for this moment, and had a place name ready that was as far away as anything she could think of. "I'm from Dahu Sett." That was a tiny collection of shacks in the Jawtooths that froze solid in the winter. Dyan had been once with her Crechemates, when they were learning about paper and logging.

"Oh yeah?" Narl wrapped his fist around the hilt of his knife and worked it out of the table. "What part?"

"What do you mean, what part?"

"I mean Upper or Lower Sett?"

Dyan didn't think there were such places. If there weren't, the question was a trap. If there were, and Narl really did know Dahu Sett, then his next question would spring the trap—he'd ask did Dyan know such-and-such a person, and she wouldn't know what to say. All she remembered of the hamlet was the lumber mill and the rows of tiny cabins.

Or, it could be an innocent question.

She shrugged. "I don't know," she said. "Just Dahu Sett, I guess. By the mill, where my old dad worked. We summered lower down, on the river."

Narl nodded. He opened his mouth to say something, and was interrupted by a knock outside the door.

"Come in," he called.

The man who entered was whip-thin and ugly, with a long scar running along the side of his nose. His cotton smock was stained, and he smelled of sweat and animals.

"You wanted me?" the newcomer asked. His voice was pinched and slow.

"I need you to go to town, Elber," Narl boomed. "Step outside with me and I'll explain." He sheathed his dagger and flashed a broad grin at his guests. "Apologies for Elber's smell. He's come from the fields."

Narl pushed out through the door with the hired man.

"Run," Aleena hissed. At the same moment, Dyan slapped the note onto the table in front of Jak. He stared at the words, then at his sister.

"What in Mother's name is going on here?" he demanded in a whisper.

"He knows my secret!" Aleena whispered back. "He controls me with it. If I left, or complained, he'd tell the Outriders! But I can't do anything to protect you—you have to run, as soon as you can manage it!"

Jak crumpled up the paper in his hand just as the door opened and Narl stepped back inside.

"Eat!" the big man urged his guests.

Jak looked like he was about to explode, and Dyan's own stomach rebelled at the thought of food. Eirig saved the situation, diving hungrily into the chunks of brown meat and white root vegetable that made up the stew.

Narl sat and took a mouthful of stew. "That's what I like to see," he said through the corners of his mouth as he chewed. He pounded the table in front of Eirig. "A boy that eats like that will grow!"

"I have no choice." Eirig slurped his food. "It takes a lot of fuel to regrow a whole new arm!"

"Well, you've come to the right place," Narl gruffed, nodding. "Her cooking is Aleena's best skill!" He pounded the table and laughed. "Well, her second best, anyway!"

Jak's hand trembled as he took a spoonful of the stew.

"I'm sorry," Dyan said. She needed to defuse the situation, before Jak's anger got the best of him. "I must have misheard. I thought you said your name was *Alyra*."

"It is," Aleena agreed, smiling with relief.

"This stew is delicious," Dyan said. "Thank you very much for sharing."

Narl looked slyly at Dyan and Jak both. "Well," he rumbled, "I guess that was the applejack talking. Still, Aleena, Alyra ... no difference in the dark, is there, Jass?" He roared with laughter at his own joke.

Jak forced another spoonful into his mouth with wooden motions. "I think a woman should be called by her own name," he said. "In the dark or otherwise."

"Oh, yeah?" Narl asked. His voice was cold and hard. "You think you have some sort of right to tell me how I should treat my woman?"

Jak put down his spoon. "There's a right way for you treat Alyra. What I think is beside the point."

Narl rested his hand on the hilt of his fighting knife. "Do you plan to teach me this right way, is that it, boy?" he demanded.

A voice in Dyan's head screamed at her to pull out the bola and intervene. One quick move, and Narl would be gone, no longer an obstacle. They could leave, and take Aleena with them. But she didn't really want to cut anyone down, not even Narl, the bully and blackmailer.

"I don't think that *is* what he meant," Aleena said, without looking up. "Anyway, our relationship is none of Jass's business, no matter what he thinks." She took a spoonful of her stew. "Now please eat."

Narl chuckled, but ate. They finished the meal in silence, other than the enthusiastic slurping and sucking sounds that Eirig made as he worked his way through two bowls of food. By the time they had finished, the light through the windows had faded to a deep, dull gray.

Narl rose from the table and stretched. "When Elber gets back, he and I have work to attend to with some of the animals." He dug inside his pockets and came out with a smokeweed pouch.

"Sick animals?" Aleena asked.

Narl shrugged modestly. "Nothing that can't be culled out. I think I'll just sit outside, have a smoke and wait for Elber. "Why don't you settle our guests? They've been traveling. They might like to just lie down now and fall asleep." He pushed his way through the door and disappeared.

"We can wait him out," Dyan suggested. She kept her voice low and they all backed away from the door, to keep their conversation from Narl's ears. "Just sneak off in the middle of the night."

"He knows who I am," Jak said.

"Well, it *is* written all over your face," Eirig reminded him. "What's he gone outside for, though?"

"He's guarding the door so we can't escape," Dyan realized. "And hoping we fall asleep, so his job is easier." She turned to Aleena. "Are there Outriders in town?"

Aleena nodded. "In town, or at one of the nearby farms," she said.

"So Elber's gone for reinforcements," Dyan guessed.

"We have to kill him now." Jak picked up one of the dinner knives and looked at it. It was a completely inadequate weapon.

"Not worth it," Dyan said. "We have to escape."

Aleena shook her head, discouraged. "That's the only door."

"No it isn't." Dyan produced the bola. "We can cut a new window out of the loft. We'll be long gone before he realizes it."

"You have to come with us," Jak said to his sister.

"I have to stay here."

"For what?" Jak's voice was bitter and fierce. "Do you love him?"

Aleena shook her head slowly. "I'm a prisoner, really. He takes from me what he wants. But it's a hard life, and with Narl it's more or less a safe one, as long as I submit. And I can't leave. He'll tell his Outrider friends who I am."

"Then we kill him," Jak concluded.

"Too dangerous." She shook her head again. "Besides, you need someone to cover for you. I'll tell him you've gone to sleep, and he won't realize you're gone until he climbs up to drag you out."

Dyan didn't wait to hear any more. She grabbed her dinner knife, climbed into the loft, and began working on creating an exit. Eirig joined her.

"I don't want to lose you again," she heard Jak say.

"Shut your mouth," Aleena told him, "and grab as much food as you can."

The rough irregularity of the log wall let Dyan get her fingers and the bola's monofilament into its depths. She was soon planing away long chunks of wood. Eirig helped by gouging the tar-and-hair chinking out of the logs, creating new entrances for the bola. In only a few minutes, Dyan had a hole big enough to stick her arm through. Carefully, slowly, she proceeded to carve out a person-sized gap.

"What happens when he realizes you helped us?" Jak asked.

Eirig went out the gap first, letting himself down onto the slope behind the house.

"Don't you worry about that," Aleena told him. She practically pushed him up the ladder, looking over her shoulder at the door. "Whatever he can do to me, I've had worse."

Dyan dropped out the open gap and onto the ground. Eirig squatted in tall dry grass behind the cabin, clutching a dinner knife in his fist. She dragged out the shoulderbags behind her and handed one to the one-armed boy.

"Sorry we have to leave the spears," she said to him.

He waved her off. "We'll be fine," he whispered. "So long as we don't get attacked by anything fiercer than a beefsteak."

Jak wormed out after them. There were tears on his face, and Dyan felt her heart snap in two at the sight.

"Up the canyon," he whispered. "Quietly."

They slipped off the shoulder of earth on which the cabin squatted and crept into a narrow, white-walled canyon. Dyan led the way and walked as fast as she dared, holding the bola in one hand just in case.

"Stop!" she heard Jak whisper behind her, and she turned around.

In the darkness of the evening and the shadow of the canyon she could barely see, but after a moment of squinting she realized that Jak was scrambling into an angular shadowed cut leading up one side of the canyon.

"What are you doing?" she hissed, but Eirig was already following his friend, and she had no choice but to go along.

On all fours, she felt her way up the cut. It started as a slope, became a twisted ledge to which she clung like a cat on a tree branch, and then became a funnel out of which she crawled onto lumpy sand. Her fingers and knuckles were scraped, and stiff brush clawed at her arms and face. In the darkness, she bumped into her friends, then drew back and climbed up onto her haunches.

Figures waited at the gate of Narl's meadow. Standing as they were in the narrow stone mouth, Dyan couldn't see any detail, but she could make out slight twitching motions in the shadow, and then the gate swung open.

Four of the figures crossed the meadow too fast to be on foot, and a fifth lagged behind. Scattering sheep bleated their objections, and Dyan realized that the four figures rode mounted on horses.

"Holy Mother," Eirig whispered.

"Shh!" Jak poked him in the ribs.

Under the bright stars of early evening, the figures gradually came into view. Dyan noticed their hats first, round and broad-brimmed, and then their long, flapping coats.

"Let's get out of here," she whispered.

"Not yet." Jak was glued to the scene.

The riders pulled up in front of Narl's cottage and Narl himself stood up. Only a hundred feet or so away in the darkness, Dyan could clearly see his face by the light of the smokeweed cigarette.

Aleena's bully of a husband stepped forward and spoke to the Outriders, but his words were too low to hear.

"He's whispering because he thinks we're in the cabin," Dyan said.

"Shh."

Three of the riders dismounted. They stepped forward into the light of the cottage's windows, cast by the fire within, and then Dyan saw that two of them wore Outrider's coats and hats, and the third was covered in a Magister's cloak. At the same moment, the two Outriders removed their hats.

Dyan gasped.

"Holy Mother!" Eirig and Jak cursed together.

The two dismounted riders were Shad and Cheela.

CHAPTER SEVENTEEN

Zarah," Dyan whispered, looking down at the hooded figure and willing it to reveal its face. Something about the Magister-cloaked person felt terribly wrong. She didn't think Magister Zarah would have betrayed her, not unless she had been forced to. It seemed ridiculous effort to go to, to warn Dyan off a week ago only to hunt her down and kill her now.

The thin, scarred figure of Elber caught up to the riders and the Magister pulled back her hood.

It wasn't Zarah. The woman in the black cloak was jowled and blonde. She had a drooping nose and one eye that seemed to blink rapidly in the darkness, but her face, on the whole, looked kind. She looked compassionate. She looked like a Magister.

And then Dyan realized she had seen the Magister before. She had seen her at the Hanging, watching Dyan in the crowd. The Magister said something inaudible and gestured to Shad and Cheela. They went into the cabin, Elber trailing behind.

Narl drew his knife. It glinted yellow and cruel in the firelight.

"I should have stayed," Jak muttered.

Dyan put a hand on Jak's arm. He was taut as a bowstring and trembled. "It'll be fine," she told him.

She knew she was lying, but it was a lie she had to tell. She wished she had her bow to hand, and arrows. In the darkness, they'd never see her attacks coming.

She shook her head to clear it.

Shad emerged from the cabin. He held Aleena, one hand on the nape of her neck and the other pinning her arm behind her back. She hung slack-limbed, letting him push her, and Cheela came out after them.

"They were here," Shad said. "They're gone."

"That's my woman you have there." Narl tossed his cigarette to the dirt and ground out its spark with his heel. "They can't be far," he growled. "Up the canyon or on the mesa."

Shad didn't release Aleena.

"We'll attend to the outlaw Jak and the renegade Aleena in due time," the Magister said. The tone of her voice was patient and warm, though the words promised death. "There are prior orders of business to attend to."

Narl looked slightly uneasy. "I'd rather not get paid until after they're captured," he said. "Alyra, get back in the house!"

Shad didn't release Aleena, and she didn't go anywhere.

The fourth figure eased its horse a little closer into the light. This one, too, was cloaked and hatted like an Outrider. Narl held the tip of his knife pointing down at his own feet, but it looked to Dyan like he shifted slightly as the horse approached, bringing the weapon in front of himself defensively.

"Your woman's an outlaw, Narl," Shad said. His voice was hard. He seemed tall and unflappable, like the funvid Outriders. "And you knew it."

"Mother," Jak murmured.

Narl's face contorted in the yellow light. He opened his mouth to frame what looked like a denial, but shifted and tried a sheepish look. "I suspected she was," he admitted. "But how could you ever be sure about something like that? And a man doesn't want to go accusing his own Goodwife of being an outlaw without being sure. Especially when she's such a good hand at planting and lambing." Narl grinned roughly. "And such a warm comfort on the winter nights, if you know what I mean."

"I do," said the Magister coolly.

The mounted Outrider's arm flashed up and down in the shadows—

and Narl's head spun off his neck, thumping softly into the dirt.

Aleena screamed.

Jak trembled. Dyan could hear his teeth grinding.

"I can't bring myself to feel too bad about that one," Eirig whispered.

Narl's body toppled forward like a felled tree, not bending at the knees or waist. When it hit the ground, blood spurted out the trunk of its neck, painting dark streaks—black in the dim light—on the packed earth.

"Bola," Dyan whispered.

Elber ran. He sprinted past the Magister and towards the sheep meadow. For a moment, Dyan thought the Systemoids might let him go, or he might get away for lack of their caring.

But the mounted Outrider's arm flashed again, and Elber's torso fell off his legs, severed completely through at the hips. He hit the ground with a sound that seemed too loud for his scrawny body, and began to scream. His screams and Aleena's clashed in awful cacophony until the unknown Outrider rode over to the thrashing hired man, pulled out his monofilament whip, and cracked it down once.

Elber fell silent, cut completely in half again, and this time through the lungs.

Aleena stopped screaming.

"Let her go," Jak muttered, and picked up a rock in his hand.

Eirig put his hand on Jak's to restrain him, and Dyan wasn't sure what she should do.

"Aleena, daughter of Rosyn," the Magister said. "You've stayed hidden a long time."

Aleena sagged. "I've always known one day the Outriders would kill me," she said. Her voice wasn't defiant. She sounded resigned.

"Capture or kill," Shad corrected her. He and the Magister both sounded kindly.

Dyan felt sick to her stomach.

"I'd ask you where the outlaw Jak and the renegade Dyan have gone," the Magister said, "if I had any hope that you'd tell me anything useful." She paused and licked her lips with the tip of a shockingly red tongue. "Do I have any such hope?"

Aleena spat on the ground.

"Cheela," the Magister said, nodding.

Cheela grabbed Aleena by her upper arm and dragged the girl away from Shad.

"I love my brother," Aleena called defiantly to the Magister. "He's smarter than all of you put together, and he's probably stealing horses from old Orvyl Rich in Marsick right now. You murderers will never catch him."

Dyan had one bola, but she looked down at the party below her and despaired. The Magister and all three of the Outriders would be fully armed. Even if she managed to eliminate one of them, she would reveal her position. The others would kill Aleena anyway, and then Jak, Eirig, and Dyan would be easy targets.

Jak thumped the rock in his hand against the dirt, snorting in frustration. He'd made the same calculation, Dyan guessed.

"Outrider-designate Cheela, my child," the Magister said. "You've heard all the words before. Take your prey, and become Blooded."

Cheela threw Aleena away from her. Jak's sister stumbled, and at the last moment her composure broke again. She turned to run, as Elber had—

Cheela snapped her whip, once—

and Aleena collapsed, dead.

Air hissed softly out between Jak's teeth. Dyan looked at his face and saw tears streaming down it. She reached an arm across his shoulders and squeezed him in something like a hug. He sobbed, once, softly, and relaxed into her one-armed embrace.

"Well done, Cheela," the Magister said. "The Outriders will have more ceremony for you later, back at Buza System. For now, I am instructed to give you this." She produced something from under her cloak and handed it to Cheela. Cheela took the object, bowed gratefully, and attached it to her belt. It looked like a long knife.

A vibro-blade, Dyan thought.

"You could have told me," Shad said.

"You're a good Outrider, Shad," the Magister said. The warmth was gone from her voice. "That's enough work for one person. Don't try to be a Magister, too."

"They carved a hole out of the back of the cabin," Cheela said. "The shepherd was probably right. They've run up the canyon."

"We'll find out." Shad reached into the bandanna around his neck and pulled up goggles, seating them over his eyes.

"Stay down!" Dyan hissed, and all three of them ducked lower. She kept her head up just high enough to keep an eye on the action below.

"Can he see in the dark with those?" Eirig whispered.

Dyan nodded. "There's a nightvision setting and a heatvision setting," she said. "Either one of those is bad for us."

"Outrider Lorne," the Magister said, "stay here in case we miss them and they double back." She swung into her horse's saddle. Cheela and Shad followed her example, and then Shad led the way around behind the cabin.

Jak picked up his rock again. "We only have a few minutes," he whispered. "I'm going to jump the Outrider."

"We can run," Eirig suggested.

"No." Dyan took the bola from her boot. "I'll take him."

She crept forward to the edge of the mesa.

Below her, stone flowed down in steep, liquid slabs to the cabin and the packed earth around it. The Outrider activated the locator switch in his bola holster, dropped easily from his horse and walked in her direction.

She prepared to attack. Could she really do this? It wasn't a fight, it was murder from ambush.

But Outrider Lorne wasn't an innocent. Outrider Lorne had just killed two men, and now wanted her dead, too.

Lorne bent down to pick up the glowing red light that was his bola.

Still Dyan hesitated.

"Dyan," Jak whispered. "They killed Aleena."

Dyan let fly.

Lorne collapsed silently in a shower of his own blood. Because he was crouched, the bola cut through his neck and his legs in a single cut, and his various parts sagged out from the center like a blooming flower of bloody meat. His horse whinnied, startled.

"Come on!" Jak whispered. He grabbed Dyan's hand and pulled her after him, forward over the face of the slope.

Her boots skidded and scraped on the stone. She thought she would fall, but once she was on the face of the slope she discovered

it was less steep than it had seemed. The scritching of her boots'
soles sounded like thunder in her ears, but so did her heartbeat, and
surely, she thought, that must be inaudible to other people.

"Mount up!" Jak whispered.

Eirig climbed into the saddle of the Outrider's horse. The horse
trembled, nervous and balking at the smell of blood, but submitted.

Dyan steeled herself. If Shad and Cheela caught up with them,
she couldn't be unarmed. She found her own bola, grabbed both
of Lorne's, and then pulled the Outrider's body back by the
shoulder to get his whip.

The body twitched as she touched it, and more blood spurted
from the stumps of its neck and thighs. Dyan felt sick, but at least
she couldn't see Lorne's face. She steeled herself and grabbed the
monofilament whip. Lorne's goggles lay there in the gore as well,
and she picked them up.

In a last-second moment of inspiration, she plucked the
Outrider's badge from his chest, too.

Jak rode up to her on their Nemapi horse. He'd bridled it, but
didn't waste any time putting on a saddle. "Now!" he hissed.

Dyan scrambled up behind Eirig with her precious blood-
stained loot, and they started across the meadow.

"Where do we go?" Eirig asked. His voice quavered slightly.

"You heard Aleena," Jak said. "She practically suggested we go
rob Orvyl Rich. Without a third horse, we'll travel really slow."

"I heard her," Dyan said. "So did everyone else."

She was thinking about Shad. Cheela was a killer more than
anything else. She delighted in the shedding of blood and was good
at it. But Shad was at home in the wilderness. He was a tracker and
a survivor, and now that he had full Outrider's gear he could see in
the dark. She needed to do something to obscure their trail.

"Open the gate," she told Jak.

He rode ahead towards the meadow's entrance. Dyan
wondered exactly how much time they had.

"What are we doing?" Eirig asked. "If I'd known this was going
to be the slow horse, I'd have ridden with Jak."

"Give me the reins," she told him, and without waiting for his
cooperation, she took them.

Narl's sheep lay in warm woolly clumps about the edges of the meadow. Her arms wrapped around Eirig to hold the horse's reins, she galloped at the nearest knot of them. They scattered, bleating, and she charged them in the direction of the gate.

"This is noisy," Eirig pointed out. "I thought we were trying to sneak away!"

Dyan ignored him. She ran at another bundle of sheep, and then a third, nudging them all in the direction of the open gate. Other sheep had awoken on their own now, and much of the herd flowed bleating for freedom.

That was all she was willing to risk. Shad and Cheela would have to get off their horses, and they would climb carefully, to avoid any possibility of ambush, but any moment now they would arrive at the top of the mesa and see Dyan running away with the sheep.

If they hadn't done it already. Dyan couldn't turn around to look, and she was out of bola range, so if the Outriders had already spotted her, they might be racing back for their horses. Or they might already be on their horses, chasing after her.

Jak met them at the gate. He turned his unsaddled horse awkwardly, to point it in the same direction they were headed. "Like sheep?" he called as they ran neck and neck.

"Lamb stew," Eirig laughed. "Wahai specialty."

His joke made Dyan sad. It reminded her of Aleen's stew, and Aleen's sudden murder at the hands of Cheela and the Magister, and her own order to Cull Jak, and every other thing that had turned upside down and wrong in her life in the last two weeks.

Jak fell quiet, too.

"They'll be able to follow us by our heat trails," she said. "In the day, when it's hot, that will be difficult for them. Right now, in the evening's cold, our horses leave great red streaks of heat across the ground, when the Outriders look with their goggles."

"So we run with the sheep," Jak said. "That way they have a harder time following our tracks."

"For how long?" Eirig asked.

"As long as we can manage it," Dyan said. She handed the reins back to Eirig. "Stay on the main road for now," she told him, "but try to drive little packets of sheep off the track. They'll have to check all the trails, and that will slow them down."

She fumbled on Outrider Lorne's goggles, thumbed them to heatvision setting and looked back, just before the bend of the road blocked the sight. She saw a slice of the meadow, red-warm from the passage of the herd, the blazing cabin and the mesa. On top of the mesa, running away from her, she saw two human figures. Shad and Cheela.

Five minutes, she estimated. She had five minutes' head start.

Hopefully, with the sheep trick, she could buy a little more time. Even if she were lucky, it wouldn't be more than a little.

CHAPTER EIGHTEEN

T hat way!" Dyan pointed.

A cluster of sheep tumbled away from the road and down towards the river. Eirig turned and followed after them. Dyan was about to remind him to try to stay exactly behind the sheep, but he was clever enough that he didn't need the warning.

Jak raced in a quick loop around the road, hallooing to scatter the little herds in all directions, and then he was on their tail. The ground dropped steeply down into the Snaik Valley. The river's edge was thick with straight-trunked, silver-barked trees, and Eirig headed for them.

The trees would help, Dyan thought, but they would only add a small delay. Jak pulled forward beside her and Eirig, as the last of the bleating sheep fell away, and they crashed into the thicket. They slowed their horses to a brisk walk.

Dyan heard shouting in Narl's canyon, probably in the meadow. They had gained a few minutes, she thought, and she tried not to let it go to her head.

"We have to get among other people!" Dyan told her companions. "Or animals. We have to hide our heat signature!"

"Marsick's this way!" Jak turned his horse and ducked to slide beneath a thick branch. "I don't know anything else around for miles."

The trees hid them from the heatvision goggles, Dyan hoped, but they slowed the pace of travel. She continued to hear occasional yells, and tried to guess what they meant. In her imagination, as she batted aside branches and squeezed through the trunks, Shad and Cheela cursed, chasing down one knot of sheep after another. In reality, Dyan had no idea.

In the daylight, she knew, the trail she was leaving would be visible to the worst of trackers, and Shad would follow it like a signposted highway. By then, she hoped to be far away.

She wasn't as confident in her evasion efforts as she'd have liked. This was the stuff Shad was good at, much better than she was. She needed something else.

In a sheltered depression right on the edge of the water, surrounded by huddling gambol oak, she stopped them.

"Jak," she said. "I want you to ride up into those trees, ride around in them in a circle, and then ride back. Stick as close as possible on the return to your original path. Okay?"

"Okay," Jak agreed. He surged through the woods into a grove above the depression. Through Lorne's goggles, he looked like a bulky red monster, thrashing around in cool green darkness.

Dyan quickly dismounted and opened Outrider Lorne's saddle-bags.

"What do I do?" Eirig asked.

"Hold still."

Dyan quickly found the bottle of liquid petrofuel and a sparker. She snapped dead, dry branches from the underside of one of the oaks, broke them up, and tucked them into a rocky niche on the riverbank. By the time Jak and his horse returned, she had squirted the branches with a little petrofuel and lit them with the sparker. She shut her eyes in the moment of sparking to avoid being blinded by the flash of heat in the goggles.

"We're not making camp here." Jak inflected his words somewhat like a question, and also somewhat like an order.

"No," she agreed. This was no time to have a fight about who was in charge. "We're going to slow them down by making them think this"—she pointed at the fire—"is a fake camp, and that"—she pointed to the trees where Jak had trampled in a circle—"is where we are lying in ambush. They'll waste fifteen minutes at least, and maybe more, before they figure out we've moved on." She was making the number up, but it might not be wrong.

"They'll just see our trail, won't they?" Eirig asked. "I mean, since they can see in the dark and all?"

Dyan shook her head and pointed again. "Here's where we go into the river."

She hoped she was right. She hoped that by the time Shad and Cheela got this far, some of the heat of the passage would have faded, and it wouldn't be immediately obvious where they had gone. In any case, she didn't have a better idea.

"Okay." Eirig walked his horse into the river. Jak followed.

"Make for the trees on the other side," Dyan suggested. "And we need to be quick. While we're out here in the river, we're exposed."

She let Eirig guide the horse and turned at the waist to look behind them. This was a gamble; if anyone looked in their direction and could see, they'd stand out like a fire on the river. She saw the flame she had just lit, blazing bright on the riverbank. She saw the heat of Narl's cottage like a faint glow over the rock of the mesa. She saw lots of sheep, each a little red pinprick in the night. To her relief, she didn't see anything that looked like a mounted rider, not in the trees or on the slope above.

Her tricks had worked better than she'd hoped.

In the middle of the Snaik, the water was high enough to soak Dyan's thighs. She worried that it might get deeper still, and become a real problem, but the riverbottom began to rise again, and a few minutes later, they sloshed out of the water on the far bank.

"Into the trees," Jak urged them.

They went as deep as they could into the thickets and turned to follow the river downstream towards Marsick. Now Dyan worried that she had been too clever by half. Her fire and false ambush trick might work against her. It might attract Shad's attention, tell him where she had crossed the river, and let him pick up her trail again.

No, she thought, that was ridiculous. He'd follow her trail as far as the river easily enough, with or without the fire. The fake ambush might not slow him down, but it certainly wouldn't speed him up.

The trees on this side of the river ended in a split rail fence that ran right to the edge of the Snaik, enclosing a large pasture of dozing cattle. They had reached the edge of Marsick, Dyan realized. They weren't safe, they weren't home free, but they were alive. And it felt like she was winning.

"There'll be a road up here to our right," she said.

"Don't we want to go through the pasture?" Jak's words were definitely a question this time, and a deferential one.

Dyan felt pleased. "We do," she agreed.

She took the reins as Eirig dismounted. The one-armed boy pulled two parallel rails out of their sockets to open a gap in the fence. When Dyan and Jak had ridden through, he mounted up again, this time behind Dyan.

They rode slowly through the cattle, and hunched low over their mounts. From far away, Dyan hoped, they wouldn't look like riders at all, but like grazing animals awake in the middle of the night.

Her heart began to feel lighter. She even sang a little, though the only song that would come to her was the one to which she didn't really know the words. "Sally, she married a soldier, a Captain named William Lee ... hmmm, hmmm, hmmmm-mmmm, Sally always loved me."

At the top of the pasture were a barn, a cattle shed, and the farmhouse. Eirig dismounted again to open the gate.

A light snapped on in the darkness and Dyan started, almost falling off her horse. Had Shad and Cheela seen them and circled around by the ford? She struggled to pull the goggles off her eyes, seeing flashing spots.

"What in Mother's name are you doing in my field?" barked a rough, scratchy man's voice. "You touch my cattle?"

Then Dyan realized that the light wasn't the bright white of a light stick, but the yellow of a petrofuel lamp. She could even smell the burning petrofuel. The light shot out in a beam so she couldn't see the holder, but that just meant it had shutters around the sides.

"We're no rustlers," Jak said. "Just passing through."

"Passing through the wrong blasted property!" the rancher snarled. "I'm armed." A long, slightly hooked knife blade flashed in the lamp's yellowish beam. "And my hired men are on their way.

Get off your horses. We're going to go have a little talk with the Sheriff."

Jak hesitated.

Dyan had an idea. "We're Outriders," she said in the sternest voice she could muster. "On Buza System business. Is this really a fight you want to pick, Landsy?" She flashed Outrider Lorne's five-branched tree badge in the lamplight.

The rancher guffawed. "Or you could be a thief. Either way, the Sheriff'll sort it out."

Dyan held up Lorne's whip in her other hand. "I think I'd rather sort it out right here," she said.

"Mother's teats you do!" The cattleman laughed. "What you'd rather do is get away to Silvertoon so you can sell your loot!"

Dyan struck with the whip.

She didn't have Cheela's skill with any of the Outrider's weapons, but that didn't mean she wasn't good. She was trained, like any System Crecheling was, to be completely at ease with the monofilament whip, capable of defending herself with it. That meant, first and foremost, the skill to use it without cutting herself in half, but it also meant accuracy. It also meant knowing how to strike with the filament only partially extended, so as to strike a near target without automatically slicing through whatever lay behind it.

She cut right through the lamp and the tip of the farmer's knife, the whip's counterweight *snicking* neatly back into its home at the end of her blow.

Lantern wreckage, knife blade and petrofuel hit the ground in a sound that was part *clunk* and part *splash*.

There was a moment of stunned silence.

"Mother!" the rancher hissed. His feet crunched on the earth as he backed away several steps from the fuel burning on the ground.

"So we'll be moving along now," Eirig said. He opened the gate. "You go ahead and tell the Sheriff you saw us. Maybe he can get you a new knife."

They rode past the farmhouse and found themselves on a dirt track, wide and gravelled flat. Other farmhouses dotted the road on both sides and in both directions. Dyan helped Eirig up onto the horse's back behind her and turned towards Orvyl Rich's store and the other buildings at the center of Marsick.

She managed to keep from laughing out loud until the farm-house was well behind them, and then she restrained the laugh into a choked giggle. The few passersby in the darkness, mounted or on foot, ignored her slight outburst. Eirig patted her on the back.

The realization that they were almost the only people on the streets of Marsick sobered her quickly.

"Shad will track us in the daytime," she said. "We have to make more distance, and we have to stay out of sight." She pulled her goggles onto her face and looked back across the river. Her vision was obscured by distance and by intervening farm buildings and trees, but she didn't see any heat-giving presence on the other side of the river that didn't seem to be a sheep.

Did that mean that Shad and Cheela had crossed the river already and were close behind them? Were they hidden in the trees because they were maneuvering to sneak up to Dyan's false ambush site, weapons in hand? Or were they following a sheep's trail up some box canyon, cursing her name?

She almost laughed again at the thought.

"The river," Jak suggested.

Dyan nodded in agreement. "But we can't just ride out into the ford now. We'll be visible for miles."

They rode up the hill and out of Marsick. This far, Dyan felt reasonably safe. They should only be visible as heat signatures, and there were fires all around them, buildings and farm animals that would show through heatvision goggles as warm red blobs.

Once over the hill, she breathed even easier. They cut off the road through more pastures, riding faster and down towards the river. When they reached the Snaik again, they were around the bend from Marsick and definitely out of sight of Narl's canyon or the false ambush. They rode into the shallows and turned down-stream, towards Nemap on the Lull Sea.

The night became colder, but their continued movement kept Dyan warm. She hummed to herself and looked over her shoulder a lot. She saw deer in the valley, and smaller animals, but no pursuit. She wanted to talk with Jak, but once the excitement of the chase was over he slumped into himself, riding with that sunken-chested, evasive body posture he had had when she had first seen him. She whispered short questions to him about how he was managing without an actual saddle, but his answers were grunts.

She didn't dare mention Aleena.

She asked Eirig to sing the song to her, the one about Sally and William Lee and the unnamed singer who loved a woman he couldn't have. Eirig sang it once, and while she was trying to sing it back to him, he fell asleep on her shoulder.

Dyan contented herself with humming softly, checking to see that they weren't being pursued, and following the river. Their heat signatures behind them wisped immediately off the cold river and disappeared.

It seemed like they had been riding all night, but eventually the valley widened and the Snaik flowed into the wide, flat pan of the Lull Sea. The fires and bodies of Nemap on the shore burned bright through Dyan's goggles, and she hesitated.

"We could camp here," she suggested, looking at the long grass and scrubby desert trees around them.

"I don't know about Nemap," Jak said, "but Ratsnay Station kept its gates shut at night. Shut and guarded."

Dyan pondered that question. "Would the guards at Ratsnay Station open the gates for an Outrider?"

Jak nodded, his head a bobbing light.

Eirig didn't wake up when Dyan dismounted, but just slumped forward over the saddle. The night air was chilly on Dyan's skin as she stripped down to her underthings for the second time in front of Jak. This time he didn't look away.

"You're beautiful," he said. He sounded sad.

She laughed, trying to lighten the moment. "You can't even see me. *I* have the nightvision goggles."

His laugh was harder-edged, and he pointed at the sky. "You've stared so long through those things you've forgotten the moon and stars," he said. "I have more than enough light to see you by."

Dyan put her System clothing back on, shirt, trousers, and coat, and she pinned Outrider Lorne's badge to her chest. She left the goggles on, because she still wanted to check for pursuit and because they helped disguise her face. Not that she thought anyone in Nemap could possibly recognize her, but she felt more comfortable with her eyes hidden.

Nemap's gates were shut and barred from the inside. A heavy woman on the stockade wall leaned on her spear and squinted down at Dyan in the light of long torches punched upright into the earth at intervals around the gate. Dyan shut off the heatvision to avoid burning her eyes from the glare.

"You from the System?" the woman called.

"Outrider!" Dyan snapped back.

It was enough. The guardswoman and her colleagues opened the gate and let Dyan and her friends in. Dyan paid for two stalls in a stable with Scrip rectangles she found in Outrider Lorne's saddlebags, and rather than spend more and risk contact with more people, they shoved a yawning gray dog out of its place and bunked beside the horses.

Eirig curled up into a ball in the hay and continued sleeping.

Jak lay flat on his back staring at the ceiling. When Dyan reached out and touched him softly, and sang to him all that she knew of the Gallows Song, he crawled over next to her and pressed himself against her body.

He fell asleep instantly, and in his sleep, he wept.

CHAPTER NINETEEN

In the morning, when Dyan opened her eyes, Jak lay on her breast. His breathing was regular and his eyes, though red and puffy, were relaxed in sleep. She ran her fingers through his hair and wondered what was next.

"Sausages," Eirig said.

"What?" Dyan snapped her head around, startled by the intrusion into her solitude, and found Eirig climbing over the wooden gate into the stable. Over the earthy, pungent smells of horse and hay, Dyan's nose detected juicy, hot sausage, and her mouth began to water.

Jak sat up, rubbing his face. Eirig dropped into the stall with three wooden skewers in his hand, and on each skewer, a taut, sizzling piece of meat.

"How did you pay for those?" Dyan wondered.

"Who did you steal these from?" Jak asked at the same moment, grinning his approval.

"Ah, now you shame me," Eirig objected. He handed them each a skewer and took a careful bite of his own sausage. "I worked for these. You two were still asleep when it got light, so I walked around and found an innkeeper. She had three sausages she didn't want, and a pile of wood she needed chopped."

Dyan tasted her sausage. She burnt her tongue but it was sweet and savory at the same time, pork with some sort of spice she thought might be fennel. "Is this Basku?" she asked.

"How did you chop wood with just one arm?" Jak wanted to know.

"Just like I did with two arms," Eirig explained. "Only slower."

"It's not Basku," Jak answered her question. "Basku sausage is red, and really spicy."

Dyan didn't care. She had eaten a full dinner at Aleena's cabin, but the night of riding had left her ravenous. She wolfed the meat down, ignoring the scorching twinges in her lips and tongue as she ate it. She finished before either of the boys did and immediately wiped her hands on the straw and stood, to avoid staring at their food and giving them the idea that they should share.

"We need to get out of here," she announced. "We need to get more distance between us and the Outriders, and get somewhere we can disappear and be safe."

"The Wahai," Jak said. "Across the water."

Dyan nodded. "Let's pack up and go find a boat."

The morning was already warm and they led their horses down the dirt streets of Nemap to its wharf. Chickens scattered out of their path as they went, and mangy dogs on the run from boys with sticks. Dyan picked straws from her coat and tugged her clothing into position. She couldn't very well wear her goggles in the daytime and she wished she had an Outrider's bandanna, but she tried to make herself look as orderly as possible by the time they reached the shore of the Lull Sea.

Jak and Eirig seemed to be accepting her lead without question, but Dyan questioned herself. She wanted to get across the Lull and into the Wahai, and she thought they'd need the horses there. But she wanted to get there quickly, and disrupt the physical trail, if possible. She didn't think Shad could track her through Nemap, but she wanted to be sure.

So she needed a large boat, large enough to carry horses. She found one.

It was a wide, flat-bottomed craft, with outrigged pontoons and piles of tradings goods. Dyan saw sacks of grain and stacked hides, but manufactured goods predominated: boots and shoes, saddles, horseshoes, coats, shovels, hammers, axes, sawn boards, and so forth.

Three brown-skinned, wiry men wearing cotton trousers and nothing else finished loading goods into the boat and checked its lines and sail. A heavier man with a prominent Adam's apple in a sag-fleshed neck checked over a list of his cargo, making adjustments with a bit of charcoal. He squinted at Dyan when she cleared her throat.

"Outrider Zarah," she said. She tried to speak with authority, but felt a twinge of embarrassment at using Zarah's name. She hadn't meant to do so, it had just come out when she realized she had to introduce herself.

"My cargo's clean," he snapped back.

"I need passage to the other side of the Sea," she said. "I don't care about your cargo."

He relaxed visibly. "What do you mean?" he asked, looking over her shoulder. "Do you mean just for you?"

"Me, those two, and the horses," Dyan said. "I can pay."

The merchant's eyes narrowed. "That's refreshing."

"Not much," Dyan hastened to add.

He chuckled sourly. "That's more like it." He sighed and scratched his head, staining the whitish thatch with black from the charcoal he still held in his hand. "Look," he said, "I'm running short on time. If you can have your prisoners help with the loading, I'll get one of my men to clear a space in the hold for the animals."

Dyan tried to think like a hard-nosed Outrider. "You expect help loading and Scrip, too?" she pushed.

The heavy man bowed his head. "Whatever Buza System thinks my services are worth," he said quickly, "I am happy to agree." Then he turned and shouted harsh-sounding words to his crew in a language Dyan didn't understand.

Prisoners? Jak mouthed to her, but he and Eirig piled timbers and hand tools, and a few minutes later one of the nut-brown crew opened a large hatch in the deck. Clucking and saying words Dyan didn't understand, he took the two horses from her and led them up the gangplank and down into the hold.

When the last barrel of nails was roped into place, the crew untied the ship from the wharf and raised the yellow-white sail. A stiff breeze tugged the sail out and scooted the ship slowly out from the wharf and into deeper water. The Wahai Mountains, blue-brown and snow-hatted, seemed larger by the minute.

Jak and Eirig sat quietly by Dyan on crates in the aft of the ship's deck, and she pretended to watch them closely. Once the ship was safely out of Nemap, its skipper joined her, offering her half of a round wheel of soft bread.

"Thank you," she said. "They haven't eaten for a couple of days." She tore herself a piece of the bread and passed the rest to Jak and Eirig.

"Going the wrong way, aren't you?" The trader chewed bread in his cheek as he talked and looked closely at Dyan's face. "With prisoners, I mean? Usually, you Outriders kill them on the spot. And when you don't, if you transport them anywhere, it's back to Buza System, not out into the Wahai."

"They're not exactly prisoners," she said. She tried to be tough like Cheela, and quiet like Shad. She didn't like the trader's curiosity, but she thought that was okay, because a real Outrider wouldn't like it, either.

"Oh yeah? What are they, then?"

She didn't want to rebuke the man or give him any other reason to hate her, or even remember her. Instead, she changed the subject. On a whim, inspired by the fact that she was crossing the Lull Sea and entering the Wahai, she asked: "Why don't you sail west?"

"Beg your pardon?" The merchant looked confused. "I assumed you were going to one of the trading posts. If you want to go to the Dam, I can take you, but I'd rather do it on my return trip."

"I don't mean the Dam," she said. "I mean beyond the Dam. You're a sailor. Don't you ever get tired of sailing back on forth on this tiny sea? Don't you ever want to sail west on the Snaik as far as it can go, until you come to the ocean?"

He squinted at her, eyes glittering and dark. "Are you asking me if I'm a *smuggler*, Outrider?"

Dyan forced a laugh. "I meant to ask if you were an *explorer*. Haven't you ever wanted to sail west and see what you could see?"

The trader spat over the gunwale and into the water. "I've known men who've done that," he said slowly. "Those who weren't killed by the Shoshan, or bandits, or wild animals, came back with stories of nothing. Hundreds of miles of nothing at all."

"Anything else?" Dyan asked.

He shrugged. "Wild stories of ruins, some of them. Ruins on the shores of the ocean. From the days of the Cataclysm, I guess, but I don't know, and I don't really care. Because here's the thing, Outrider." He stared at her with a sour eye. "I don't care about exploring. I don't care about any ocean, I don't care about any ruins and I don't care about the Cataclysm. What I care about is making a profit, and that's why I sail the Lull Sea. The crazies out there herding sheep and mining and the crazies on this side farming and making furniture are all the same—a bad year will ruin them. Insects in the crop mean the farmer starves. Sickness in the hooves of the herd means a cull, and death comes even to healthy animals. Bad luck on your stream, or claim-jumpers, means a miner dies a solitary death. The only one who prospers in all this, the only person who always prospers, is the trader. Because no matter what, all the crazies need someone to run around between them, carrying their goods to each other and making a profit. That's what I do because that's what I care about." Dyan felt his eye boring into her forehead. "Making a profit."

"Well," Dyan said, "to each his Calling."

She handed several rectangles of Scrip to the trader, careful not to look too closely at them or show her uncertainty at how he would react. He didn't look at the Scrip either, just took it, slapped two fingers to his forehead in a sloppy salute, and returned to the work of bellowing at his crew.

"Thank you for making me *not exactly* a prisoner," Eirig said when he was gone. "My old dad would be proud. I've finally become what he always dreamed I'd be."

"Well done," Jak told her. He reached over and squeezed her hand, and his expression was one of real gratitude.

"Why were you asking him about the west, though?" Eirig asked. "If that was small talk, it's small talk like I've never heard before. I'm used to hearing *so, Ira, how are the chickens doing this year? Oh, the poultry are fine, Jeet, but you know I've never really recovered from that cough and now half the kids have some kind of gut worm.*"

Dyan wanted to giggle, but didn't think it would look right in her Outrider costume. Instead, she shrugged and smiled. "I just wonder," she said. "The Magisters never taught us anything about what might be downriver on the Snaik, except for exactly the same things the trader just told me. Bandits and wild animals, ruins, lands so blighted by the Cataclysm that it isn't safe even to pass through, and that sort of thing. But I wonder if that can be true."

"What do you mean?" Jak scratched behind his ear.

"I mean, the world's a big place. I can tell you from geology and physics that the world is a ball about twenty-four thousands miles around and about seven thousand miles through the center. That's an awful lot of space. Can it really all be destroyed, wasted, nothing? Can Buza System and the settlements really be all that there is? Or might some of those ruins that I've been told about really be populated?"

"Holy Mother," Eirig gulped.

"Other Systems?" Jak asked.

"Maybe," Dyan said. "Or maybe human settlements without Systems. Just ... you know ... people, without anyone from a System coming out to Cull their children. Just people living together."

Eirig's eyes were wide with astonishment. "The earth is a *ball?*"

"Uh ..." Dyan was uncertain what to say.

Jak punched his friend and Eirig laughed.

"My old dad always told me that the world was shaped like a giant turd," Eirig said. "He was such a traveler, I assumed he knew what he was talking about."

"*Life,*" Jak said, "not the *world.* Your old dad always said that *life* was a turd."

"Isn't it the truth, though?" Eirig shook his head. "And it's the very best people who always get the worst part of the turd, isn't it?"

He put his arm around Jak and grinned. Jak grinned back, but there was a tear in his eye.

"Well," Dyan said, "it's too bad the world isn't shaped like a turd. A cylinder would be much easier to map than a sphere."

"Ah, you misunderstand me again," Eirig said. "That's my fate, I guess. No, the world isn't shaped like a *human* turd, you see. It's a cowpat, a great big cowpat of a world, and we're all on the underside of it, smashed against the ground."

"Are there maps?" Jak asked. His eyes still glistened, but there was a hard fire behind them now.

Dyan shook her head. "I never saw any maps. The Cataclysm

changed the face of the earth, we were told, so the old maps were pointless, and no one sent out from the System has ever returned with the information to produce a new one. I know place names, from pre-Cataclysm history, and I can tell you a little about where they are. Sayatil and Portolan should be west of here, for instance." She considered. "Maybe those are the ruins the trader is talking about. They were supposed to be large cities. And somewhere away to the south was Satulak. But the country's capital, back before the world broke, was in a place called Washatun, which was far away to the east."

"On the other side of the Jawtooths," Eirig said, "or my old dad would have mentioned it."

"Much further than that," she corrected him. "I think ..." she tried to remember stories that might have any bearing on how far Washatun might be. The Cataclysm had so thoroughly changed things that most historians didn't bother studying anything that happened before it. Or maybe they didn't have the information. But she remembered legends of people in carts and wagons, coming to Satulak and Buza on foot over many months from Novoo and Chakag. And Washatun was much further away still. "I think maybe so far that it would take years of walking to reach it."

"Years!" Jak whistled low. "How did they possibly control everyone?"

"Control?" Dyan was startled. "What do you mean?"

"Don't you think that makes sense?" he asked. "Buza System controls everything in the Treasure Valley, and all the settlements around it. But as powerful as the System is, it couldn't control something that was a year's travel away."

Dyan struggled for an answer. "Lots of things were different before the Cataclysm," she said. "I think they traveled much faster. And even faster than travel was information sharing."

Jak frowned. "What do you mean?"

"I mean ... even though a messenger might take a year to cross the country, there were tools to send messages much faster. Maybe instantaneously."

"That can't be true," Jak said. "Can it?"

"Sure." Dyan didn't know herself, of course, but she had read books and enjoyed lectures on history and folklore. "And they had weapons, things that could kill at a distance, even a great distance. They had weapons that caused explosions, and weapons that could melt buildings, and weapons that could kill a person at a great distance by penetrating him with a bit of metal."

"Pistols," Jak said. "Guns."

Dyan was startled. *Pistol* was one of the words in the Gallows Song, and she hadn't recognized it. She thought she'd heard it at Ratsnay Station, too. "What are pistols and guns?" she asked.

"There are ruins out by Ratsnay Station," he told her. "Pre-Cataclysmic. Everyone knows they're haunted. They call it Farkill, because the ghosts there can kill you at a distance. Everyone knows to stay away."

"I don't understand."

"*Pistols* and *Guns* are the names of specters that kill people in the ruins. *It isn't safe to play with Guns*, that's what mothers in Ratsnay Station have been telling their children since ... since forever. There are stories about how Guns bites children with his long metal tooth when they try to play with him, even from far away. Pistols is something similar. *It isn't safe to leave Pistols lying around*, they say. You have to bury Pistols, the stories go, put him in a *safe place*, or he may bite you with his steel tooth."

"Yeah," said Eirig, "but that's *ghosts*."

"Is it?"

"Could it be?" Dyan asked. "Could Ratsnay Station be sitting on pre-Cataclysmic weapons and not know it?"

Ahead, a long wharf and a trading camp fast approached.

CHAPTER TWENTY

I don't know why you care about Pistols and Guns," Jak said, as they rode south out of the Shoshan trading camp.

Jak had haggled with the Shoshan barterers, a trio of solemn-faced old men with canny looks in their eyes and hair braided in long queues down their backs, for a saddle to replace the one they had lost at Narl's and Aleena's cabin. The Shoshan had never spoken a word that Dyan could understand, and had conducted the entire negotiation using gestures. Two colored blankets, one blue and one yellow, lay side by side across a heavy wooden table, and Jak and the Shoshan had made offers and counteroffers by placing objects on the blankets, the yellow holding the items Jak would surrender and the blue holding what the Shoshan were willing to give in exchange. The traders had shown no interest when Jak had offered one of the monofilament bolas, but had let shine through a glimpse of excitement when Outrider Lorne's goggles had been offered. Eventually, Jak had come away with a saddle, several waterskins full of water, strips of dried meat pounded with berries, and the blue blanket itself.

"I'm not sure I do," Dyan countered thoughtfully.

They left the Shoshan and the Nemapi merchants haggling in silence over finished goods and rode south through crunchy yellow grass. Dyan rode behind Jak on Outrider Lorne's horse, and Eirig rode alone on the Nemapi beast, which, when the two stood shoulder to shoulder, looked like a pony. Ahead of them, the hills bulked up, the broad valleys narrowed into canyons, and the Wahai proper began. The sun pounded down without mercy, and Dyan was sweating.

"You're not really a killer," Jak said.

"Neither are you."

"Ah, but *I* am," Eirig interjected. "Bloodthirsty as old Guns himself, they all say it."

"I do what I have to do," Jak defended himself. "And anyway, you're plenty capable of slicing up man and beast with those monofilament weapons of yours without going chasing after ghost stories. Which is probably all it is."

"Pulling his pistol, he shot her," Dyan sang. "That doesn't sound like a ghost."

"It doesn't sound like a pre-Cataclysmic weapon capable of making things explode, either. *He shot her,* that's all the song says. Did he *melt* her? Cause her entire settlement to *burn to the ground?* It almost sounds polite, the way the song has it. Maybe he administered medicine."

"But then they hang him."

"Well … okay," Jak conceded. "But you can't give too much weight to old songs, especially when you don't understand them."

"I don't really care about Pistols," Dyan said. "But what if this ruin had other things? Information, for instance, about life before the Cataclysm? Or about the Cataclysm and what caused it?"

"I don't care about the people who lived before the Cataclysm. I care about people who are alive," Jak said. "Death is where I draw the line. You die, I stop caring about you."

Dyan bit back words about Aleena, or about his father or Eirig's, or about his friends who had been Culled. She stifled her own feelings, too, about Wayland and Aleena. She tried not to remember how it had felt to watch Outrider Lorne crumple to the ground dead, a complete stranger she had had to kill in order to survive, at whose death she had felt relief.

"What about maps?" Dyan asked. "What if the ruins of Farkill had a map that showed us the way to Satulak, or Sayatil, or Portolan?"

"More ruins," Jak dismissed the suggestion.

"We don't know that," Dyan said. "No one knows that because, as far as I can tell, no one's been to those places since the Cataclysm. At least, I've never heard of it, and no one will admit to knowing. And even if they are ruins, what if they're still places where we can just be together, and not be followed by the System? Wouldn't that be worth it?"

"Is there another girl in this picture?" Eirig asked. "Or do I get to play the heroic character of the fellow consoling himself with his one remaining hand for the rest of my life?"

"What are you talking about?" Jak turned beet red.

"Ah, don't make the mistake of thinking I'm an idiot," Eirig said. "Lucky for all of us, I'm not the jealous type."

"Anyway," Jak continued, trying to get off this subject, "I told you I've been into the ruins, and I didn't see any maps."

"Yeah?" Dyan asked. "How much of it did you explore? What were you looking for, and how did you look?"

"I wasn't exploring," Jak said. "I was proving I wasn't a coward. I did what you have to do—I stayed the night with Guns and Pistols."

"And did they bite you?" Dyan mocked him slightly.

"No," he admitted. "But the wind was pretty fierce. Farkill is out in the flat middle of nowhere, and a lot of the walls are punched through, so bad weather just comes right on in."

"And did you do this, too?" she asked Eirig.

He nodded. "I'm no coward."

"So in other words," Dyan summarized what she was hearing, "you hunkered down behind a wall and slept all night."

"That doesn't make me sound as heroic as I felt at the time," Eirig said. "But it isn't wrong."

"I didn't see any maps," Jak admitted, "but maybe they're there. It's a big place, and Pistols and Guns could be keeping all kinds of secrets. Do you want to go look?" He pointed straight ahead down the canyon with his whole arm. "We could just ride south, straight through the Wahai and turn left. We could be back at Ratsnay Station in a couple of weeks. We'd have made a nice big circle."

"Maybe I do," Dyan said. "But right now I want to find a place to stop early and make camp. I'm exhausted."

They followed a deer trail and found a box canyon, high above the floor of the main canyon at the top of a long sandy slope. They ate dried meat and drank water without a fire, and as the sun began to go down, Eirig loudly volunteered to stand the first watch. He took a field lens with him and disappeared.

Jak said nothing, but sat and held Dyan's hand while they watched the stars come out together. Later, when he had fallen asleep, she covered them both with a microfiber blanket and lay awake, wondering what to do until Eirig stumbled back into camp, singing in a very loud voice.

In the morning, she taught Jak how to shoot with a bow. Once he had mastered basic posture and fingering and how to aim, she had him sink arrows into the trunks of a couple of old trees until nearly midday.

"This is fun," Eirig commented as he chewed on his noon strip of meat and watched. "But it doesn't seem as useful as the bola."

"It's much more useful," Dyan disagreed. "You can hunt with the bow."

"Oh, I've seen what one of those things can do to a horse," Eirig said, pointing to the bolas that rode now on Dyan's hips. "I expect it would do more or less the same thing to a deer, and the meat would be entirely edible. Besides, *I* can't hunt with a bow."

"You'll never make your own bola in a pinch, though," Jak pointed out. "Not that slices people in half, anyway. And if you mess up with the bow, you won't take off your own limbs."

"Aw," Eirig grumbled. "Where's the fun in it, then?"

"I'll teach you to use the bola, too," Dyan promised. "We have three of them, it would be good to share. Besides," she looked at each of them playfully, "you'll need something to defend yourselves against the mighty Pistols and Guns."

Jak looked at Dyan with long and serious eyes, until she felt herself blushing and looked down. "Okay," he agreed. "Back to Ratsnay Station it is." With that agreement, it felt like their journey again acquired direction.

They rode several miles that evening, following the canyons south. Game was plentiful but water wasn't always easy to come by, so they filled all their flasks and skins at every opportunity. As the sun set and the narrow canyon's shadows became the darkness of night, Dyan rode around a bend in the path and saw they were not alone.

There were five of them, and they looked rough. Even if there had only been one or two, she would have been wary, but she definitely didn't want to get into a fight with the odds against her. She had the reins of the horse, with Jak mounted behind her, but she let one hand drift down and rest on the bola at her hip.

They wore wool serapes, but not the colorful, bright weave of the Basku. Their outer garments were long and brown, the dirt and dust pounded into the wool only serving to make them even closer to the color of the canyon's rock walls. They were all men, and unkempt. Ragged beards of various lengths fouled their jawlines, and hair that shimmered with grease spread across the backs of their necks. Two of them rode with spears in their stirrups, pointed at the sky. They all had swords or axes. Two lean dogs with patchy dark fur slunk along in the middle of the band.

It might have been her imagination, but Dyan imagined she could smell them as soon as she saw them, a hundred feet away. They stared back at her with expressions that suggested that they, in turn, found her repellent.

"This sort of makes me feel like we should have started with the bolas rather than the bow," Eirig muttered.

Then Dyan realized that she was still dressed as an Outrider. She even still had Lorne's badge pinned to her chest.

There was no time to back down now. She held her head high and took the bola from its holster, just in case. She held it in her left hand, discreetly invisible from the men as she urged her horse to pass them on the left, their rights. This would make it harder for them to draw weapons and attack her, she thought. Especially the spears.

The man in front spat on the ground, but didn't draw a weapon. The others growled, frowned, or stared with beady eyes, but Dyan kept her head high and stared them down. The power that forced the men back was in her uniform, she realized, and not her own gaze. Still, she had to put on a good face, or even the uniform of the feared Outriders wouldn't be enough. She wished she could Jak's face, but he was fierce and she was sure he was giving stares as tough and menacing as he got. The two dogs snarled back at her, but they also held their attack.

She heard low grumbling as she passed the last of them, and then behind her she heard Eirig yelp, "Hey!"

She turned around. The last of the men had leaned over in the saddle and grabbed Eirig's saddlebag. With his stump, Eirig struggled to stop the man from stealing their supplies, but without fingers there wasn't much he could do.

Then the man drew a knife.

The dogs barked.

His knife was a long weapon, hooked forward and jagged-looking, with great scallops like bite marks in the blade side. He raised it—

"Hey!" Dyan yelled.

She raised the bola over her head and the bandit looked back at her. He grimaced and exhaled through his nostrils.

Behind him, his four comrades stopped and turned around.

"There's five of us, Outrider," the bandit growled. "You gonna kill us all?"

The dogs growled, too, and one of them barked again.

Dyan knew that a shot through all five men with her bola was possible. She also knew it was very hard, and that as soon as fighting broke out, she would be the target of every one of the dangerous-looking ruffians.

"Only if I have to."

She and the bandit stared at each other, and she curled up her lip to show her disdain.

One of the men in the back of the line shouted something she didn't understand. The bandit in front narrowed his eyes in hatred and practically threw Eirig back into his own saddle. Eirig slipped, but caught himself with his one hand. He glared at the bandit and said nothing.

Without a word, the outlaws turned their horses around and kept riding.

"Holy Mother," Eirig breathed.

Dyan turned to Jak to calm herself and saw that, without her noticing it, he had armed himself with one of the bows.

"Come on," he said. "Let's get some miles behind us and find a place to sleep."

Dyan's heart was still racing fast an hour later when they chose their site. She set a false camp like she'd done outside of Marsick, lighting a small fire on a shoulder of hill over a bend in the canyon. The fire threw up a feeble orange light against the wall beside it, but in the darkness of the canyon that light looked immense.

They led their horses into the real campsite. It was a crack in the canyon wall that never quite turned into a real canyon itself, but after thirty feet of cutting back into the stone, ascended sharply over boulders, desiccated tree trunk fragments, and other rubble. They let the horses crop what grass they could in the canyon for half an hour after they rubbed them down, and then led them deep into the crack to hide.

Dyan stood watch. She kept the field lens pressed to her eye, scanning the star-shimmering darkness for signs of movement and trying to keep her ears tuned to the chirruping rhythms of the night.

Jak and Eirig lay down. Jak kept a bow and arrows beside him, though in the darkness Dyan thought he was likely to shoot friend as foe. Soon both boys were breathing regularly, and Dyan continued her watch alone.

Probably, she told herself, the bandits wouldn't come back. If they had really wanted to attack, they would have done it on the trail. She played back the incident in her mind and wondered whether it would have been better if she hadn't been dressed as an Outrider. Had she provoked them? Or would they have been even more prompt to seek a confrontation if she hadn't been wearing Outrider Lorne's badge?

She had always had a romantic idea of the Wahai, she now saw. Its reality was dirty men who robbed you because they could, and because they wanted to. Was life in the System or in the settlements worse than that, even with the Cull? And would life in Satulak or Sayatil possibly be any better?

Click.

Dyan's heart stopped. She probed the shadows around the false fire, looking for motion or silhouettes that didn't belong. The sound could have been a falling rock, knocked over by the breeze or by time or by a passing animal. It could have been the hoof of a deer, striking the dry creek bed. There was every reason to be cautious, but no reason to be panicked.

Click.

There it was again. Dyan wasn't sure she trusted herself to throw the bola in the darkness. She drew her whip instead, planning to keep the filament extended as little as possible, and use the weapon more like a sword than like a whip.

Click.

This time the sound came from right next to her, and she knew it was a pebble, hitting the ground. Was someone throwing stones at her? Or were they falling off the top of the canyon wall?

She had a terrible feeling, and she looked up—

just in time to see shadows swarming down the crack above her.

CHAPTER TWENTY-ONE

Jak!"

Dyan hesitated. In the near-pitch darkness, she was afraid of hitting Jak if she started laying about her with the whip. Then she heard the heavy thud of one of the bandits dropping to the earth, and she knew she was out of time.

She aimed high, way over her head. She snapped the whip, letting it ride out to its full extension straight ahead of her and up with an overhand flick of the wrist.

A scream split the darkness, followed by more thuds. Warm liquid sprayed her face, and a stinging cloud of something that might have been rock chips. She heard grunting and struggling just feet away from her in the crack, and knew it had to be Jak or Eirig wrestling with a bandit. Blind as she was, she couldn't risk trying to help. A few inches to the wrong direction with her whip, and one of the boys might end up losing another limb. Or a head.

But she had the light stick in the pocket of her coat, and she grabbed it.

"Mother!" she heard, and "Blast you!"

Horses whinnied in surprise and panic, deeper in the crevice.

Dyan pulled out the light stick. She snapped it on.

"Ha!" Jak yelled. A bowstring twanged.

A confusion of bodies collapsed to the sand to one side of the crack. Eirig must be in there somewhere, Dyan thought. She couldn't tell if there was one bandit on top of him, or two, and though she saw the feathered tail of an arrow protruding from the mass of flesh, she didn't see who had been hit.

Jak crouched near the opposite wall of the crack, jittery and gray in the beam of the light stick, and he had a bow. Just as he nocked a second arrow, a bandit jumped him from the darkness. Knife held high, he plowed into Jak and knocked him to the earth.

Dyan heard motion above her before she saw it, and she drew back her whip to strike again—

a hand grabbed her wrist and yanked her back. She heard the bark and growl of dogs.

"Dyan!" Jak yelled.

Thumping sounds.

Her attacker ripped the whip from Dyan's hand and sent it flying into the night. A hand gripped her face, stinking of sweat and filth.

She bit it, and the hand let go as a string of foul curses filled her ears. She lost her grip on the light stick. As it fell, its beam swung wildly, and Dyan saw thrashing limbs and faces twisted into snarls. She lunged forward with her head, trying to butt the bandit in the face. What she struck felt hard, but more like muscle than a skull. Then she took a punch in the jaw and fell back, lights flashing before her eyes.

"Not much good without your whip, are you, Outrider?" the man sneered. He punched Dyan again in the belly. She doubled over in pain. Her stomach hurt so much from the blow that she could barely feel the dog's teeth that sank into her calf.

Dyan grabbed for her bola, but a hand caught her wrist.

"Only I don't think you're an Outrider at all." The man dragged her to her feet and slammed her against the canyon wall. "See, I met this trapper yesterday, and he was all excited about an Outrider selling her gear to the Shoshan post. He didn't know why an Outrider would ever want to do that, but he didn't care, because it meant he got a fancy new set of eyewear."

He slammed her against the wall again. She heard scuffling, and a cry. A dog bit her again.

Dyan felt stunned, the breath knocked out of her and her vision flashing. She could barely hear the words her attacker was saying, but she stared into his face from only inches away. Even in the indirect glow of the light stick's beam, shining away from her where it lay on the ground, she recognized him. He was the man she had faced off with earlier in the day. Also, she could see that he was now wearing an Outrider's goggles.

"He didn't really want to part with it," the bandit growled. "But I persuaded him."

In the space between them, under Dyan's chin, he held up a hooked and scalloped knife.

Dyan heard another twang, but it seemed far away and it didn't help her. She felt herself fading, and when the bandit drew his knife arm back to swing his weapon like an ax, the only resistance she could muster was a feeble wiggle.

WHAM!

Something crashed through the darkness in front of her, huge and fast and animal. The bandit disappeared, swept away under the charge of this new thing. Dyan wondered whether there were bear in the Wahai. She slipped to her knees, dimly glad that the dogs had disappeared.

She toppled forward forever, breath shallow in her nostrils. When forever ended and she slammed cheek-first onto the sand, the force of the blow punched her eyes wide open. In the confused and dim light, she saw a flurry of hooves trampling her attacker, and above it, mounted on Outrider Lorne's horse, Eirig.

A bow twanged again, and a scream that Dyan realized she had been hearing continuously for a minute or more cut off.

The world revolved slowly around her, the confusion calming. Two dogs barked and growled. She heard another twang of the bow, and the two growls became a single whining yip. Then a heavy crunch silenced even the yip.

The night air was cold.

"Dyan?"

She felt gentle fingers touching her throat and lips, and then Jak rolled her over onto her back and took her into his lap. "Are you awake?"

She nodded. Her vertigo and the sense that the world was a chaos of motion and darkness receded. She heard hoofbeats and then Eirig appeared.

"They're all dead," he announced.

Dyan felt sick. "When did the world become all about death?" she asked.

Jak shook his head. His big head blocked out the already narrow strip of stars. "It always was," he told her. "Only we didn't know it."

"We're going to need to move camp," Eirig said. "Unless you want to sleep in puddles of blood." He stood and started away. "I'll gather up our stuff."

"I don't want to be part of it," Dyan told Jak. "Not like this. There must be a way to live without killing all the time."

"I agree," Jak said. "What are you going to do about it?"

Dyan felt her calf and found torn fabric and blood. "I want to go away," she said. "I want to go somewhere where life isn't like this. Where people don't have to kill each other."

"I thought Ratsnay Station was that kind of place," Jak told her. "But I was just a kid then."

Dyan shook her head. "We can't go there. Our presence would put your mother's life in danger."

"We'll get her later," Jak suggested.

"I want to find a new place," Dyan continued. "Maybe in Sayatil, or Portolan, or Satulak. A place without a System. Or if there is a System, a small one, that doesn't kill people."

"That doesn't break up families," Jak agreed.

Dyan hesitated. "That's really what I want," she said. "A family."

"I'll be your family," Jak said instantly. "Will you be mine?"

She found his hand in the darkness and squeezed it.

Jak helped her to her feet and they surveyed the scene. With their light sticks, they found five bodies: two sliced in half, two shot with arrows, and one trampled to death by the horse. If Dyan hadn't felt so numb, she'd have been ill.

With all the bandits accounted for, no one worried about moving the camp very far. Dyan let Jak load her into one of the saddles and lead her to a rock overhang around the bend, and there he treated her leg with supplies from the medikit. He was still checking her for other cuts and bruises when she fell asleep.

A bright, hot sun cracked her eyelids open, and Dyan was lying in a furnace. She sweated and trembled, and though she realized after a moment that she was lying in the shade of a thorn tree, the light of the sky blazed all around her, rebounding off the orange rocks of the canyons and melting her flesh.

"Water," she rasped. Her own voice sounded ten thousand miles away.

"Ah, and the outlaw queen lives to ride another day." Before she could actually see Eirig she felt a metal flask pressed to her lips, and cold water crashed into her mouth like a hammer. The water was too much and too cold, and she choked. Still, when Eirig pulled the bottle away, her lips, tongue, and throat felt much cooler. She also felt better for his simple presence, his shadow muting the light as he leaned over her.

"Jak?" she asked. She meant to ask a more complex and elegant question, but she didn't feel like there was enough of her left to phrase a complete sentence.

"Jak's looking for a better campsite," Eirig told her. "You may have noticed that you're not well. He and I agreed we should get you to someplace more sheltered, and off this highway of rascals."

"Thanks, Eirig," she managed to say.

"Jak really wanted to be the one to scout a new camp," Eirig told her. A soft breeze ruffled his hair; it felt like sheets of ice on Dyan's exposed skin. She realized that she was propped up lying against a saddle and was covered with a microfiber blanket. She pulled the blanket tight up under her chin. "I think he felt he owed to you. Maybe he thinks he let you down."

Dyan shivered. "What if we got attacked while he was gone?" she managed to ask.

Eirig dismissed her worry with a snort. He held up a hand, and after her eyes took a moment to focus she saw that it was one of her bolas. "I don't actually know how to use this," he said, "but at least if I tried I'd put us both out of our misery quickly. Besides, I saw what you did to those robbers last night, and I have no doubt that if any of their like tried anything again, you'd make short work of them even in your sleep."

Dyan's laugh was weak, but genuine. "You're a good friend, Eirig," she said. "You can be in my family anytime." She stretched out a boiling hand and patted Eirig softly on his knee before drifting into sleep again.

Dyan missed most of the move to a new camp. She awoke twice to find herself sitting in the saddle under a hot sun, Jak behind her and holding the reins of Lorne's horse as it plodded along. When she woke up the third time it was night, and though the burning in her skin had passed, her throat felt like she had swallowed acres of sand.

She patted around in the darkness and found that she was lying against a saddle again. She grabbed the horn of it and pulled herself into a sitting position. Her entire body trembled and ached and the muscles of her arms felt like loose strings.

"Water," she heard a voice. She was surprised to realize it wasn't hers.

It was Jak. Moonlight shining down on them both revealed him sitting beside her, holding out a water flask. She took it and drank.

"Thank you."

"Eirig made a sort of soup by boiling dried meat," he said. "It's not as disgusting as you might think."

She nodded, and he passed over a small metal cup, warm to the touch. She drank, found she could only handle a few sips of the salty broth, and set it aside.

"Where are we?"

"We didn't go far at all," he told her. "This little canyon has one great virtue, which is that it is hard to find and hard to get into. I think we managed to get up in here without leaving tracks."

"What are its vices?"

"Don't worry about its vices," Jak said. "That's *my* job."

"What's *my* job?"

He took the cup of soup and moved it away from the nest of blankets on which she lay. "Your job is to go to sleep," he said.

She nodded and lay back down again. She watched Jak watching her, and beyond him a shadowy recess that might be an overhang of stone, and below him a stand of trees, waving back and forth in the moonlight like the five fingers of a twitching silvery hand.

Dyan awoke again and this time found herself alone. Her skin felt fragile as a paper, crispy to the touch and warm, but she was able to wobble to her feet. If the boys had abandoned her, they had left all the gear behind; one saddle was on the ground, and blankets rolled roughly and stacked against the stone base of the overhand, and cooking gear, food and medikits. The canyon was short and boxy, with high walls and a stand of trees in the center of it. One of the horses cropped at tall grass growing around the trees.

She felt thirsty and looked around for a water bottle. She was unsteady on her feet, but in a couple of minutes of staggering around, she was able to dig all through the equipment. No flasks, no waterskins.

She checked the canyon again.

"That's the vice," she said to herself. "No water."

Jak and Eirig had gone to get water, that had to be it. They'd taken one of the horses, because there were lots of water bottles. Looking around the canyon, though, Dyan felt alone. The walls loomed impossibly tall about her and she felt sick. She had lost everything and everyone, except Jak and Eirig, and now she might be losing them, too.

She'd go down the canyon, she resolved. She checked herself over. She was dressed in her Outrider garb, other than her bare feet and a bandage wrapped around one calf. She pulled on her boots and found her weapons, tucking them gingerly into place. She double-checked the campsite to be sure she hadn't missed any water containers. Finding none, she bent to pick up the saddle.

It was too heavy; she couldn't lift it.

"Holy Mother," she murmured.

She sat down on the saddle, light-headed. She should wait. They'd be back. There was no sign of violence, and the idea that the two of them might have ridden off together on one horse, abandoning her, was ridiculous. If they wanted her dead, they'd have taken both horses. If they wanted her alive, they'd have left water bottles.

They were coming back.

But she couldn't wait.

Wincing at each step and keeping her hand by her belt and the whip that hung there, she shuffled out of the canyon.

The top of the canyon, by the campsite, was a box with earth, trees, and grass in it. The exit from the back led into a long sluice of rounded orange stone. A channel dug through the bottom of the sluice, but it was dry. It had probably been carved by run-off water during millennia of rainstorms, Dyan thought, or maybe there had once been a spring and it had dried up. The sun pounded on her from above, and pounded off the rock on which she walked, hammering her a second time in the face.

The sluice turned and wound around a tower of red rock, then struck into what looked like a much larger canyon, on a shelf above the level of the floor. There she saw Jak and almost cried out in relief—

but stopped.

Off to her left she saw the second horse tethered to a wiry tree, no thicker than her wrist, that sprouted stubbornly out of an earth-filled crack in the stone. To her right, at the edge of the rock shelf, lying on his belly and looking down at something, was Jak.

Whatever he was watching, he was obviously hiding from it.

CHAPTER TWENTY-TWO

yan felt delirious with relief, and in her imagination her skin suddenly cooled. Jak had the horse.

But he was hiding. Something was wrong. Where was Eirig?

Dyan crouched down and tried to creep quietly, rolling her feet from heel to toe as she walked. She felt like a giant, tromping great thundering holes into the ground, but she couldn't have been that loud in others' ears.

She was almost to Jak before her boot sole scuffed the stone and he turned to look at her. He beckoned her to join him, and shushed her with a finger across his lips.

Dyan meant to continue creeping on her feet but stumbled. She caught herself, mostly silently, she thought, and then wormed forward on her belly to see what Jak was looking at. Insects of fear gnawed at her stomach in anticipation.

What she saw felt like a punch in the eye.

A spring of water gushed out of the rock at the foot of the shelf on which she stretched out. It bubbled maybe fifteen feet below Dyan's head. Water bottles, skins, and flasks lay on the ground around the spring, some filled and some empty. The cliff face was sheer below Dyan, though off to the right, where the main canyon wall came down past the shelf to the ground, there was a slide of stone that was less steep.

"I can't help you." Eirig knelt at the spring, holding a flask in the crystal stream of water to fill it. He coolly kept his back turned to the three figures whose appearance nearly made Dyan's heart stop.

Cheela, Shad, and the Magister from the Hanging and from Narl's cabin, the jowly blonde-haired woman with the drooping nose and one fluttering eye. They all rode big Outrider horses, fully kitted-out for the wilderness.

And Cheela rested her hand on her whip handle.

"Don't think I don't recognize you," Shad said evenly. "You're the boy who intervened at the Cull this year, at Ratsnay Station."

Eirig stoppered the flask by pinching it between his knees and putting the stopper in with his one hand. "Sure," he agreed. He set the flask down. "I didn't recognize you at all, actually, but my arm here"—he waggled his stump around his own ear—"did, and it reminded me that you're the Mother-blasted son of a goat who killed my friend Dimon. Took his head clean off his shoulders, as I recall. He bled a lot." He picked up a waterskin.

"So what?" Cheela was belligerent.

"You have a good memory." Shad's voice was flat, maybe a little sad. Dyan was shocked to see him. She had felt so proud of all her tricks and evasions, and they had failed. What had gone wrong? Had Shad been closer behind her all the time than she had imagined?

Or had her disguise worked against her? She thought of the trader on the ship, who expressed surprise at being paid by an Outrider, and the bandit with the nightvision goggles, who didn't think she could really be an Outrider at all if she was willing to sell her equipment.

Of course, the bandits' fresh bodies—the ones sawed neatly in half by monofilaments—must have been a clear sign to Shad that he was hot on Dyan's trail.

Eirig turned to kneel again at the spring, filling the waterskin. "And now you're going to kill me, too," he said. "Take my head off, I suppose. Ah, you can't deny it. I heard your Magister, didn't I? She said you would not only hunt us down, but kill our families if we told."

"Blazing right," Cheela muttered.

Eirig finished the waterskin and stood again. "Go ahead," he told them.

Shad raised his eyebrows. "You want to die?" he asked.

Dyan pulled both bolas from their holsters and held them quietly in her hands. She didn't think she could throw them safely from a position lying on her stomach, and she was afraid that the moment she stood, she'd be spotted. So she might get off one shot. She might not even get off one, she felt so shaky and fragile. She asked herself which of the three she should target.

"No," Eirig said. "All in all, I guess I don't. But my friends moved on and left me, thanks to this." He waved his stump in demonstration. "I can't hunt, you see? Can't shoot a bow, can't fight, can't even really get into the saddle by myself. So they left me here and headed out on their own."

Eirig said his words like they were a joke, straight-faced. He was a good liar, Dyan realized, and she felt perversely proud of him.

In her heart, she wanted to kill Cheela or the Magister. It was totally unreasonable, but she had a feeling that Shad didn't really condone what he was participating in. It wasn't fair, it denied Shad responsibility for his own actions, but she had to believe that some part of him resisted what he was being made to do. She had to believe it because … she just had to.

"Because you're a cripple?" Cheela sneered. Dyan remembered that it had been Cheela who had taken off Eirig's arm, as well as the head of his horse, back at that first deadly encounter.

"Life's hard, isn't it?" It wasn't really a question. "They left me by water, at least. And there are little animals here to trap, and pine nuts."

The Magister narrowed her eyes at Eirig. "And whom did you tell about the Cull, Landsy?"

"Landsy," Eirig chuckled. "I kind of like that. It makes me sound like I'm connected to something, and can stand on my own two feet, doesn't it? Like I'm solid as these rocks, and not just some mutilated kid without a home."

But Dyan knew that if she could only kill one of the three, that one had to be Shad. He was the tracker, and if he survived, whether he liked it or not, he would track Dyan down.

"Don't waste my time with this," the Magister said. "I have no tears to shed for you. Your life is hard. So is mine. So are all the lives that the System exists to protect, and who are you to decide that it is wrong for the System to pluck a few withered flowers to protect the entire garden?"

Eirig shrugged. "I'm nobody," he admitted. "Just a kid who doesn't think his friends deserve to be murdered."

"Whom did you tell?"

"Does it matter?" Eirig asked. "I don't have anyone left for you to kill. My old dad's long dead, and you already killed Aleena, who was like a mother to me. Now what? Are you going to threaten to kill Jak and Dyan? You're trying to kill them, anyway." He shrugged. "No, I'm happy they're in love, and they rode off without me. They can go have a good life somewhere, and you can take off my head and put me out of my useless misery."

Shad grimaced, and Dyan felt a twist in her gut.

In love?

"I have a plan," Jak whispered softly into her ear.

"We can't leave Eirig."

"Eirig came for me. I'm not going to leave him."

"Aren't you going to tell me what you have in mind?"

"Be ready," Jak said. "Get Eirig and get out of here."

"You dying is no better than Eirig dying," Dyan whispered. "In fact, it's worse." She grabbed his hand.

He squeezed her hand tight, once, and drew her to him and kissed her. "No time," he whispered and began his move.

Jak backed away on all fours and then quietly rose to his feet. His shoes, cut of soft leather, were much quieter than Dyan's riding boots, and he tip-toed along the long shelf of stone and over to the horse. Untethering the animal, he gave Dyan one last look and nodded at her.

Then he led the animal away.

Dyan couldn't worry about Jak. Instead, she crouched on the stone on all fours, bola in each hand, and watched the scene below.

"Hooves," Shad said, tilting his head to one side. "Do you hear?"

Cheela drew her whip, but the Magister maintained her hawklike focus on poor Eirig. Dyan tried to relax, to breathe consciously and be ready for whatever came.

She shifted her balance to free one of her hands and readied a bola. In her mind's eye, she aimed it at Shad, and she imagined hitting him with it.

The sound of Jak's horse approaching became louder. From a slow scrape of horseshoe on stone it changed to the faster beat of a canter.

"Perhaps," the jowly Magister smiled slowly, "your friends have not quite abandoned you after all."

Eirig scratched his head. He looked for all the world like he didn't care, and was completely calm. "Or maybe it's more bandits," he said. "I guess if you folks are as good as Dyan is with those whips of yours, you might not be too worried."

Shad palmed a bola and moved away from the spring, laying his body beside a clump of tall grass on a low rise of sand. Propped up on one elbow, he waited for the horse.

"This is your last chance," the Magister said to Eirig. "Tell us where your friends are."

Eirig shook his head slowly. "Maybe that's them," he said. "I have no idea."

The Magister moved fast. From somewhere under her cloak she produced a bola. Dyan had barely noticed it clutched between the woman's thumb and first two fingers when the weapon was already spinning through the air.

Thwack! The bola and its counterweight struck the stone behind Eirig and splashed down into the spring—

along with Eirig's other arm, severed near the shoulder.

Inside her head, Dyan screamed. Nothing came out of her mouth.

Eirig stumbled. His feet, boots stolen from Wayland's dead body what now seemed ages ago to Dyan, slipped in the muddy sand around the spring, and he fell forward onto his knees.

"Now do you have anything to say?" The Magister's smile looked maternal and generous, but her eyes glinted hard and bright and her voice was cold.

"Mother blast you to blazes," Eirig murmured.

"Enough of him," the Magister snapped her fingers. "Here comes another."

Cheela drew her whip and cracked it in one fluid motion. The invisible line sliced through Eirig vertically and he split apart like a gourd opened with an ax. One moment he knelt in the mud mouthing his defiance, and the next he was a mess of blood and flesh, watered by the little desert spring.

Dyan felt a scream about to explode within her. She jammed the meat of her own thumb into her mouth and bit down on it, hard.

Shad rolled over in his ambush-ready position and stared.

At that moment, Jak rode into view around the corner. Too late.

"Eirig!" he shouted. He immediately wheeled his horse around. The horse protested loudly, but turned, and with a great kick of its hind legs raced away, carrying Jak up the canyon.

"After him!" the Magister snarled.

Shad continued to stare. He looked surprised and disgusted.

"What?" Cheela asked him. "I did what an Outrider has to do."

"Capture or kill," Shad said. His voice was heavy and bitter. "We can sometimes capture them, Cheela."

"Not this one," the Magister said. "The Cull is a sacred thing, Outrider. It is to be protected from defiling by Crechelings and by Landsmen alike. Their knowledge is defilement, and threatens the System. He had to die, for the same reason his friends must die. For the same reason Magister Zarah will die."

Cheela arched her eyebrows defiantly at Shad. He shook his head and staggered to his feet. He looked as shaken as Dyan felt.

Magister Zarah?

Dyan ripped her thumb out of her mouth and looked at it. She had left deep teeth marks in her own flesh, and it hurt. She didn't think Jak had seen Eirig die. He had been in view for only a split second, and she thought he would have reacted strongly to his friend's death if he had been aware of it. He probably expected now to lead some members of the System party away so that Dyan could rescue Eirig. Instead, they would all chase after him.

And Dyan couldn't help. She was on foot, and by the time she ran up the sluice to retrieve her mount, it could all be over, and Jak could be dead.

"After him!" the Magister snapped again.

Cheela raced to her horse and leaped into the saddle. Shad followed. His footsteps seemed heavier than usual, but he shook his head at the last step and swung easily into his seat. "Gee yap!" he cried, and both their horses sprang into motion after Jak.

As the Outriders disappeared out of sight around the side of the shelf, the Magister walked towards the spring. This was her chance to even the odds, Dyan realized. The smartest thing she could do was to hit the Magister by surprise with her bolas, right now, before she could see what was coming.

Only she had heard this Magister say that Magister Zarah would die. Because she had not kept the secret of the Cull. And Magister Zarah had spoken very privately with Dyan on a cold night above the Snaik River, about the Cull and about life, and she had let Dyan go.

Dyan absolutely had to know what had happened.

She stood. Distracted by kneeling to retrieve her own weapon in the gory mess that had once been Eirig, the Magister didn't see her. Dyan whipped one bola around her head and slammed it down into the spring immediately in front of the Magister's face.

"Stop!" she cried.

The Magister froze, retreated a pace, and looked up.

Dyan raised her second bola over her head.

"Disarm yourself," she ordered the Magister. It felt profoundly wrong to be giving an order to a woman in the black cloak of authority, but she forced herself to do it.

The Magister slowly drew a whip from under her cloak and tossed it to the sand. She followed it with a bola, and then she held her hands out to Dyan, palms up.

"Step away from the spring," Dyan told her. "Stand by the pine tree, and put your hands on your head."

The Magister slowly complied. "My name is Haika," she said.

"You have no name," Dyan said. "If you move, I'll slice you in half. If you doubt my nerve or accuracy, you can ask Outrider Lorne."

She walked sideways to the rockslide where the canyon wall swept down past the edge of the stone shelf and fell into the spring. She took slow steps and kept an eye on Magister Haika.

The Magister stood calmly and held her hands carefully on top of her head as she'd been told. "Outrider Lorne wasn't looking," she said. "You killed him from behind."

"From above," Dyan said. "Get your facts straight, or I won't be able to take you seriously." She planted her feet carefully on the rockslide and left herself skid down it. She kept her eyes on Haika the entire time and wished she didn't feel brittle and overheated.

How far away was Jak now? And was he still running?

"I don't doubt your skill," Magister Haika said. "But when you were instructed to Cull Jak, son of Rosyn, a person whose name you knew and whose face you could see—a *person*, not an abstract fact, not a shadow—you balked. So you see, I do doubt your nerve."

"Don't expect your face to save you," Dyan said, finally catching solid footing on the floor of the canyon. "You're not nearly as good-looking as Jak."

The Magister smiled gently. "I'm warned."

"Good. Now it's time for you to answer some questions."

CHAPTER TWENTY-THREE

Why don't you come home, instead?"

The question caught Dyan by surprise.

"I ..." She hesitated. "I don't believe you."

"Would you want to come back to the System?" Magister Haika smiled softly. "If you could?"

"I killed Outrider Lorne," Dyan said. "I don't think Buza System will take me back, even if I wanted it to."

The Magister continued to smile, though her smile looked tighter at the corners. "You're not listening to me. I asked if you could, would you return?"

Dyan shook her head. "I'm asking the questions!" She forced her mind back into its earlier train of thought. "What happened to Magister Zarah?"

Haika pursed her lips. "I'm afraid that Zarah's old transgressions have finally caught up with her."

"What transgressions?"

"I see," Haika said. "You are worried about Zarah. Understand this, my child. Zarah is doomed, no matter what you do. The question isn't what you can do to help Zarah. You can't do anything. The question is what you can do to help yourself."

Dyan felt sick. "I'm not your child."

"You could be," Haika said. "You could be an Urbane, and my fellow Magister."

Dyan hesitated. What if it was true? What if Zarah had done something that doomed her, and there was nothing Dyan could do to help … but Dyan could accept Zarah's offer, return to the System, and become a Magister as she had long hoped?

"And Lorne?" she wanted to know.

Haika smile became hooked and biting. "There are only two living witnesses to Outrider Lorne's death," she pointed out. "We can't hide the death, but if there were only one living witness, he … or *she* … would have to tell the System who had killed the Outrider."

"You don't think I'd let you kill Jak," Dyan blurted out.

"I think you will do the killing yourself."

"No." The bola in Dyan's hand felt hot and slick with sweat.

"My child, my child." Haika's voice was gentle. "You cannot be a child any longer. It is time for you to become an adult."

"I've killed," Dyan said. She felt guilty saying it. She felt like she was trying to get credit for the Cull without participating in it. She felt like she was betraying Eirig. She said it anyway. She'd have said anything to save Jak. "I killed Lorne."

Haika only shook her head.

"Let Jak go," Dyan said simply. "I'll come home."

"Don't you see?" Haika spread her arms, a gesture of explanation that made her look very much like a Magister. "The Landsman can't go. He can't tell his fellows about the Cull. It's not my choice, Dyan. I don't want this Landsman hurt any more than you do. He simply has to die, I have no choice in the matter and neither do you. If you accept that his death is your task, at least you can make sure it's painless."

Dyan struggled. Her arm, holding up the bola, felt heavy as lead. "You killed Eirig."

"The one-armed Landsman had to die for the same reason. I had no choice. You must understand that. I know that when your hand is forced, you, too, do the necessary thing."

Magister Haika smiled and her voice was soft. Dyan felt tired, her skin crispy and hot, and her head spun a little. Haika's words made some sense to her. She had killed Lorne when she had to. She would kill others if she had to. It wasn't her fault or her choice. She was being forced.

And then, wavering in the heat-shimmering air between her and the Magister, she thought she saw Eirig. Eirig looked directly at her and winked.

"He wasn't one-armed anymore by the time you finished with him," the phantasm quipped.

Eirig wasn't a nameless one-armed Landsman. He was her friend, and when he had had no choice, he had chosen anyway, and stood up to Magister Haika and the Outriders. He had done it and taken the consequence, which was to die. He had done it to protect Dyan.

And Jak.

"Tell me where Magister Zarah is." She shivered, cold despite the heat.

"Zarah isn't a Magister anymore," Haika told her. "She's a prisoner, and will die in the next Hanging."

Dyan choked.

"Why?" she asked. "What do you mean ... you said earlier, she defiled the Cull? What do you mean?"

Haika's face took on a curious expression. It wiggled slightly, like she was keeping something funny to herself. The look made Dyan want to punch the Magister, but it passed quickly. "Former Magister Zarah let you go," she said. "She let you choose to flee the Cull with the Landsman youth."

Dyan was astonished. "How could you know that?" she asked. "Was someone following her? Did she confess?"

Haika laughed. "Every Magister is recorded," she explained. "All the time. The Magister's Calling is too important to leave any room for human weakness." She let her arms fall by her sides. She took a slow step forward.

Dyan felt rivulets of sweat running down her back. "Why are you telling me this?" she asked. "You said I'm still a child."

Haika nodded, and rubbed her biceps under her cloak. "Very good," she said. "I'm telling you this because either you will make the right decision, complete the Cull and become an Urbane—in which case you will become a Magister as you have been Called to be, and this knowledge is appropriate for you—or you will make the wrong choice, in which case you will die, and it won't matter what you know."

She took another step.

"So ... this conversation is being recorded right now," Dyan said. "By what?"

Haika held the five-armed tree medallion with one hand. "The recording device is in here," she said.

Dyan heard the words and they felt like a cool breeze coming down the canyon, refreshing her with a sudden realization. She felt strength flood into her trembling limbs.

"But that means," she said, "that when you told me that no one would ever know that I killed Outrider Lorne ... you were *lying*."

Haika said nothing.

"There is no deal," Dyan said. "You just want to distract me with this talk. It's all lies." She took a step back. "You just want to kill me."

"Look," Magister Haika started and moved closer again.

"Stop!" Dyan clenched the bola tight in her fist and raised it over her head.

"Wait!" Haika raised a hand. "Wait ... please." She slowly removed her medallion of office, raising its chain over her head and then dropping it aside to the ground.

"It's Zarah," she said. "Don't you understand?"

"What?" Dyan's arm sagged in surprise.

Haika attacked.

Dyan had not seen her palm the bola, but there it was, flashing in the Magister's fingers as she snapped her arm over her head to throw. Dyan had no time to do anything but hurl herself backward. The bola sliced through the air over her head with a *whooshing* sound and she heard the crunch of boots on the sand.

Dyan hit the ground hard and rolled. She flung her body to the side, trying to avoid the attack that she thought must be coming—
only it didn't.

She tumbled to her knees, bola at the ready, and saw Haika snatching her whip off the ground. The Magister wheeled to face Dyan. She was faster than she should have been, for a woman with so much extra flesh on her frame.

Haika spun her arm around and Dyan snapped off a shot, flinging her bola at the Magister's upraised arm.

Haika cracked her hand down and Dyan flinched, expecting to be sliced in two. Instead, nothing happened. She hesitated from surprise for a moment, and Haika stared down at the whip in her hand.

The counterweight was gone.

Splash!

A chunk of stone from the lip of the shelf where Dyan had lain to witness Eirig's murder fell off the front of the cliff and dropped into the spring. The rock broke apart as it fell, some of it throwing up gouts of water and some of it thunking heavily on top of Eirig's mutilated form.

She had cut the weapon in two, Dyan realized. The line of her bola had crossed the line of the whip in midair, severing them both. It was sheer luck that the detached monofilament line hadn't sliced through her in its flight.

Haika must have reached the same conclusion at the same moment—she roared in rage and hurled the whip handle at Dyan. The blunted stump banged into Dyan's shoulder, and Haika dashed for the spring.

Two bolas lay in the cold pool, under the rubble that had once been the cliff face and the gore that had once been Eirig. Dyan couldn't let Haika get to them. She drew her own whip and snapped it at the Magister.

Out of intuition or calculation, Haika dove to the ground at the last moment. Dyan's whip snapped through the air over her head, carving a shower of stone chips out of the cliff face. Dyan drew back her arm again as the whip's counterweight snicked home, aiming to slice right through the large middle of the cloaked woman—

Haika rolled back and threw at her.

Dyan ducked, fearing and yet already resigned to being cut in half. The thrown object thumped into her and she stepped back, stumbling on the lowest end of the rockslide. She lost her footing and crashed to the ground—

losing her grip on the whip handle.

As she sucked in a lungful of air, she saw the object that had struck her. It wasn't a bola, or even a rock.

It was Eirig's severed arm.

Dyan screamed. She couldn't tell whether her scream came from rage or pain, and didn't know if she would even be able to tell the difference at this point. She grabbed for the whip and couldn't find it.

She hurled a rock instead, but it wasn't a big one and it bounced off the Magister's back. Dyan lurched to her feet, picking up a bigger rock with both hands and charging. She screamed, raising the rock over her head and bringing it down as hard as she could on Haika's head.

Except that Haika twisted at the last second and Dyan missed. The rock thudded hard into Haika's shoulder and she fell back, with Dyan on top of her.

For a blind moment, Dyan could make out nothing but flailing arms and legs. She heard a growling sound and didn't know who was making it. She felt hands at her throat, with fingernails digging into her flesh, and her mind focused.

She knelt over Magister Haika, punching the larger, older woman in the face and shoulders repeatedly. The Magister had her hands around Dyan's throat and squeezed, and Dyan felt the air in his lungs running out. Her vision began to blur.

Dyan picked up a rock.

Haika squeezed tighter.

Dyan smashed the Magister. Dyan's arms and hands felt broken from the force of her own blow, which jarred loose Haika's hands and knocked Dyan off and to the ground. She lay stunned, beside the still Magister, and felt sand and pine needles dig into her skin.

Then Haika groaned.

It wasn't over. Dyan needed something to end the fight, permanently. She hit the locator switch on her bola holster—one of her bolas was destroyed, but the other should be in the spring. She raised herself to her hands and knees, moaning from pain and effort, and looked into the water. She couldn't see the light. That could only mean that the bola was buried under the fragments of rock.

"Blast and blazes," she muttered.

Haika's hand shot out and grabbed Dyan's wrist. Her fingers were tense and strong, claw-like, and her nails dug into Dyan's skin. Dyan looked at the Magister, and saw blood streaming down over her face from a gash in her forehead. Dyan had caused that wound, she realized.

And no amount of blood flow would hide the anger in Haika's face.

"Vixen," she snarled.

Dyan punched the older woman again, right in her bloody forehead.

Haika fell back with a yelp.

Dyan hit the locator switch on Haika's holster.

She immediately saw one of the Magister's bolas. Its locator light winked red, and Dyan reached for it—

but stopped. The bola sat in a red, bloody mess that had once been Eirig.

He wouldn't care, she tried to tell herself. He would want her to grab it.

But she couldn't force herself to do it. Instead, she shambled to her feet and stared at the rockslide.

There, above her head among the red rubble, winked the light of the Magister's second bola. Her legs screamed with pain. Her skin burned. Her tongue felt like a toad in her own mouth, and she tasted blood. Dyan kicked herself into a lope, and ran for the bola.

Behind her she heard scrabbling sounds. She hit the slide and stumbled forward onto all fours. Like a dog she pushed forward, scraping her hands and breaking fingernails on the rock as she dragged herself up it.

Her hand closed around the bola and she rolled over onto her back.

Haika knelt in the blood and bone mess of Eirig, blood smeared on her forearms as she snatched the other weapon.

Dyan jumped to her feet. At the same moment, the older woman stood.

They both raised their weapons. Dyan snapped her arm in a throwing motion—

Haika threw—

but Dyan didn't release the bola. Instead she let herself fall down and forward. She hit the ragged rocks hard, pinching her ear and bruising her shoulder, but the cracking sound behind her and the shower of rock dust that rained down on her told her that Haika had thrown and missed.

Dyan somersaulted forward and came up in an unsteady crouch.

Haika charged. She raised her arms like a wild animal's, talons extended.

Dyan threw the bola. It snapped through the top of Haika's head, and winged off into the pine trees, scattering severed branches and clouds of yellow-green needles as it went.

Haika ran three more steps. Dyan staggered aside to get out of the way, and when the Magister collapsed onto the stones of the rockslide, she was dead.

CHAPTER TWENTY-FOUR

For a moment, Dyan could do nothing. She sank back onto her haunches and then sat, with a rough bump, onto the rockslide. She felt the sun on her skin, which burned her but failed to warm her inner core. She felt cold.

Cold and very, very tired.

Magister Haika was dead. Weight dragged Dyan's body down and pressed on her chest, making breathing difficult. The sun's light suddenly seemed much too bright, and she shivered and hid her face in her hands.

Magister Haika was dead, and Magister Zarah soon might be. And if she died, she died because of Dyan, because she had let Dyan go.

Even worse than that, Jak might die, too, and for the same reason.

She forced herself to think. Jak was outnumbered two to one by enemies with better weapons. He'd outwitted Cheela and Dyan before, back on the Snaik River, but that would only make Cheela more wary this time. He'd need help, if he wasn't dead already.

And Dyan wasn't sure she could help him. She trembled in all her limbs, dry as a bone in her mouth and eyes, and she burned and froze at the same time.

She stood.

First, she would deal with the recorder. With blocky, puppet-like steps, she crossed to the sand where Haika had laid her symbol of office. She picked up the five-armed tree medallion and examined it. It looked solid at first glance, made of some ceramic or metal Dyan couldn't immediately identify. When she looked closer, she noticed that in the joints between the trunk of the tree and its arms were tiny pinprick-sized holes.

To let in light and sound to the recording device, she guessed.

She dropped the medallion on the sand and limped back over to the rockslide. She tried to avoid looking at it, but couldn't help seeing Magister Haika's corpse with its open brainpan. She'd bled surprisingly little from having the top of her head severed, less than she had from the face wounds Dyan had inflicted.

Dyan shrugged off a feeling that was half-fascination and half-revulsion. She bent at the knees and picked up a rock the size of her own skull, and then turned and carried it back to the medallion. She knelt, stared down at the little device, and raised the rock over her head.

Dyan meant to cover the medallion, to render it harmless. But something unconscious in her body took over, and when she brought the rock down she slammed it. At the same moment, she burst into tears, and then raised the rock and smashed it down again. And again and again, until the Magister's emblem of office was cracked into pieces and pounded deep into the sand, and Dyan lay huddled on the top of the rock, weeping.

She came back to herself a few minutes later with a deep panic and a sense that she had run out of time. She collected her whip, and the three bolas she could recover, resetting them to respond to the locator switch in her own holsters. She had no plan but to race to catch up with Jak. Hopefully, she could at least even out the odds a bit, or at least give him a chance not to die alone.

She was about to climb onto the back of Magister Haika's horse when she had an idea. Stiff and shaky, she shrugged out of her Outrider's coat. After a moment's hesitation, she draped it across Eirig's mutilated body, shedding a fresh burst of tears as she did so.

Then she set about stripping the Magister's body.

Haika's glazed eyes accused her of theft and murder, and she ignored them. She peeled away the woman's cloak and then her clothing, leaving her exposed, limbs askew and head gaping open. Stripping down to her own underclothes, Dyan felt weak and alone, but as she stepped into the Magister's trousers, tunic, and boots, and finally pulled the cloak about her shoulders, her strength returned.

Haika's horse shied away and whinnied nervously as Dyan approached. She patted its neck to calm it before climbing into the saddle. Then she pulled her hood over her face and rode up the canyon at a quick trot.

She was significantly smaller than the Magister, so her sleeves sagged, her trousers were tucked into her boots and, when she stood, her cloak dragged on the ground. In any case, the tiniest glimpse of her face would give her away, so the disguise would gain her only a very little time at the most.

The tracks were impossible to miss. Three horses galloped up the canyon, disturbing sand and grass and shrubbery. Dyan couldn't gallop quite as fast as they had, but the trail was wide and obvious and she cantered quickly.

There were opportunities to turn, to get off the sand and onto rock, but Jak hadn't taken them. He'd stayed in the center of the main canyon, obvious and enticing and fast. He hadn't been trying to escape, Dyan realized.

He'd been trying to lead the Outriders away, so Dyan could ambush Magister Haika and rescue Eirig.

Had Jak planned on surviving? Dyan wondered.

It didn't seem like it.

Still, he'd ridden far. She followed the trail several miles, crossing and recrossing a shallow brook that flowed out of a side canyon and zig-zagged across the sandy floor. As her strength flagged, she rounded a corner and saw the Outriders.

Three horses waited tethered to a thorny bush on the near side of a bend in the canyon. On the far side, across the stream, a stand of huge cottonwood trees dotted a raised bank and pressed up against the canyon wall. Cheela stood back from the trees, staring up at the wall behind them.

Shad had his whip out, and was systematically chopping down trees with it. With two flicks of his wrist, any trunk lost a wedge-shaped divot from near its base and quickly toppled over.

Cheela turned at the sound of Dyan's approach and waved a lazy salute. "Magister Haika," she greeted Dyan, and then turned back to watch the cliff.

Dyan looked up the cliff face and saw Jak. A ledge creased the stone below the tops of the trees where the face of the wall retreated in steps from the brink. Jak had climbed up there, Dyan guessed, and now squatted, shielded in part by the tree branches and by the ledge itself. A thrown monofilament bola would slice through wood and stone as easily as flesh, of course, but if either the bola or its counterweight struck anything solid in midair, the bola would be knocked off course.

Which was why Shad was chopping down the sheltering trees.

Dyan rode up to Cheela's side.

"He's up there, Magister," Cheela said. "He can't get off the cliff, so once we get down the trees, we can pick him off at our leisure. Or starve him out."

Dyan dismounted, carefully getting down from her horse on the side opposite Cheela. She walked around behind Cheela, palming one of her bolas.

She only had one shot at this, and then she would find that she was the one who was outnumbered two to one, with Jak up in the treetops unable to do anything about it.

Cheela chuckled, an ugly, gargling sound. "Or just ride away and leave him to the vultures."

Dyan wrapped her arms around Cheela's chest from behind.

Cheela started and began to raise her arm to struggle—

but froze when she saw that Dyan had pulled out the bola's counterweight with her other hand. A wire of death stretched invisible in front of Cheela's chest, an unseen and unstoppable garrote. If Dyan so much as stepped backward, Cheela would fall apart in two pieces.

"Magister?" Cheela asked in a small voice.

Shad snapped his whip and another tree groaned as it collapsed sideways. The cottonwoods mostly lay in a heap of splintered lumber now.

"Guess again, my child," Dyan growled.

"Blazes!" Cheela snapped.

"Drop your whip and your bolas and your vibro-blade," Dyan whispered. "And do it really slowly. I'd hate to stumble, and get blood all over my fancy new clothes."

Shad took down another tree, oblivious.

Cheela carefully drew her whip and dropped it on the ground, followed by her bolas and her knife.

"Good," Dyan approved. "Now cover them with sand."

"I don't have a shovel," Cheela sulked.

"Use your boot," Dyan told her. "Unless you want me to cover them with your headless corpse instead."

Cheela kicked sand over the weapons, careful not to get too close to the monofilament garrote. Dyan's hands trembled, and she realized she didn't have the strength to drag this confrontation out very long.

"Well done," she said. "Now stand on them."

Cheela stood on her own buried weapons. "You'll die for this," she snarled.

"Death isn't a consequence," Dyan said. "We all die. The consequences of our choices are all the things that happen between the moment of choice and the moment of death."

"I'll kill you myself. I should have killed you on the Snaik."

Shad took down another tree. Only one remained.

"Yeah," Dyan agreed. "Probably you should have. Now call Shad."

"Shad!"

Shad stopped and turned around. He looked puzzled, and Dyan remembered that she still had the hood down, obscuring her face. Also, he probably couldn't see the bola, so to him she probably seemed to be Magister Haika, resting her feet by leaning on Cheela's back.

"Magister?" he asked.

Dyan shook her head back, letting the hood fall away from her face. Cheela sucked in a sharp breath at Dyan's movement, but Dyan was careful not to bring the monofilament into contact with her prisoner.

"Dyan!"

The look on Shad's face was one part surprise, one part anger, and one part something else that Dyan couldn't identify. She didn't have time to think about it now, or time to look up at the cliff and try to see Jak's reaction, about which she was more curious.

She rested her elbows against Cheela's sides to try to keep her arms propped up.

"What do you want?" Shad asked.

"To kill us, you idiot!" Cheela snapped.

"I don't think so," Shad said slowly. "I think if she wanted to kill us, we'd already be dead."

"I don't want to kill anybody," Dyan agreed. "Too many people have already died."

"You know about ... the one-armed boy, then," Shad said.

"Eirig," Dyan agreed. "I also know about Outrider Lorne, because I killed him. I killed Magister Haika, too, just a few minutes ago. This is her clothing I'm wearing. I don't want any more deaths, but don't think I won't happily kill you both, if I have to."

Shad nodded. "So what do you want?"

"Drop your weapons."

He did.

"Kick sand over them and stand on top of them," Dyan ordered him. While he did as she had told him, she risked a glance at the last cottonwood tree. Jak had already leaned out from the cliff face and climbed into its branches. He was coming down fast, falling as much as he was climbing.

"So you were watching at the spring," Shad said.

"Yes."

Jak was almost to the ground now, moving a little slower so he wouldn't fall and impale himself on a stump or a splintered branch.

"I'm afraid I can't leave you any horses."

"What?" Cheela hissed.

"I understand," Shad said. "We'll be fine."

"Not that she cares," Cheela growled.

"True," Dyan lied. "I don't care."

"Are you going to go after Magister Zarah?" Shad asked.

"What do you mean?" Dyan remembered again that Zarah had been imprisoned because of her, and was going to be executed at the next Hanging. That was little more than two months away, she realized, and knowing the number of days made her feel sick. "I'm not interested in revenge," she bluffed. "She only did what she thought she had to do."

Cheela laughed out loud.

Jak splashed across the little stream and headed for the picketed horses.

"Zarah's your mother," Shad said.

Dyan froze. Her vision swam in and out of focus and she almost lost her balance and fainted before she managed to draw another breath.

"Why would you say that?" she asked.

"Because it's true, you blasted vixen!" Cheela snapped. "Didn't you wonder why she would let you go?"

"But ..." Dyan was dumbfounded. "I don't have a mother."

"Did you think you hatched from an egg?" Cheela taunted her. "Everybody has a mother!"

Dyan looked into Shad's eyes and saw that, whether or not it was really true, at least Shad believed it. "How would she know?"

"She's been watching you all along." Shad shrugged.

"That's not allowed," Dyan said.

Shad shook his head. "Of course not. I guess her superior Magisters knew, or maybe they just suspected. And they let her be your Magister for the Blooding, to see what she would do."

"And when it went wrong, she let me run," Dyan said softly. In hindsight, Zarah had almost *encouraged* her to run. Why had she done that? She must have known she was putting herself at risk.

And how had she not realized she was being recorded while she did it? Maybe the knowledge that the medallions were recorders was restricted to senior Magisters, or to certain Magisters anyway.

There was so much, Dyan realized, she didn't understand about the System.

Jak gathered up the reins to the three horses and joined Dyan.

"I can't give you a headstart," Shad said. "I can't promise any mercy." He looked sad.

"I don't need your mercy," Dyan said. "I'm taking your horses instead."

Jak mounted one of the Outriders' horses, still holding the reins of the other two.

"I'm going to kill you," Cheela repeated herself.

"I'll leave you your weapons," Dyan said, "so I suppose you're free to try. But right now you're going to run over and touch that tree trunk."

"I'm sorry about your friend," Shad told her. Their eyes met, and Shad looked away. Then he looked at Jak, too. "I'm sorry."

Cheela snorted.

"I'm sorry about all my friends," Dyan said.

She carefully raised the bola over Cheela's head, keeping the line extended so that it remained a threat. Cheela stepped out of Dyan's grasp, shuddering.

"Go," Dyan said softly.

Shad and Cheela turned and jogged across the brook. While they splashed through the water, Dyan climbed into her saddle, and then she and Jak rode away. Before the young Outriders had returned to their cached weapons, Jak and Dyan were around the corner of the canyon and out of sight.

CHAPTER TWENTY-FIVE

here's Eirig?" Jak asked.

Dyan restrained a sob. "They killed him," she managed to get out. "Just as you were riding away."

They rode in silence for long minutes.

"Thank you," he finally said. Then again, a few minutes later: "Thank you. I thought they had me back there."

"I'm glad they didn't."

They kept riding.

"I don't know what to do with the body," she told him, as they cut through the bola-mangled pine trees and up to where Eirig lay.

Small animals scattered away from both bodies as Dyan swung a leg over the saddle and dropped off her horse.

"At home, we'd bury him," Jak said, and shook his head. "But ..."

"What do you do in an emergency?" she asked.

"We'd burn him." He dismounted and looked over at Magister Haika, who was a little worse for wear for the nibbling at her face and hands of wild dogs. "Her, I don't care."

"I do," Dyan said. She reached out and took his hand. "Not as much, of course."

"Poor Eirig," Jak said. He picked up the Outrider's coat and stared with a steady eye at the mangled remains of his friend. Dyan couldn't bring herself to look without flinching, so she looked at

Jak instead. "This is all my fault," he said.

"It's no one's fault," Dyan corrected him. "Not yours, anyway."

"No?" Jak's voice was bitter. "And if I'd just gone along quietly with the Cull?"

"Eirig made choices," Dyan said, "and those choices had consequences."

"He stuck up for me and lost his arm."

"And he saved your life, too. And he stopped me from becoming a murderer. And then he saved both of us."

"A kindness for which your friends killed him." Dyan must have looked uncomfortable at that description, because Jak sighed and squeezed her hand. "I'm sorry," she added.

Dyan felt more fragile than ever. A breath of wind would have whisked her away. "We don't have much time," she reminded him.

Dyan poured petrofuel over Eirig's body before Jak covered it again. She also soaked the coat for good measure.

"Do we ... sing?" she asked. "Or anything?"

"There are prayers to the Holy Mother," Jak said. "And songs." He took the sparker from Dyan's hand and lit the mound of coat and flesh that had been Eirig on fire. "I don't remember them."

The flames whooshed high immediately. Dyan knew funeral dirges of Buza System, but none of them seemed appropriate. Instead, she sang the song she had learned from Eirig, and despite her exhaustion and pain, the words all came to her.

> *"Sally she married a soldier,*
> *A Captain named William Lee,*
> *And I guess in his fashion he loved her,*
> *But Sally always loved me.*
> *Now I sit by this stone and remember*
> *Her blue eyes and tresses of gold,*
> *And how we said when we were younger,*
> *We'd be together when we grew old.*
> *Oh, sweet Sally,*
> *Dear Mrs. Lee,*
> *Your footsteps are gone,*
> *But your memory lives on,*
> *And you'll always be Sally to me."*

It was all she could get out, and it seemed to fit, more or less. She thought Eirig would have enjoyed it even more because her sung farewell to him made him sound like a woman named Sally, with blue eyes and blonde hair. She still didn't know the name of the song, and she wondered whether it had been written about real people, some doomed couple who lived and were separated by death before the Cataclysm.

Jak mounted his horse. "We don't have long."

Dyan poured out the rest of the petrofuel on the dead Magister. A lizard scurried away as the liquid splashed down on it, but ants and beetles continued to crawl on her flesh without taking any notice. Dyan took one last look at Magister Haika. Without her robe, her smashed medallion, or her weapons, she was nothing. She was an unlovely and unintimidating corpse, missing the top of its head and only half-dressed.

When Dyan sparked Haika's body, the insects burned with her.

Both burning corpses stank, but in Dyan's mind all the stench came from Haika. She remounted, shushing her skittish horse and patting it on the neck. The gesture didn't do much for the animal, but it helped calm Dyan.

They rode north, away from Shad and Cheela and back towards the Lull Sea.

Late that afternoon, Jak directed them across a bar of stone and up a side canyon. "They'll hit this place in the dark," he explained. "If it doesn't throw them off completely, it should at least slow them down."

Dyan nodded, too tired and sick to do anything more.

"They're still Outriders," Jak pointed out. "And we're still on the run."

"Maybe we always will be," Dyan said. The thought made her feel defeated.

Their path led them up a knife-edged ridge as the sun set and down into a broad, grassy valley on the other side. Two well-trodden trails intersected in the middle of the valley, quartering the world between them, and they camped well back from both of them, in the notch of a hill that made the wind whistle over their heads.

Jak sat up for the first watch. Dyan lay awake what seemed like a very long time, watching a yellow moon creep up through the notch and slowly dominate the field of glittering, indifferent stars.

Then she woke up, her face scratched by the wad of wool blanket on which her head rested.

"Let's go south," Jak said to her. He squatted on a saddle, huddled into a microfiber blanket.

She sat up. Her body ached all over. "South?" She stretched. "Satulak?"

"If you want, sure," he agreed. "But we wouldn't have to go that far to get away from the System."

"Ratsnay Station?"

"That's more east than south, really. I was thinking—look, we could just find a place in the hills somewhere with water, and make a go of it."

"Farm? Herd sheep?"

"Both. Whatever."

Dyan hesitated. "Are you asking me to be your Goodwife?"

"Yes," Jak agreed. "I haven't said it in a very romantic way, I know. But I don't think it would be a very romantic life. But we'd be Goodwife and Goodman."

Dyan considered. "Is that even possible?" she asked.

Jak nodded. "There are people who live out in the hills alone. One here, another there, I mean, and no one bothers them."

This was news to Dyan. "Who is *no one*?" Dyan yawned and tried in vain to chase fatigue from her head. "You mean that people from Ratsnay Station don't bother them?"

"Yes, that. But also the Collectors."

"They don't contribute to the System?"

"I guess not. I suppose they're so small it's not worth the effort."

"And outlaws?"

Jak shrugged. "It isn't perfect. But you're great with those weapons, and we'd choose some place really out of the way. We'd be fine."

"We'd be hunted," Dyan said. "By the Outriders, and by any outlaws who happened to learn of our existence."

"Satulak, then."

"I would like to go to Satulak with you," Dyan agreed. "Or Sayatil, or Portolan. But there's something I have to do first."

"What's that?"

"Magister Zarah. The woman who ... who came to Ratsnay Station to Cull you."

"I remember." Jak's voice was hard and his eyes narrowed in the bright morning sun.

"She came to me on the night after we left the Snaik River ..." She fumbled for a better description, "the night after Wayland ... died."

Jak's eyebrows shot up his forehead. He opened his mouth as if to say something and closed it again.

"She let us go," Dyan told him. "Looking back at it, I think she almost told me to run, to get away."

Jak shook his head. "That doesn't make any sense."

"While you were climbing down the tree this afternoon," she continued, Shad and Cheela told me that Zarah ... Zarah's been imprisoned. She's going to be executed."

"For what?"

"For letting us go."

Jak frowned. "Why would she do that? She must have known the System would consider it treason, or at least some kind of crime."

Dyan took a deep breath. "Magister Zarah is my mother."

Jak stared.

"I only found out today," she told him.

"You mean that your System friends told you?" He looked skeptical. "The same ones who chased me up a tree and then tried to chop the tree down?"

"Yes," she admitted. "But it's the only explanation that makes any sense to me."

Jak looked at her a long time, and then laughed. "Okay," he said. "North it is. Do we have a plan?"

"No," Dyan said, and thought about Shad and Cheela. "But I think we have a head start."

ABOUT THE AUTHOR

D.J. BUTLER (Dave) is a novelist living in the Rocky Mountain northwest. His training is in law, and he worked as a securities lawyer at a major international firm and in house at two multinational semiconductor manufacturers before taking up writing fiction.

Dave writes speculative fiction for all audiences. In addition to his steampunk, urban fantasy, and science fiction novels published with WordFire Press, he has a forthcoming steampunk fantasy series to be published by Knopf. Look for *The Kidnap Plot* in spring of 2016.

Dave is a lover of language and languages, a guitarist and self-recorder, and a serious reader. He is married to a powerful and clever woman and together they have three devious children.

Read about all of Dave's fiction projects at:

http://davidjohnbutler.com.

OTHER WORDFIRE PRESS TITLES BY D.J. BUTLER

Rock Band Fights Evil:

Hellhound On My Trail

Snake Handlin' Man

Crow Jane

Devil Sent the Rain

Our list of other WordFire Press authors and titles is always growing. To find out more and to see our selection of titles, visit us at:

wordfirepress.com